The feminist CEO and

the arrogant SHEIK

A. C. Mabrano

Bethany is an intelligent businesswoman who inherits her family companies and becomes the CEO of a powerful conglomerate. She believes in equal rights and also equal responsibilities for her employees.
For her expansions, she makes many contacts with influential men.
But she was not prepared to find an arrogant opponent, Omar, one Sheik that comes from the mysterious lands in the deserts, the birthplace of the petroleum empires.
This romance is about these two people whose chances to mix are like water and oil.
And still, the blood is racing in their veins and their hearts have already accelerated.
Will love overcome prejudices?

For my sweet nieces.

I find you handsome... you find me.

Paula Braga, poet

Chapter 1 - The Escape

INTRODUCTION

The first reports of the Arab civilizations and the beginning of the tribes of the powerful sheiks bring emotions, struggles, conquests... Everything for the survival of those ancient peoples.
And love, could it survive?

IN THE DESERT
Now:
Bethany was hidden among the luggage of the cart. She could hear her brother talking to the head of the caravan that he had hired. It was a vibrant and cheerful voice. Scott was very protective, but even so, she was afraid.
She had everything to lose if she was discovered. Her life. And her son's. The baby slept peacefully in her arms. Looking at that angelic calm, Bethany managed to smile for the first time in weeks.
Her son. Her love. He fully filled her heart and it was worth all the sacrifice she made to protect him.
"Are you warm enough, little sister?" He still called Bethany by her childhood nickname.
"Yes, Scott. But I would like to stop for a while to feed the baby."
Scott smiled and nodded. He immediately gave the order to the members of the caravan. They were crossing the desert regions of the Arab world, heading for a region far to the south. Scott had business with some of the tribal leaders there.
These tribesmen did business to survive. Just like their parents had done, and their grandparents, great-grandparents, and other ancestors. But there was no record of any of that. Writing had not been invented at that time. As well as almost nothing in the world that accompanies the writing.
It was all very rudimentary in those desert places, however, the willpower and determination of those men, made possible the formation of several villages that today have become busy cities.
It would be a good hiding place for Bethany and her baby.
The cunning for trade and the fighting force against the enemy tribes had passed from parents to children, countless times.

Bethany had heard many stories about these fascinating events. And today she was part of that chain of influencers who commanded most people's lives there. Those willing to follow confident leadership.

And that was because Bethany was the wife of Sheik Omar Sahid al Maliq.

The facts that Bethany intended to pass on as an inheritance to her son, and everything she knew about the past, came from stories told as treasures.

These commercial links were true heritages. People's very survival depended on strengthening these contacts and not making mistakes that overthrew others, in that region so difficult to live.

Everyone in the caravan was excited about the stop and started preparing and distributing food. There was a mix of people, but most were from the Maghni tribe, which meant 'singer'.

These people were very happy. Where they were, fun was guaranteed. Even the simplest task was performed with singing and laughter. As that vast desert was a place of many conflicts and wars, this quality was a real fuel for them to face tragedies.

Not to mention sandstorms, which destroyed many lives and goods.

The people of that region were always under reconstruction.

So it was fortunate to have an ally or friend from the Maghni tribe, to be able to do everything with joy.

Scott had a good friend from that tribe, the head of that caravan. His name was Habibdul, a young man with a strong and attractive voice. He always stood out at meetings and parties. He was frequently asked to contribute with his music. He sang from war hymns to pleas for the love of some more attractive woman.

He had already had his share of passions, but he had not yet formed a family, like many young people his age.

All protective, Scott sat next to his sister. While the baby was being fed, they listened to Habibdul, who softly sang a ballad from his childhood, which he had learned from his grandfather.

The baby was almost asleep and Bethany, calmer with the song, leaned against her brother's shoulder and gave herself up to the memories of when she first met Sheik Omar Sahid al Maliq.

CHILDHOOD
Past:

Bethany's grandfather was the billionaire Christopher Worthgold. A ruthless man, considered to have a heart of steel, he only softened in the presence of that sweet and beautiful child, his granddaughter and only heir.

He had warned her that they would receive visitors from a very distant country. They were powerful men with different customs. Their clothes were special and their customs could surprise her.

He explained to Bethany that they were from the desert regions.

"The country of the camels, grandpa?" Old Worthgold laughed a lot at the naive child's description. Bethany was only nine years old.

"Well, I believe that our Arab friends, would not like to think that way about their country."

"Why not? Camels are very beautiful animals. And useful. I studied about them at school."

"You are very smart, dear. Now go get ready, so they know that we also have princesses in our country."

Bethany kissed her grandfather and followed the nanny. She was very obedient. She did not care about Arab customs, because for her, her grandfather was the real prince.

FIRST SIGHT

Past:

"Where are you taking that bird, girl?"

Bethany looked and saw the young boy who was staring at her with curiosity. He must have been about ten years old. She was nine. She did not recognize him from the surroundings, but her grandfather had warned her about foreign visitors.

However, this boy was not wearing different clothes, as her grandfather had suggested. He was wearing jeans and a T-shirt.

"I will release the bird in those trees to see if it can already fly. It had injured the wing and I fed it for a while until it got better."

"Nonsense. The bird will not make it. I am Omar, son of Mohamed al Maliq." He was very proud of his father, who was the sheik of his tribe. It was the equivalent of a king's position in a monarchical country.

"I'm Bethany. Do you want to go with me?"

"Let's go."

And from then on, while the visit lasted, they walked together everywhere, while the heads of their families were together closing deals.

When they reached the trees, Bethany put the bird down and said a few words to encourage it to fly.

Omar, beside her, watched in silence.

Then he was taken by surprise when, for the first time in his life, he heard Bethany sing. She had that gift. In a soft and charming voice, she managed to transmit calm and joy.

The little bird seemed to have felt all this energy coming from the girl because it had stirred a little and flew.

It was as if the bird had received vital fuel. It flew high and far away.

The girl raised both arms in a happy waving of goodbyes.

All her gestures were delicate and matched with the music she continued to sing.

Bethany surrendered to the moment and did not realize that Omar was also supplied with all those feelings. Something moved very deep in the boy´s soul and connected him to her in that inexplicable way that happens to some people, even though they are not even fully aware of it.

"The little bird did it, did you see it?" She addressed him, smiling broadly. Her stare was deep and true.

Although too young to know this, they would become husband and wife, respected and beloved leaders of the Al Maliq tribe.

Chapter 2 - A sea of sand

Now:

Some tourists claim to know the desert. They spend two weeks sunbathing by the swimming pools with extravagant shapes, found in several luxury hotels, and think they have become Bedouins. But the Bedouins are nomadic peoples of the desert, who move rudimentary through the sands as far as the eye can see, under a scorching sun.

Their survival depends on a lot of resistance to difficulties, the ability to defend themselves against dangers, and the capacity to face a sea of sand.

Bethany would never have the vanity to declare that she knew the desert, because she lived a life of luxuries and riches, protected from the least discomfort anyone could imagine.

She thought it was foolish to declare herself an expert in the desert, as it would be as if, after watching some dance performances, she declared herself a ballerina. You don't become something, just by looking at it. Great efforts, adaptations, and a huge amount of talent are needed.

And those qualities, Bethany recognized in the people who traveled with her, in that caravan heading south. Their sun-tanned cheeks spoke of a tan acquired with great hardships, in the drudgery of life, far from beaches and pools.

These people had searching eyes as if they expected to face danger at any moment. Their survival instincts led them to act with caution. Everything was very well calculated, from the routes to follow, to the quantities of water and food to be consumed.

So, when Bethany received a smile from one of these people, she felt all the sincerity and kindness it contained.

Some people traveled as a family, in groups formed by couples, or brothers and even parents and children. But in the caravan that Scott had arranged to transport his sister and her baby, there were no children. The distance to be covered was very large and the difficulties, which could be overcome by adults, were perhaps extreme for a child.

Not to mention the many dangers that these travelers had been through before.

So Bethany took great care of her son Benjamin. She tried to wrap him up well, to keep him hydrated and away from very noisy activities, such as hammering stakes at dusk, to set up the tents in the improvised camp.

But wherever Bethany moved, she felt her brother Scott's watchful eye and that gave her security and comfort.

On one of the first nights of the long journey, Scott had approached his sister and brought a young woman, whom he introduced to her.

"Bethany, this is Adjia. I hired her to accompany you and the baby during our trip."

"It's not necessary, Scott."

"She speaks our language. She is nineteen and is traveling with her parents and two brothers. When we reach our destination, Adjia will marry a well-known fabric merchant."
"Ah, you are engaged. Nice to meet you, Adjia."
"The pleasure is all mine, madam."
"You can call me Bethany. This beautiful sleeper here is Benjamin. He is a year and a half."
"He's a beautiful baby."
"I will leave you two talking, while I go to get us some water." Scott walks away.
"Don't you prefer to travel with your family, Adjia?"
"No, madam. The boys are messy and don't leave me alone."
"How old are they?"
"Amin is fifteen and Haidar is seventeen."
"So you are the oldest?"
"Yes madam."
"You're not going to call me Bethany, are you?"
"No, madam."
The two women exchange sweet smiles and Adjia is no longer so nervous about their meeting. She recognizes kindness in Bethany's eyes.

ANOTHER KIND LOOK
Past:

Bethany was a cheerful child. She lived in a mansion, had beautiful clothes and an enormous amount of toys.
At school, she lived surrounded by little friends who could not resist her sense of humor and creativity. She invented creative games that were a mixture of paintings, magic tricks, and puzzles. Everyone could participate. She had a generous heart.
On her birthday, which was always celebrated at school, because her grandfather was very busy and traveled frequently, her friends were the ones who got gifts.
Bethany had a nanny, Lucy, who had stayed with her even after she was no longer a baby. Lucy provided the cake and decorations for her parties, checked her school supplies so they were always in

order, and helped her with small feminine tasks, like braiding her hair or choosing what to wear.

Bethany obtained her grandfather's consent, which was given with pleasant laughter, and Lucy went to buy toy trucks and dolls for the child's friends. They were like birthday favors and were very pleasing to the children.

Naturally, on arriving home after the party, Bethany found her own birthday present. A pony or a dollhouse in the garden, custom made for the size of Bethany, who sat at the toy table and served an imaginary tea to Lucy and a dozen dolls.

All of this contributed to her happy and healthy childhood, but there were moments of sadness, caused by her mother's visits.

The arrival was always cheerful. Bethany ran into her arms and received many kisses and hugs. She even slept on her mother's lap and the patient butler took her to her own bed, when her mother, Michelle, signaled him.

Her grandfather was out of sight on those visiting days.

Bethany did not complain, because her mother participated in all of her childhood activities. They strolled together in the garden looking for insects, gave names to all her dolls, and Bethany was even allowed to skip school to be with her mother.

These visits took place throughout Bethany's entire life since she was a baby. That is why she already knew that when her mother's face started to get very serious and sad, the time to leave was near. She tried hard to tell jokes and cheer her mother, but she realized that the smiles she got on those occasions were not natural.

The mother started to explain something about being together one day and the child did not understand well, after all, they were together now.

Michelle told her that everything depended on the 'lawyers' and the child feared these men because the mother spoke in a very serious tone.

Then the day of departure would come and it was always very traumatic. Bethany clung to her mother, who did not hide her sadness, sobbing and promising to return soon.

The butler, the chauffeur, and some security guards always had to separate the two of them, who were hugging and crying. When they were finally able to place the child in Lucy´s arms and Michelle in the car that would take her outside the mansion, the child's cries could be heard from a good distance.

In those moments, caused every three or four months during the visits, Bethany was inconsolable. She sensed something bad about the situation, but she couldn't understand what it was.

Not even Lucy could cheer her up. Bethany sat huddled and quiet until Mrs. Longsmith, feeling very moved, approached the child. She was the housekeeper of the mansion and because she was elderly, she did not follow the games with running around in the garden, as Lucy did.

But she always offered the child sweets and juices and told many stories from fairy tales. She was like a grandmother to the child, who corresponded her love.

Mrs. Longsmith, only on those occasions, would put Bethany in her lap, and more than offering explanations and solutions, which she did not have, she listened to the child's outburst. Bethany told her about her fears and pains. She always asked Mrs. Longsmith to talk to her mother and ask Michelle to live in the mansion.

The housekeeper rocked the child, kissed her hair, and promised that everything would be fine.

Somehow, Bethany looked at her intently and believed in her promises.

Because Mrs. Longsmith had a look of kindness.

Chapter 3 - Panic in the palace

Now:

The sheik Omar Sahid al Maliq's palace was imposing and sumptuous. Inheritance of a wealthy family for generations, it had been modernized by the current sheik, providing all the comforts that money can buy.

Its facade was imposing and impressive, however, it showed all the charms of a building made to shelter dreams.

The walls were of an almost shining white, in undulating lines, common to Arabian taste, and rose to great heights until they gave way to towers and ceilings of gold.

On the main dome, a flag with the family's coat of arms identified who the majestic palace belonged to.

There were more than two hundred rooms spread over several floors. All the expensive furniture attested to the good taste of its owner.

After three weeks of business travel, the sheik approached his valuable property. He was proud of his possessions and all he had achieved.

But he was absolutely convinced that his most valuable asset was in the palace's master suite. His wife Bethany.

She was the cause of his breathing, the reason for his joy, and the fuel that moved him. He loved her passionately and showed that love at all times. There was electricity between them that lit up a room.

The sheik's magnetism found equal strength in his wife's personality. The woman who made him happy and presented him with his son, Benjamin al Maliq, heir to his kingdom, his power, and all his material possessions.

When he thought of the baby, Omar's smile expanded. The son was beautiful, which was natural, given his lineage of royalty and the stunning beauty of Bethany. But the boy also proved to be very smart for his age. From an early age, he recognized his father and jumped into his arms, making Omar proud and happy.

Bethany sometimes laughed at her husband's comments, "Look, Bethany. Ben follows your movements with his eyes.

"He is probably hungry, Omar."

"Ben is an observer. Our son will move the world."

"He has already moved my world, for sure."

"And you have moved mine, Bethany." While saying this, the sheik approaches the wife and kisses her lips softly.

"Do you want to give me the boy, Omar? I will get him to sleep."

"No. Today Prince Benjamin goes to sleep listening to the stories of his ancestors." And the sheik sat in a comfortable armchair, with the sleepy baby in his arms. For about ten minutes he told stories of kingdoms and adventures. Then he was silent because his wife was lodged at his feet and when Bethany saw the request in the eyes of her husband, she started to sing a beautiful lullaby. It lulled the boy to sleep and filled the man's heart.

The three-week trip had been too long for him. But his uncle had insisted on his presence and prolonged his stay abroad, creating a series of problems. This had irritated Omar, who was determined to take serious action on his relative's attitude.

But at the moment, he didn't want to think about it. His arms almost ached from the need to hug Bethany.

He hurried up to the royal quarters, only to find them empty of the beloved presences. The servants, when questioned, looked confused and terrified. They just answered his questions about his wife's whereabouts, with a confused 'I don't know'.

It was unacceptable. Tired of the incompetent people, Omar went to interrogate his butler Amin, since he had been requested by the sheik, to manage the needs of Bethany and the baby.

Omar was blunt because he felt irritated again.

"Where are Bethany and the baby, Amin?"

"They ran away, my lord."

The sound of shattered objects thrown at the walls and the sheik's violent screams were heard throughout the palace.

This increased the panic that had settled in the place since Bethany's escape.

There would be harsh consequences for those involved in this situation.

A LINE OF CAMELS

Now:

Scott had stayed at the end of the line to watch his group traveling at a slow pace since the heat was too much. He followed a group of about thirty people, well organized for the long march to the final destination. Some of them cooked, others set up camp. About ten fighters always traveled with the group, in case of an attack to plunder.

There were highwaymen on these roads. They lived on it and were merciless. They had been vomited from the society of the surrounding villages, due to their inability to live with others. They were noisy, disheveled, and had a rotten odor. It was never pleasant to meet such a bunch.

But Scott was prepared for everything. Very accustomed to these trips, there were no surprises for him. He prepared for eventualities. His sharp mind played a game, the prize of which was survival in this hostile world.

He always sent three men ahead two days in advance. But it had already happened that these scouts had died up ahead and the villains had caught up with their group, which was marching towards them, without knowing it. He had won hand-to-hand combat in those past fights, but it was more exhausting.

Scott had now improved his strategy. The scouts left two days ahead, but after one day, one of them came back. Two kept going. They took turns with a fourth man who hurried forward while the first one rested. One of those two must be getting back by then. In this way, he always had two scouts ahead and every day one had to be back.

That way they would know that not every scout had been killed upfront. If no one returned within that time, they would deviate from the route.

It was a game. Almost foolproof. But, of course, there were always surprises. That was what gave commercial trips an extra flavor, apart from the profits they provided. It kept Scott alert and happy.

But not this time. His cargo was too precious. His sister and nephew were worth everything to him.

In this trip, all precautions were taken, both for the way ahead and for the possibility of being followed.

He didn't believe an attack was possible, he was surrounded by people he confided in.

Scott had fighters of the highest skills and friends who would give their lives for him, as he would for them. Many were related to each other, cousins and uncles who had become accustomed since childhood to fight together and protect themselves.

Even so, Scott did not risk letting his guard down. This wasn't a trip on which he was going to rest much. He would sleep on some other occasion. He never thought about the possibility of dying on the way. He was a winner. And a survivor.

But even surrounded by the best fighters, his sister traveled anonymously. Scott did not want the fact that the sheik's runaway wife traveled with them to spread widely.

She was hidden in the wagon, during the journey, and in the tents furthest from the main group, at night. She also wore simpler clothes, which somewhat disguised her royal posture.

On this trip, for personal contact with Bethany and her baby, Scott had chosen only four or five people, of his highest trust.

Chapter 4 – A girl with a dream

Past:

Michelle Clarkson was a very pretty girl. She worked at the municipal library during the day and went to study business administration at the School of Commerce at night.
She was punctual and organized at work. Her love for books showed, in her indications to the library members, that often asked for her opinions. Michelle also got good grades at school.
She was working hard and educating herself because she had a dream. Mainly it consisted of leaving her home, because her parents drank a lot, the house was always a mess and the shouting and cursing were constant there.
Fortunately, she was never beaten by them because the parents entertained themselves hitting each other. Many times, Michelle had to clean their mess after they had broken furniture and glasses and went to the bedroom or the nearest sofa for a drunken slumber. She was used to it since it had been happening her whole life, nonetheless it made her sad.
When she saw families hugging in the park, or showing interest in what one was saying to the other, she was sure she was never going to have that with her parents.
Her neighbor was a retired teacher and gave her a lot of good books. Michelle absorbed ideas from great people that had overcome challenges as sickness or poverty.
Abraham Lincoln, Marie Curie, Martin Luther King and Thomas Edson became role models for her. She talked to the old teacher and asked her if, in the current days, success could be obtained, as it was shown in those biographies. The teacher said yes. And the formula was the same, work and studies.
So Michelle made her plan and was living it. She was saving money from a job that she loved and she studied business administration. Her first step would be to get a place for herself, even a room in some boarding house would suffice. Then, with skills from her college education, she would try to find a position in some store and work hard to become a manager in the long run.

This would make it possible for her to think of having her own family someday because she loved kids.

She often read stories for some kids weekly at the library in her free time.

Michelle was really a good girl and life seemed to be rewarding her efforts, after her harsh start in a difficult family.

A BUSINESSMAN

When Tom White entered the library and asked Michelle´s help to find some books about international trade, she didn´t think much about it.

Many business people used the library and she was used to seeing well-dressed men. She found him handsome and polite, but it was a normal thing. The only difference was the way he talked to her when he was living, "Thanks, sugar. See you tomorrow."

Michelle´s attention was caught by the intimate way he said that. As if he was asking her on a date. And she liked when he called her sugar. Michelle was not used to compliments, she never even heard the tender words that most children hear from their parents. The guys at school also didn´t flirt with her, because she always dressed with simplicity and wore no makeup. She didn´t have any time or money for vanity, while other girls who were surrounded by suiters seemed to have both.

Then, being realistic due to a lifetime of disappointments, she concluded that he said that because he didn´t know her name. It made sense and calmed down her accelerated heart a little.

But the next day brought new compliments and a rose. It was the first one she had ever received, even being already nineteen.

"Hey, beautiful. Can you help me find some more books?"

"Sure, Mr. White." His name was on the library card.

"Call me Tom, please. I am not that old at twenty-six, am I?"

"Of course not, Tom."

This went on for a week and then, when Tom had finished his book search he asked Michelle to go out for a coffee.

During this first date, Tom said beautiful and pleasant things to her. She was soon infatuated with him. He courted her for a month, taking her out every day after school. She even missed some classes which got her teachers worried. One of them even had a talk with her to check if everything was alright. But she assured the teacher that it was just a schedule conflict and nothing else.

Because she had a great memory and a quick mind, the teachers always encouraged and helped her. Everybody believed she was going to achieve her goals of success because she was not shy in sharing her dreams of a better life. Many students talked about their reason for doing this course and their choices for the future.

A DIFFERENT DREAM COMES FIRST

When Tom kissed her mouth for the first time, he noticed that Michelle was very inexperienced and he made her tell him the truth. In fact, it was her first kiss. Instead of being disappointed like she thought he would be, he changed his words from sugar and sweetie to my love.

She was surprised and delighted. Michelle loved Tom with all her heart now. And not only because he had showered her with flowers, nice chocolate, and beautiful dresses. It was more because of his intent look and tender words. She believed in everything he said and every promise he made.

Soon their dreams were the same. Basically, get married, have kids, and open a business together. He had a great amount of money to invest because he had saved during some years working with import-export trades.

Six months had passed since their first encounter and Tom already knew all about her troubles at home. One day, when she was feeling down, after a violent scene at home, he suggested that they got away from all this.

Michelle instantly said yes. She thought he was proposing to her. Then he was celebrating her decision with kisses and telling her that he would buy the tickets for their trip and she was too embarrassed to change her mind.

On the way to a tropical island, Michelle confessed to herself that she was happy about her decision. She saw no problem in inverting the things a little because she was sure that after this honeymoon, they would soon be getting married.

In fact, this trip was for Michelle, a glimpse of what a good life could be. She felt so important when she entered the airplane. Tom was holding her hand the whole time but she was not afraid. She felt as if she was inside a dream. She sat by the window and looked at the city from a distance. Everything looked so peaceful from up there, that it was almost impossible to imagine that inside of one of those tiny houses she was seeing, her parents were destroying objects and trying to kill each other.

At the island she walked in the white sands and entered the crystal-clear waters of the Atlantic Ocean, feeling blessed for having Tom in her life.

The hotel was very beautiful and shining. Their bedroom smelled of flowers and the sheets were clean and soft.

Michelle learned all about love on that island and it became her favorite place in the world.

When they returned home, they kept seeing each other, and she spent many nights in his apartment. Tom convinced her to do that, after buying her an engagement ring. It was a simple one, but worth everything to her because it was a symbol of their love and a promise of future happiness.

Three months after their sort of honeymoon trip, Michelle was holding the test that confirmed her pregnancy.

Chapter 5 – Starting a family

Past:

Tom had not been as excited as Michelle imagined he would be when she told him about the baby.

"Tom, don´t you want to be a father?"

"Of course, I want to be a father, sugar. It is just that I didn´t expect it to happen so soon."

Tom had gone back to calling her 'sugar', after their trip. She really didn´t mind it that much, it is just that Michelle missed hearing him call her 'his love'. Tom had never said the complete sentence to her anyway. Maybe after the baby was born, he would find the perfect occasion to say: 'I love you'. She expected fervently for that.

"I think this is the perfect time for us to start a family, Tom."

"And you may be right. It is not that I don´t want to. The truth is that I had plans for us."

"What plans?"

"I was thinking that we could travel the world for a couple of years. I wanted to show you some romantic places, and now, with the baby coming, it will have to be postponed."

"Oh, Tom. You are the best. Maybe we can still do it before the baby is born. I mean, I am only at the beginning of my pregnancy, so we still have some months to enjoy ourselves. If we get married now, we can travel on our honeymoon."

"That is a great idea, sugar. The perfect solution."

The next morning, Tom was surprised to witness how nauseous the pregnancy had made Michelle. She rushed to the bathroom with just enough time to throw up there, instead of making a mess in the bedroom.

Tom looked thoughtful while he watched her dealing with her morning sickness because she didn´t have time to even close the bathroom door.

Luckily, she was feeling better when Tom left her at work. During her lunch break, Michelle bought the first clothes for their baby and she could hardly wait to show them to Tom.

He didn´t appear to pick her up after work and as she was riding the bus to her parents´ house, Michelle thought she should ask Tom about the possibility to move to his place for good. Soon her belly would show and she wasn´t sure what her parents´ reaction would be since she was still single.

When she called him after dinner, the call went straight to voicemail. Two more days passed without any word from Tom, but Michelle was not one of those undecided people who would wait indefinitely. She took a bus after work and went straight to his apartment.

The doorman was very polite and answered her questions patiently.

"He doesn´t live here anymore."

"It is impossible. We were together at his apartment here just a couple of days ago."

"Right. He moved away this morning."

"Are you sure we are talking about the same person? It is Tom White, from apartment 506, the one that I am looking for."

"That´s him, all right."

"I thought he owned the place."

"No, madam. It was a rental. I have the keys with me. Do you want to take a look?"

Michelle accepted that kindness and went to take a look. There must be a simple explanation. Someone was making some kind of joke or maybe it was only a mistake.

But when she opened the door, Michelle saw the empty place and she felt like a complete fool, for the first time since she had met Tom.

She walked slowly from room to room, allowing herself to grasp the reality.

And very similar to those rooms, she also was feeling empty.

A SMALL BEDROOM AT THE BACK

Michelle had to be practical, so she dropped night school and got herself a second job, waiting tables at a restaurant near the library.

She saved all the money she could because she knew that after the baby was born she wouldn't be able to take the night shift.

The things at her parents' house were worse than before. Now they took pleasure in calling her names. Michelle tried to hide her pregnancy for as long as she could. Then, they said she was gaining so much weight for being lazy which was not true since Michelle did all the housework and they only kept drinking heavily and slept most of the time.

Her dad had a pension that he received due to an injury in his arm, that had happened ages ago at his old job. It was the perfect excuse for him to never return to work. Her mother cleaned houses when she was in the mood for it, but as soon as she had enough money to buy booze, she would join her husband in doing nothing.

Those facts were reason enough for Michelle to decide to move out of their house. She didn't want her baby to grow in a place like that.

When she was six months pregnant, Michelle found a small bedroom with an adjoining tiny bathroom at the back of an old lady's house. She felt glad to be able to afford it and did her best to make it look cozy for her baby. She glued drawings of birds and flowers on the walls and hung a curtain with sunflowers design on the window.

When baby Scott was born, Michelle had organized her life to be able to show him how much he was loved.

Their place was clean, their food was healthy and she stayed with him for nights and weekends.

Michelle had found a decent daycare center near her work and all in all, she considered herself lucky.

Scott was already one year and a half old and there was happiness in his life and in the life of his mother.

AROUND THE WORLD

Michelle received postcards from beautiful places around the world. They were from Egypt, Morocco, Greece, France, and Italy. There were a couple from Mexico and one from Brazil.

The postcards were all from Tom. Also, they were always sent to the library, as if he knew that Michelle could not have stayed with her parents during her pregnancy.

It made her confused because a man who abandons his pregnant girlfriend, usually doesn't send cards. And it was not as if she could keep in touch with him because there was never a return address on those cards.

Michelle didn't know what to make of it. She had a slight impression that he was only showing off. It seemed to be his manner to make it clear to her that Michelle had missed out on all this fun when she got pregnant.

But Tom was an intelligent man. He had to know that she didn't do it on purpose. He had been the experienced one in their relationship, and since she never blamed him for anything, Michelle sure hoped that he didn't blame her as well.

Because she didn't have anyone to talk to about these things, Michelle decided to do what she considered to be the best for herself and her baby. She put it in the back of her mind. She would not suffer unnecessarily trying to give meaning to things that she didn't understand at all.

And her life followed in a comfortable rhythm. Michelle liked to work. And Scott provided her with infinite love.

Being with him gave her the energy and strength to face the struggles of life. She knew that some people were in worse situations than herself.

LARGE APARTMENT

Then one day, out of the blue Tom came back. He marched into the library where Michelle worked, making a lot of noise about his woman and their baby.

Michelle was so surprised to see him that she couldn't say a word. Tom hugged her tight and took her outside the library to give her a long kiss.

"Tom, it is crazy. I can't just go out like that. This is the place where I work, you know."

"You will just have to quit. Where is our baby?"

"Scott? He is at the daycare."

"You named him Scott… I like it. Scott White, it is."

Then he insisted that they should go immediately to pick up the baby at the daycare center. Michelle gave some lame excuse to her boss, grabbed her purse, and followed Tom to his brand-new sports Mercedes Benz car.

When Tom saw the baby, he said all the right words about his son. He mentioned how handsome he was, how intelligent he looked and he added that Michelle had done a nice job with raising Scott so far due to the fact that he was a happy and healthy baby.

"I think he looks just like me." Tom had a big smile as he held Scott close to his face.

"Yes, Tom. He really does."

After that, Tom took Michelle and the baby to a very large and modern apartment downtown. The furniture was new and expensive, also the place had a jacuzzi among other comforts.

But what certainly made Michelle's heart skip a beat was the room specially prepared for Scott. It looked like those beautiful rooms, that you only see in furniture magazines.

"You can buy anything else that you think is necessary, Michelle," Tom said that as he lay Scott, who was sleeping by now, on the crib.

"It is perfect, Tom."

And Michelle finally dropped the barrier that she had built to protect her hurt feelings and walked slowly to the man she loved, giving him a long passionate kiss on his thirsty mouth.

Tom reacted immediately, picking Michelle up and taking her to the suite bedroom, where he showed her how much he had missed her. She hardly got any sleep that night, then when the morning breeze started to move the silk curtains and the sunlight touched her face, she woke up to the view of his wonderful bedroom, wondering if she was still sleeping.

After checking on the baby, she heard Tom singing in the kitchen, but decided to take a shower before joining him for breakfast.

Michelle was delighted to find a pink robe for her in the closet and thought that she had to pick up her clothes and Scott's at their old room.

When she entered the kitchen, Tom was reading the newspaper and eating pancakes. He kissed her on the lips and poured her some coffee, while she started her meal by eating fruits.

"I was wondering if you could take me to pick up my things after breakfast. If you are not busy, I mean. Otherwise, I can leave Scott at the daycare and bring my stuff here by cab."

"Of course I can take you. And I don't know if you agree, Michelle, but I would much rather have you take care of our baby."

"It is what I most want."

"So, no more daycare for Scott?"

"Certainly not."

"And you must quit working because I can for sure provide for my family."

Michelle felt warm and cozy when she heard him referring to them as his family. Deep down she knew that they should discuss his attitude in the past. Tom had abandoned her when she was pregnant, and it was not a sign of good character.

But she was so happy now and Tom was in such a great mood that she was afraid to cause unnecessary stress. After all, things had worked out just fine. He seemed to have overcome his fears of commitment. If Tom had flaws, Michelle was aware that she was not perfect either.

After they finished eating, Tom gave her some papers to sign and for a brief moment, Michelle thought they were marriage papers.

"This is a rental contract for this apartment."

"It is indeed. You see, Michelle, I thought you would like me to prove to you how much I am investing in this relationship. Therefore, you sign these papers, knowing that I have valued you and made you take part in our decision-making."

"But you decided everything without asking me."

"I am sorry that you feel that way. We can always choose another place. Give me the papers. It is no big deal."

She saw in his face that Tom was hurt. And because it was really not a big deal, she signed the papers without saying another word. And Tom had a perfect taste, so the place was great, after all.

Chapter 6 – The beloved not-husband

Past:
Michelle was really living her dream. Since she had quit her job, it was possible for her to spend much of her time taking care of Scott and enjoying her new home. Some nights she would get a babysitter to stay with the baby because Tom insisted that they went out to clubs and restaurants.

Mrs. Chairtall was a nice old lady very experienced with babies and Scott seemed to like her, so Michelle was able to enjoy her nights out with Tom. They went to many different restaurants and tried international cuisine as well as local food.

She also enjoyed their talks, mainly because Tom was very optimistic about their future and quite often he would mention that they were headed to become very rich.

"What is your work about, Tom? I still don´t understand exactly what you do."

"It is too hard for you to understand, pumpkin."

"You could try to explain it to me, Tom. I used to do a business course, remember?"

"Have you finished?"

"No. I couldn´t finish the course."

"Just as I told you, don´t worry about these matters. A dropout like you couldn´t even start to understand the complexity of my trade."

That comment hurt Michelle´s feelings so much that she almost told him that the reason that she had quit school was to take care of his baby when Tom had abandoned them. But she decided that it wasn´t worth picking out a fight with him. They were at a very nice small restaurant and she was looking forward to trying their dessert since it was highly recommended by the chef´s guide magazine. So Michelle took a sip of her drink and continued the conversation normally, without placing blame for the past.

"I got your postcards. Is your work about import-export?"

He looked at her and said nothing. She sensed that he was furious now because he pushed his dish away and started to tear the paper napkin into small pieces very slowly. Then Tom said to her in a disdainful manner, "You sleep all day, then you don't value relaxing moments as I do."

"It is not fair, Tom. I take care of Scott. Also, I have the house chores and the cooking."

"How important you make yourself sound. I couldn't agree less. You and the baby sleep a lot and we have a washing machine among other devices that allow you to lead the life of a princess."

She didn't know what to say because she had not even complained about her lifestyle, to begin with. Michelle had only tried to show interest in his work and somehow it seemed to have offended him severely. Tom was standing up and leaving some bills at the table, so Michelle didn't have any choice other than follow him to the car.

"I am sorry, Tom."

"If I hear one more word from you, you will just walk home. I mean it. Don't try my patience even for one minute longer."

Because Michelle was used to her parents' verbal abuse for years, she recognized that Tom was behaving just like them and it went beyond reasoning. What she couldn't understand was the reason for that because somehow she had always linked this attitude with heavy drinking. They had ordered soft drinks for dinner and in fact, one of the things that Michelle had always appreciated about Tom was that he rarely drank alcohol.

When they arrived in their apartment, Mrs. Chairtall was surprised to see them back so early.

"I have just put Scott in his crib. He ate well and played a lot with his teddy bear."

"That is nice. Thank you, Mrs. Chairtall."

"You are welcome. Did you enjoy your night out? It is still early."

"We could have enjoyed the night if Michelle wasn't such a blabbermouth," By saying that, Tom made the babysitter very uncomfortable at the same time that he made Michelle feel humiliated. They were not expecting his complaint and Mrs. Chairtall grabbed her things as quickly as she could, while Michelle managed to get some money in a nearby drawer to pay her before she left in a haste.

Michelle went to check on the baby and his peaceful face gave her the courage to go to her bedroom. She would rather sleep on the couch, at least for tonight, but maybe it would make things worse.

She tiptoed to the couple's room and after using the bathroom to brush her teeth and change into comfortable pajamas, she laid by Tom's side and turned her back on him. Maybe he would apologize in the morning.

"Michelle…"

"What?"

"What I said in the car still holds. If I hear another word from you tonight, even if it is a talk from your sleep, I will kick you out of this bedroom."

"Okay."

"That is one word. Now, are you trying to make me mad?" He was holding her face by now and his other arm made her turn completely in a way that her body was facing his.

Then she moved her head from side to side, assuring him that she didn't mean to upset him.

"Better. Now show me something that you are good at."

And to her complete disbelief, he proceeded to make love to her, as if they were on the best terms ever.

But Michelle knew that love had nothing to do with this act.

MORNING SONG

Tom always woke up in a good mood. He was singing while he prepared breakfast. Michelle took some moments to consider her situation.

Not much had changed really. She had a nice roof over her head and good clothes and food for herself and Scott. But in a way, she missed their old little bedroom.

She had not suffered violence from Tom. In fact, he had been as passionate as ever. But she couldn't help finding him selfish and offensive.

Maybe she had expected too much from him. It was as if she wanted him to live a movies-love story with her.

But now she had to confess to herself that she didn't love him too. Michelle could arrive at that stage of her feelings. She had even started to love him, but he made it too hard for her to see him through pink glasses when he didn´t share his life with her. And the reason for that was that he considered her a stupid person, a school dropout.

And it hurt even more because she really wanted to have finished school. Maybe she still could, if Mrs. Chairtall could stay with Scott for school nights.

This gave her hope. Michelle stood up, took her shower then went to the kitchen where Tom was feeding Scott some baby food.

"Good morning, sugar."

"Good morning, Tom."

"I have an appointment with my accountant for lunch, so don´t wait for me."

"Right."

"Also, remember to pick up my clothes at the dry cleaners. I am starting to think that you are getting lazy."

She thought it was better not to answer that. It was just like her parents.

"I am joking, sugar. It is a joke. Are you becoming uptight, now?"

"No, Tom. I know some jokes if you are in the mood for that."

"Maybe later, sugar. I gotta go now. How about we order some pizza and have a movie night, just the two of us?"

"Sure. Have a nice day."

"You too." And Tom gave a quick kiss on her lips as well as a kiss on Scott´s forehead and left whistling happily.

MOVIE NIGHT

While Tom laughed his heart out watching a slapstick comedy movie, Michelle kept a half-hearted smile on her face.

When she thought of their situation, now that reality had hit her in the face, she had to recognize that they led a strange life. Tom never introduced her to any of his friends and Michelle, in turn, didn´t have any friends, to begin with.

She was sure that Tom had friends because he went bowling and golfing almost every week. Once she had asked to go along but he said it was a guy´s thing, so she didn´t insist. Mainly because Tom took her out a lot too. It is only that it was always the two of them and even if it was enough to content her, still she couldn´t help but imagine if this situation would be ideal when Tom got a little older.

Even for simple things, she couldn't think of a solution yet. For instance, who would they invite to Scott's birthday parties? Would Scott never experience barbecues at the park with a group of family and friends? Michelle certainly never had, but she wished a different life for her son.

She knew that he would have his school friends, but still… It seemed to her that as a mother, she should make a bigger effort at socializing, in order for her son to benefit from it.

Tom put his feet on her lap, implying that he wanted a massage, as sometimes he did. Michelle started to caress his feet and he turned to her in a great mood.

"If this guy falls again I will just write the director to congratulate him. It is the funniest movie I have ever seen."

Michelle looks at the screen just in time to see the actor taking a huge fall from a chair and spill food all around him.

"See, Michelle? I told you. What a great movie."

His laughter is so contagious that she joins him. Then, when the movie finishes because she senses that Tom is so relaxed, Michelle brings up one of the things that were on her mind.

"You know, Tom, I was thinking to go back to school. The beginning of the semester is in two weeks. So, if I can arrange things with Mrs. Chairtall, maybe I will be able to do it."

Tom stares at her. He pulls his feet from her lap and sits up straight. Michelle starts to worry about his reaction and she corrects herself.

"It was just one idea, Tom. Don't worry."

He has a big smile now.

"Michelle, it is a great idea."

"Do you think so?"

"Of course I think so, sugar. I believe you can do it."

"I will plan everything, Tom. It shouldn't interfere with the way things are working right now."

"I agree."

"It will only take an extra effort from me. I will wake one hour earlier to do school work. And I will sleep one hour later on the weeks of the tests. If the baby ever gets sick, I will just skip school that day. What do you think, Tom?"

"I like your enthusiasm. Now come here. We must celebrate it."

He sits her on his lap and kisses her with passion. She is marveled by his positive reaction and she shows her gratitude by retributing his kisses until they are both out of breath.

Michelle was so happy that she had found a solution for their tension. In the end, he really needed her to show some initiative towards the improvement of their life together. After all, he had given her clues that he thought she needed to improve her education. Michelle was glad that she could take the hint since he was just too considerate to say it straight to her face.

Every couple had a period of adjusting to do. When they knew each other better, they wouldn't have to endure such stress anymore. It would take a little longer than these few months they were together, but Michelle was patient. She wanted to do the best for Scott, Tom, and herself. She would start by trying to be a better wife.

When Tom took her to their bedroom it was a repetition of their first night there because Michelle didn't have more than few minutes of sleep. He showed her how much he wanted her, and he did it all night long.

The next day, Michelle didn't get up before lunchtime. Tom had said that she should sleep and he would take care of Scott.

"Wake me up if you need me, Tom."

He kissed her mouth and left the bedroom. Michelle went into a deep sleep and wasn't sure if Tom had entered their bedroom to get some of his clothes or if it was just a dream. After a long and relaxing hot shower, Michelle went to the kitchen to eat something and was delighted to find Mrs. Chairtall taking care of Scott. It was really considerate of Tom since she was feeling tired from last night and could use some help. Moreover, it would give her the possibility to discuss a new schedule with Mrs. Chairtall.

"Good morning, Mrs. Chairtall. I am glad to see you."

"Me too, dear. Scott has already eaten and I will take him to the park for a while if that is okay."

"Sure. It is perfect."

"Oh, before I forget. Mr. White left you this note."

Michelle was smiling when the babysitter left the apartment. She thought this love note was tom's way of showing the older woman that he cared for his wife, even though he had been rude the other night.

But instead of love words, Michelle read there: 'Out on a work trip. See you later, sugar.'

He was gone for almost three months. All Michelle got from him were the usual postcards.

She never returned to school.

Chapter 7 – Adjusting to the new life

Past:

When Tom returned from his trip, Michelle still expected some explanation or apology from him. But he offered none, acting as if he had returned from the nearest bakery.

He had toys for Scott and a bracelet for Michelle, but no explanation, whatsoever.

Since she was afraid to anger him, she accepted the situation. Tom was in a good mood and he took Scott to the park almost every day.

"This little guy makes me proud, sugar. He is just like me."

"I am glad to hear that, Tom."

Their new routine was very simple. On most mornings, the proud dad took Scott to the park that was just in front of their apartment. It gave Michelle time to clean the place and prepare their lunch. One thing was for sure, Tom disliked frozen food and for that reason, Michelle avoided it as much as possible. She liked cooking and took pleasure in trying new recipes that she found on the internet.

"You could open a restaurant, sugar. This pasta is superb."

"Do you think we could, Tom?" deep down, Michelle still dreamed of having her own business.

"What?"

"Open a restaurant? Some day?"

"Suuuure. Why not? Pass me the sauce, will you?"

"Tom. Maybe I could join some cooking classes."

"Maybe. Are you going to try that Mexican dish for dinner?"

"Is it okay if I make it for tomorrow night? I have to buy some ingredients yet."

"Even better. Today I feel stuffed. You are going to turn me into a fat guy."

And after saying that, he went to the couch with his plate because he wanted to watch some sports program. Michelle didn't mind being left alone to eat, although she was kind of sad to realize that he didn´t really mean it when he had talked about opening a restaurant. She went to check on Scott, who having eaten earlier, was taking his nap peacefully, unaware of his mother´s disappointments.

"Bring me some ice cream, sugar."

Now that could make him fat. Lazing on the couch and unable to pick up his own dessert or even a simple cup of coffee. He always preferred to order her around. But Michelle knew that these thoughts came from her resentments, therefore she pushed them aside and took him the ice cream.

"You are the best, sugar."

His words had become meaningless for her since he used compliments to get what he wanted and not because he appreciated Michelle.

In the afternoons, Tom went to work and Michelle had no idea where it was. She once mentioned it to him, "I would like to know where you work. You know, in case of an emergency or something like that."

"In case of an emergency, you can always call me. I never turn off my cell phone."

"Except when you travel."

"That is correct."

"Tom, I want to visit your office."

"I rarely go to the office. I usually meet with clients for drinks or at their companies."

"Why?"

"I am a consultant. It is better if I see what the clients are talking about. So I visit their shops and industries."

Michelle was happy to hear so much about Tom´s work for the first time.

"I thought you were in export-import trade."

"It is one of my areas of work. But I have many talents. Come here and I will show you my best skill."

"Please, Tom. I want to talk to you more."

"And I want you to shut up."

Then he started kissing her, which led to him carrying her to their room and the conversation was dropped for good. She learned that if she brought the subject back later or in the next few days, he would dismiss it by saying, "We have already talked about that."

It was not a bad life and Michelle felt guilty for allowing sad thoughts to enter her mind. The feeling of emptiness was constant in her life and she was always insecure about her clothes or her hair. She put it down to being ungrateful and tried to improve herself. Michelle watched videos on the internet and could learn about the better combination of colors for clothes and what would be adequate for formal events. Her hairdresser also showed her simple ways to do her hair for a night out.

Tom never complimented her on her appearance and when she fished for it, he would often say, "It is only you that I am taking out, not a top model. Now, don't go on all vain on me."

It was not a matter of vanity, it was really all about her self-esteem. Subconsciously, she just stopped asking Tom. However, Michelle kept struggling to improve herself. Deep down she knew that someday she would be in public with Scott, taking him to school or functions. She wanted her son to be proud of her when the occasion arrived.

On many afternoons, Tom didn't go out to work at all. He didn't help Michelle to do laundry or dust the furniture, either. On those days, he just sat down on his favorite armchair and watched his favorite TV series, while eating a lot of snacks.

Mrs. Chairtall still came three or four days a week to babysit Scott while his parents went out dancing or visiting an art exhibition.

This was her new life and Michelle had gotten used to it.

A FEVER

One afternoon, Scott had a high fever that wouldn't go away. Just to be on the safe side, Michelle took him to see the doctor. She had tried to call Tom, but because the call went to voice mail, she messaged him the news, expecting him to pick them up at the pediatric clinic.

The doctor had prescribed some medicine after explaining to Michelle that the fever was due to a sore throat and therefore she didn't have to worry.

When Tom entered the waiting area, Michelle was ready to leave. The receptionist was very kind and polite.

"Have a good day, Mrs. Clarkson. Mr. Clarkson, it was nice to meet you."

Michelle waited for Tom to correct the woman since his name was Tom White. But he just nodded to her and took the baby to the car.

"Why didn´t you say something, Tom? She called you Mr. Clarkson and that is my last name, not yours."

As Tom adjusted the little chair on the backseat of the car, he said absentmindedly, "Ah, she just thought we were married."

After they were all inside the car, Michelle couldn´t stand being quiet about it anymore.

"Do you know what, Tom? I thought we were supposed to be married too. Am I that dumb?"

"You sure aren´t smart."

"What does that mean?"

"Well, dropping out of school and all."

"That again? I don´t get it. So, people who drop out of school aren´t allowed to get married?"

"That is not what I am saying. Listen, why don´t you calm down? You are starting to scare the baby."

That was such a big fat lie. Scott was playing with his baby blanket and looking out of the window with his childish curiosity. And she was not screaming, just talking.

But Michelle decided to take a deep breath and try to calm down a little. Because if there was any truth to what Tom had said was the fact that she was not calm.

She decided to approach the subject from another point of view.

"Tom, don´t you want to marry me?"

"Of course I want, sugar. It is just not a good time, right now."

"Why not?"

"You couldn´t understand it."

"Try me."

"It is just that I want us to have a big wedding. I think of at least two hundred guests. And I can´t afford it right now."

That was a surprise. Michelle thought that men didn´t dream of wedding parties, that it was more of a girl´s thing. But she recognized the prejudice in that idea. As always, she sensed that the core of their problems was that they didn´t know each other that well.

"Sorry, Tom. I didn´t know you felt this way."

"Haven´t you dreamt of a wedding party, sugar?"

"Not really. I was always so poor that I didn´t even have a cake for my birthday."

"Oh, poor thing."

"I am only telling the facts. I don´t indulge in self-pity."

"Of course. But this is one more reason for me to insist that we do it on style."

"Okay. Do we even know two hundred people to invite?"

"Of course we do, sugar. And it will guarantee our place in high society. Don´t you want Scott to have it all?"

"The way I see it, we could start by giving him the minimum necessary for a normal life. Can´t we compromise?"

"How so?"

"We could go to city hall later this week just to officialize things. Later, when we have the money, we throw society a party."

"You know, sugar, this may be the perfect solution.

Michelle felt relieved that at least that was settled.

The next day, while she was at the supermarket, Tom packed his bag and left for over two months.

And Michelle realized that it was his way of making clear that his will should prevail. It would happen in the future again and again. His sudden departures made her lost. There was no way of contacting him. Moreover, there was an implicit threat that Tom could even not return at all.

Chapter 8 – Sunny as can be

Now:

The ride under the desert sun was not an easy one. That is why Habibdul started very early in the morning and had everybody resting when the sun was stronger. That is when the group would eat and rest. He was a strong leader and everybody trusted him.

From experience, he knew that the animals also needed their rest otherwise they would slow their pace. Owners who forced the animals too much could even make them sick or cause their death.

Scott had hired Habibdul services many times in the past. More than that, they were friends and Scott had confided in him about his hurry to arrive at their destination. But it wasn't an easy task since they needed to avoid the main roads used by traders for centuries.

Habibdul knew that soon they would be chased by the Sheik's men, so he had to use his skills to avoid the confrontation. Every night he discussed escape strategies with Scott, who was also an experienced traveler of those lands.

It had been necessary to accept some families to join their group because this would avoid suspicion to arise when they met other caravans, which was impossible to avoid. When caravans met, it was common to exchange provisions, like food, medicine, and water. Many times, the own survival of Bedouins depended on that tradition.

Scott knew as well as Habibdul, that it would take at least two or three weeks to arrive in the South and they were traveling for no more than three days now.

Bethany was resting under the shadow of an improvised tent and Adjia was by her side rocking the baby. Scott approached them and sat by his sister.

"Have you eaten, little sister?"

"I ate some fruit. All this heat makes me lose my appetite."

"But you have to eat more than fruit if you want to keep your strength."

"I know, Scott. I will try harder."

Adjia had entered the cart to give them privacy and also to lay Ben on the soft pillows that were arranged in a box, meant to be used as a crib for him.

"And you, Scott? Have you eaten?"

"Not yet. I was talking to Habibdul about our route. What about sharing some bread?"

As he said that, he took some food out from a bag he had brought to his sister. The rest of the group was either eating or sleeping.

"That is a great idea. I always feel better when you are near us."

"I never lose sight of you, Bethany."

"Thanks. I never wanted to be a burden for you."

"And you are not. You are my only sister and I would do anything to protect you. And Ben."

"What makes me nervous is the thought that by now, Omar has already found out that I ran away with the baby."

"I think so. But we have the lead of a few days. And he doesn't know where we are headed."

"He knows for sure that I didn't leave the country, since he keeps my passport locked in the palace's safe."

"I guess by now, Omar has gathered a searching group with his best-skilled men. The way I see things, you only have one advantage, little sister."

"And what is that, Scott?"

"You have me."

And that was so true. Bethany didn't even want to try to imagine what she would have done without Scott's help.

As her brother offered her some bread, he had a broad smile on his handsome face, and maybe because it reminded her of their adventures as children, Bethany was able to relax a little and smile back at him.

DISTINGUISHED COMPANY

On the next morning, the scout who came back to inform about the way ahead told Habibdul that a group of horse riders was coming their way.

Scott was informed about it immediately.

"Should we deviate or hide?"

"I don't think so, Habibdul. They are coming from the opposite direction from where we ran away. They certainly are not bandits because if that was the case they would not show themselves so openly. They would come down from mountains and attack by surprise."

"That is true, Scott. Outlaws don't just parade themselves in daylight. What did the men look like, Ibrahim?"

"They look distinguished. They look like authorities."

"Probably they are traveling on some official mission. Thanks, Ibrahim. You can go now."

The scout joined his friends and ate some food that had been kept for him from breakfast. They sure took care of each other, in a way of improving the conditions of such a hard lifestyle.

"So, we just meet these strangers and allow them to follow their way, right Scott?"

"Yes, Habibdul. I think it will be a harmless encounter. But if these men are authorities, like diplomats, there is a chance that they know Omar. We will keep my sister always in the cart until they have passed. I don't need them to recognize her and spread the news."

"Maybe they will recognize you too. From your brother-in-law's functions at the palace."

"You are right. I will also stay out of their sight, just as a precaution."

And just as they had foreseen, a very distinguished group of horsemen approached them later. They stayed for a couple of hours and followed their way. Bethany had a glimpse from the cart and seeing their clothes caused a pang to her heart. She couldn't help but remember the first time she had seen the Arabian typical clothes long ago…

DJELLABA AND KEFFIYEH

Past:

As Bethany watched those men ride away looking so distinct, it brought her memories of the first time she had ever seen Omar in those Arabian clothes.

It was on the same day that they had met in her garden, only this time they gathered for a formal dinner her grandpa was offering his guests.

The visitors were dressing the traditional tunic called djellaba and Bethany was glad for grandpa's warnings about it otherwise, she would be open-mouthed the whole time. It gave them such a mysterious look.

And to add to the exotic look, all of them wore a keffiyeh, which is like a scarf over their hair.

She had only seen those on TV and later she learned that it was possible for a man to wear it, even when he chose to dress a traditional west-style suit. It gave a kind of Arabian touch to the look.

There were combinations of colors and mixtures. Red and white, or blue and white was very common.

Except for Sheik Mohamed al Maliq who stood out from the crowd in his all-white vestments and the many jewels that adorned them. He was royalty and he sure looked like it.

Then Bethany saw Omar. The young prince looked like the heroes from the movies Bethany had seen. His robe was all-white too and the keffiyeh on his head was adorned by an emerald.

Their first encounter had left her with the impression that they could be good friends. But this time, when she saw him, Bethany felt a different kind of emotion awakening in her heart. Like some girls have crushes on movie stars, she started to develop a crush on this young man that was being raised for leadership. Omar was to become a powerful and respected sheik in his country.

But right now, Bethany could only grasp the impression of his decided walking and noticed that he was not intimidated to talk to adults at all. Even grandpa Worthgold expressed his admiration for how well Omar behaved.

"This young man certainly leaves no doubt of his intelligence and determination. He shows all signs of royalty."

"I am glad you noticed. My son, the prince Omar, is my successor and I am very proud of him."

"He has a confidence that cannot be taught. Only blood will assure those qualities. I congratulate you, my friend."

"Thank you, Worthgold. When the time arrives for Omar to get a college education, I want him to do it in western countries. The way I see it, we can spread our interests. For generations, our family has profited from petroleum, but I think Omar will be able to diversify our interests to the computer industries or communication business as well."

"That is wise, Sheik Mohamed. You know that I am all in favor of diversification. Also, my last acquisition, as I have already told you, is in the food and drinks industry."

While the adults went on discussing their businesses, Bethany noticed how Omar's hair was as black as a moonless night. His eyes were also black and she found them mysterious.

Due to the fact that she could search his eyes as she pleased, Bethany came to the realization that he was also staring at her. Luckily they were seated across from each other because she felt a need to drink up his image and Omar seemed to be trying to memorize her looks too.

Neither of them felt shy or turned their faces away. They were just too young for that kind of game. So, the dinner was perfect for them to satisfy their curiosity about each other.

Chapter 9 – Financial needs

Past:

Always when Tom left home, it became obvious that he didn't give a second thought to the well-being of Michelle and Scott.

The first time he disappeared was the only time that he left some cash in his desk drawer. And it was just enough money to buy groceries and put some gas in the car. Had she or the baby needed clothes or even medicine, there would not have been any money to provide it.

Since Tom always went overseas, Michelle felt lucky to be able to use the car. At least his postcards were from abroad because apart from them, there was no other indication of his whereabouts.

But the second time that he left, Michelle only found empty drawers on his desk. She couldn't believe that Tom would be so inconsiderate. Even if he was mad at her, baby Scott was innocent and unaware that he could starve if he depended on his father's provisions.

Michelle made a solemn promise to herself that it would never happen. She would work as a housemaid or even beg on the streets if she had to, but her son would not suffer because of her bad decisions. And she was starting to consider her decision of moving in with Tom, a bad one.

After two days had passed without any news from Tom, she checked his closet with more detail and noticed that by the number of clothes he had taken, Tom must have decided on a long stay away from home.

There were only a couple of coins inside her purse, which helped Michelle decide on her line of action. So she sold the bracelet and earrings that Tom had given her. Fortunately, he was generous with presents and she still had a valuable necklace and a watch that she could also sell if necessary.

It didn't cause her any pain to part from her belongings because Michelle was not emotionally attached to them. On the contrary, she felt relieved to be able to provide food for Scott and herself while she fervently thought of new ideas to make money.

In case she decided to take a formal job, she would have to take Scott back to daycare and she didn't know how Tom would react to both news.

She was just considering all that when the doorbell rang and it was Mrs. Chairtall.

Michelle had completely forgotten that they had arranged for the babysitter to come over every Wednesday, Friday, and Saturday at night. Because they went out so much, it was easier to have a regular arrangement, otherwise, Mrs. Chairtall could be babysitting for some other family when they called. And for that, Tom was going to pay her every week, instead of each night.

"Oh, Mrs. Chairtall, come on in. Have a seat. I feel so embarrassed for having forgotten to cancel with you."

"It is all right, dear. Did anything happen?"

When Michelle heard that question and saw the sincere concern in the old lady's eyes, she burst out crying.

"Oh, Mrs. Chairtall. Why couldn't I have had a mother as sweet as you? Why is life so mean to me?"

"Now, calm down, dear. Did anything happen to your mother?" Mrs. Chairtall was a little confused now.

When Michelle heard that question, she gave a hysterical laugh and cried even harder.

Mrs. Chairtall went to the kitchen and got her a glass of water. Then she sat patiently waiting for Michelle to stop sobbing. She took her hand and gave encouraging littles pats.

"Oh, Mrs. Chairtall, I am sorry. It is just that I don't remember seeing my mother when she was not drunk. When I called her to tell about Scott's birth, she hung up on me, after calling me some bad names."

"It is terrible, dear. I understand how you feel. I grew up at an orphanage and I seldom heard kind words too."

"And yet, you are so kind yourself. I am ashamed of myself, Mrs. Chairtall, for bringing this up. I want to be stronger because tears won't solve anything."

"We all have our bad days, dear. There is no shame in being human."

"Thank you so much. I feel better now."

"If I understood correctly, you won't be needing my services tonight."

"That is right. Tom went on a business trip. I don´t know when he will be coming back."

"Oh, I see."

"I will pay you for this whole week, Mrs. Chairtall. And then we will just have to call you when he comes back."

"Nonsense. Today is still Wednesday, there is no need for you to pay me for the whole week."

"I will feel better if I do."

"Okay. If you insist. But listen to my proposition. Since you will be paying me anyway, let me at least take care of Scott. You seem to be a little stressed and some rest will do you good. I will come on Friday and on Saturday too."

"Oh, Mrs. Chairtall, I accept your kindness."

"You can call me Nancy if you want."

"I would like that very much."

And when Michelle felt the soft touch of the pillow on her face, she realized that she had just made her first friend.

Now with only one hundred and ninety-nine more to go, Tom could have his dream party.

GETTING BUSY

Michelle felt better after her rest. She was drinking some tea and talking to Mrs. Chairtall in the kitchen.

"The biggest problem for me is to be in the dark, Nancy. For the reason that I don´t know of Tom´s whereabouts, I can´t count on him for anything. And since I don´t have a clue of when he is coming back, it is hard to make plans."

"I see what you mean."

"Let´s suppose that I get a full-time job and leave Scott at daycare. As soon as Tom comes back, I may have to quit. It would look bad on my curriculum."

"Sure. It could make it harder for you to get another good job in the future if you quit after only a couple of months."

"Then I am left with the choice of freelance jobs. I even have some practice as a waitress. They don´t pay much, but it is a start. The only problem is that if I have to pay for a daycare center, the money won´t be enough."

"Right. Look, I have one idea, Michelle. What about our previous arrangement? I keep babysitting for you on those three days a week. You can work on those nights for a while, only to be on the safe side. If the situation drags for longer, you can think of other solutions."

"But what about your payment?"

"We write the value down and Tom can pay me when he gets back."

"But Nancy… What if Tom doesn't come back?"

"I don't think you could be so lucky!"

When Michelle heard that she was so surprised to find that her new friend Nancy had a sense of humor that she was delighted to laugh at the joke.

"Now, seriously, dear. Let's take one step at a time. It is just a start, as you said so well."

"You are right, Nancy. I will focus on what I can do and not on what can go wrong."

And things went well for them. Luckily Michelle got a job at the restaurant she had worked in when she was pregnant. Fridays and Saturdays were busy nights and the tips were good. She opened a savings account in her name and it gave her a sense of security. Even knowing the amount was not huge, it was better than nothing. Nancy enjoyed babysitting Scott and she started to sleepover because she knew Michelle could use a friend. Thankfully the boy was very healthy but like any other caring mother, Michelle worried about being alone in case something happened to him.

It was a comfort for her to have Nancy around. The old lady also loved cooking and when she slept there on Saturday nights, she made sure to prepare a delicious Sunday lunch for all of them.

After three months of this happy arrangement, they were not even mentioning Tom's name. And then he came back.

HIS MOODS

This time Tom came back in a bad mood. He was quiet and had a constant frown on his face.

Michelle kept her distance. It was on a Monday afternoon that he crossed the apartment door and it gave her time to let Albert, the restaurant manager, know that she was quitting. He understood her situation and said that she could come back anytime, which was a relief for Michelle. Albert was the son of a single mother himself, and this was the reason for him accepting her working there when she was pregnant. He had a lot of temporary staff and they respected him and liked him for being so understanding. Michelle promised to keep in touch.

Later she called Nancy only to let her know that Tom was back but assuring her that she should come to babysit normally on Wednesday.

By now, Nancy had her own key to the apartment, so it was good to know that Tom was there because then she made sure to ring the bell.

"Well, Mrs. Chairtall. What a surprise."

"A good one, I hope."

"Of course. Come in, please. Michelle, look who is here."

"Oh, Mrs. Chairtall. Welcome. You know Tom, I forgot to mention to you that I kept our agreement with Mrs. Chairtall. It was a chance to go out to the laundromat or the supermarket while she kept an eye on Scott."

"No need to explain. Only the best for my boy. Now, since we already have the babysitter, let's go out and have a nice dinner."

Michelle wanted to scream at Tom for being so false. How could he say that he wanted the best for Scott when he left his son unassisted, for a long time?

He gave on her nerves because Tom seemed to find it necessary to pass an image of a caring father while he acted otherwise. Strangely it was as if he believed his own lies.

But as always, Michelle chose peace over war. While she got ready, Tom paid Mrs. Chairtall the overdue salary and agreed to pay one month in advance when she suggested it.

After that night out, Tom's mood improved much and he went back to his routine of taking Scott to the park and asking Michelle to prepare exotic food for him.

By now, Michelle thought more about the near future and she took Tom to the supermarket with her more than once. The reason for that was that when she went on her own, he gave her only one or two hundred dollars to shop for the needs of a week.

But when Tom was with her, she made sure to stock food and goods. She bought dozens of baby food and snack packs as well as cans of regular foods. Michelle filled their cart with milk and juice gallons and was sure to purchase all the cleaning products for the apartment in abundance.

Tom thought it was funny but never complained of the amount spent when he passed his credit card to pay for all those items. He just said jokingly, "Are you preparing for the event of a war."

Michelle smiled at him and made sure to cook his favorite food for a couple of days, even without his asking for it.

She also had the idea to take some online courses on how to illustrate children's books and create beautiful book covers. Michelle chose the best courses and they were expensive ones. So she made sure that Tom paid the yearly fees in advance. Because she could choose her hours of online studying, she always did it on the afternoons that Tom was out.

When Scott was two years old, Michelle chose a very nice kindergarten to take him to in the afternoons. It was a premium place, extremely clean, and with an outstanding staff. They took monthly payments, but again, Michelle made sure that Tom paid the whole year in advance. He called her neurotic but she didn't mind because he paid for it all the same.

Money was not a subject of fights for him. He bought nice clothes for the three of them and purchased a new computer for Michelle, saying that he was glad that she could entertain herself with games and cartoons at home.

Because Tom had started to act very possessive and jealous of Michelle. One night, after unfairly accusing her of flirting with some waiter at a new restaurant they were at, he broke some dishes back at the apartment and screamed a lot. She locked herself in Scott's room and tried to calm him while his father made much noise and punched on the door.

Of course, the next morning Tom had left for another month. This time Michelle felt more prepared to deal with his absence. It wouldn't be an exaggeration to say that she even enjoyed it a little.

Chapter 10 – Search group

Now:

Sheik Omar al Malik was surrounded by the men he trusted the most. This group was composed of his personal assistants Nahim and Youssef, his secretary Zyan and his cousin Khaleb, who once had risked his life to protect Omar.

"Did you gather the information that I asked, Zyan?"

"Yes, emir. We have questioned the housemaids and found out that the shaikhah left three days ago. She didn't take any of her valuable belongings. Only some simple clothes for herself and the baby."

"Right. I imagined that. Did you find out if my brother-in-law was with her?"

"He made an appearance on the day before the escape and stayed few hours. But when the shaikhah left with the baby, her brother was not with her."

"He probably came in advance to discuss the details with her, cousin."

"I agree with you, Khaleb. Nahim, how many men have you gathered for the search?"

"One hundred and twenty, emir. We intend to send them in two separate routes."

"Make it three routes. I want every piece of land searched."

His assistant agreed with him and went out to give the new instructions to the waiting men. They were soldiers, experienced in many battles and they would give their lives for their Sheik.

"Youssef, gather fifty more men, that must prepare to leave tomorrow. That is the group that I will join personally."

"Yes, emir."

When Sheik Omar was alone with his cousin, he told him about his worries.

"You know Khaleb, I am sure that Bethany isn't aware of all the dangers that may come her way. Otherwise, she wouldn't have Ben going on such a dangerous journey. I fear for their lives."

"Because she is not from these parts maybe she thinks that it is just a matter of crossing the desert to visit some Oasis. That the only worry will be to avoid sunstroke. But there are dangerous men who could kidnap her to ask for a treasure hansom."

"I know. Bethany must have been desperate to have acted on such an impulse. I will find out what or who was threatening my wife, Khaleb."

"Is that why you didn't leave with today's searching groups?"

"Exactly. I want to have a detailed look through her things. Maybe I can find a clue or an indication of what direction she went. Even if I miss one day, it could save valuable time."

"There are things that only your eyes will be able to perceive, cousin. I wish you luck. Now I will join the first group that leaves."

"Be careful, cousin."

"I will, Omar. I hope to bring back your family."

"If you manage that, I will be forever grateful to you, Khaleb."

They say their farewells for now and while Khaleb goes out of the palace, Omar enters Bethany´s bedroom and opens her closets to take a look.

Her perfume fills his senses and he misses her so much that it is almost a physical pain. His hands touch her many dresses and gowns, which make him remember the first time he saw her dressed formally for a dinner. They were still children.

LIKE A PRINCESS

Past:

Omar was used to joining his father for his many business trips. Being the only child of Sheik Mohamed al Maliq, he was being prepared for succession one day.

His father had interests in the modernization of their country. Sheik Mohamed believed that it was possible to maintain their traditions and promote their culture at the same time that they provided the population with equipment and appliances that could facilitate their lives.

So, the visits to western countries were frequent and Omar knew that he would spend some years there when it was time for college.

He had also assimilated much of western culture and costumes from hundreds of movies and cartoons that his father encouraged him to watch. There was a private movie theater inside the palace.

But the first time Omar saw Bethany, he was not ready for that. She seemed to have a deep connection with nature and her voice had transported him to a dreamland, the first time she sang in his presence.

That same night, Omar saw Bethany dressed like a princess from the many cartoons he had seen. She had an angelic face that always smiled at him. Her hair was blond in the same color of the desert sand that Omar loved so much. Her green eyes were sparkling and sincere. Everything about Bethany looked soft and elegant. Her satin dress was long and embroidered with some sparkling material that looked like diamonds to him.

He realized that she already looked like a princess, but Bethany could become a real one by marrying him. He knew that they were both young but Omar would wait a lifetime for her if it was necessary.

Love was a rare thing and since it had happened to him, Omar decided that he would not ignore it.

He silently vowed to himself that if he was to be the leader of his country and nothing less than a sheik, Bethany had to be his wife and a shaikhah herself.

THE PASSAGE OF YEARS

They met only two or three more times during childhood. And it was as if they hadn't been apart at all. Even their games were continued as if they had not been interrupted.

It was easy and fun to be with each other. They made it very clear to anyone that could have an interest in the matter. So, during his visits, they were inseparable. Omar asked her to sing for him every day and Bethany was happy to oblige him.

"I wish you can visit me in my country. There is so much that I want to show to you."

"It is my biggest dream to visit your kingdom."

"Can't you ask your grandfather to take you?"

"I will make sure to ask him."

"And I will teach you how to ride. We will explore the Oasis in the desert as well as the nice things that our developed cities have to offer."

They kept daydreaming and making plans about the future.

"Omar, can we go to other places on the planet, as well?"

"Where do you want to go?"

"I have always been curious to go on a safari. Also, I would like to see the pyramids in Egypt."

"I will take you to those places, Bethany. Believe me when I say so."

"I believe you, Omar. Oh, and I have always been curious to see how the Eskimos live. And visit the wonderful Amazon forest in Brazil, that is called the lung of the world."

"My sweet Bethany. Even if you ask me to take you to explore the moon, I will find a way to make it happen."

And he said that with such intensity that Bethany felt like the luckiest person in the world.

When the time came to say their farewell, Omar looked into her beautiful green eyes and simply stated his feelings,

"One day, I will marry you, Bethany."

Deep down Bethany felt like it was not just one of those things that some boys say to impress girls. It sounded like a promise to her.

LONG SEPARATION

Suddenly Omar's country was involved in a war that lasted some years. Sheik Mohamed al Malik was so intent in the war effort that he put aside his interest in innovation.

His visits to western countries for the purchase of machinery completely stopped.

The war presented the sheik with a large bill and a great loss of friends and family.

This meant that Omar and Bethany had to be apart for many years and would only meet again as adults. They missed each other and longed to be together but her grandpa would not take her to a war zone. And Omar's father couldn't abandon his people who counted on him at this tragic moment. Many families lost their loved ones and were threatened to live in slavery if the enemy managed to take the power.

The expected victory came for sheik Mohamed al Maliq and his devoted warriors. Many years of peace would follow.

When the time for college arrived for Omar, his father sent him overseas to get modern education and get acquainted with the latest technological gadgets and appliances.

After more than a decade apart, Bethany's image was like a distant memory for the young prince. And Omar was for her, only a childhood sweet dream because Bethany was sure that he had moved on and probably had a harem by now.

Nonetheless, destiny said otherwise.

Chapter 11 – Working mom

Past:

Mrs. Chairtall had told Michelle how proud she was of the way she was handling a difficult relationship.

She was patient with Tom´s eccentricities and never picked up a fight with him. At all costs, Michelle wouldn´t allow Scott to grow up amid a violent family. Mrs. Chairtall witnessed her struggle to guarantee some reliability for her baby.

When Tom was absent, Michelle had a schedule that she followed with much effort. She would study online every morning, and then do house chores, while Scott was entertained by his favorite TV cartoons. He stayed in his bin with many toys and stuffed animals. In case he got tired of TV and asked for his mommy, Michelle would pick him up and play with him, or share some fruits and milk. He liked to fill her mouth with food and since she made funny faces to him, Scott laughed a lot on such occasions.

Before lunch, she took him to the park, which he loved. Tom had got him used to this, which Michelle considered a healthy activity.

When Scott went to kindergarten in the afternoons, Michelle took that quiet time to work on her designs. The illustration of children´s books was not easy, therefore it paid well. Two or three publishing companies were using her drawings by now and she was starting to make a name for herself in this field. Her excellent taste showed in her work.

Her saving account showed a respectful number by now, even though it was far from the millions that Tom had always said that they would have someday.

Michelle was not greedy. Her main goal was not to live in fear of starvation for herself and her baby.

Mrs. Chairtall noticed all that and more than once complimented Michelle on her achievements.

"Maybe you don´t need to work as a waitress anymore, dear."

"I know you are right, Nancy. But I might as well do it while I am young and healthy. It is always extra money. Also, it is good for me to be out of the house for a while."

"It is just that I worry about you being out at night, dear."

"I hadn´t thought of that. I guess it is because I never had anyone to care about what I did or where I went."
"I care, dear."
"I know, Nancy. What about this? Maybe I keep only the weekend shifts. What if I stop going to the restaurant on Wednesdays and I take you and Scott out instead?"
"Me?"
"Of course you, my friend. You will be our guest of honor."
Mrs. Chairtall was so touched by these words that it was impossible for her not to shed some tears.
"I guess I never had anybody who cared about me too, dear."
"I care, Nancy. I care a lot."
Then this new routine started for them. Every Wednesday they would go to a pizza place, or a famous fast-food restaurant. Sometimes they dined at home and went out for delicious desserts at fashionable bistros and cafes.
By now they were very close friends and had learned a lot about each other´s life. Nancy admired her young friend more and more each day. On a quiet Sunday afternoon, while Scott took his nap, she told Michelle,
"You could have so easily given up and become an alcoholic like your parents, dear. Instead, you are proving to be a fighter and a winner, if I may say so."
"Thank you, Nancy. I think that the whole difference is that Scott means everything to me. I don´t think my parents ever felt anything for me. Many times, they didn´t even acknowledge my presence in the house."
"Well, dear. It is their loss. It proves that they don´t understand how lucky they were by having you. Some people are just incapable of loving."
"I never thought about that at the time. I was busy trying to survive. If I didn´t learn very quickly to cook I would just starve. There was never anything in the fridge except for booze. I used to hide some slices of bread under my bed, and I knew it had to last for many days, sometimes a week."
"That is so sad."
"When I was eight or nine, I was able to handle cans and I learned to use the stove. My life improved because I could open cans of peas or

corn and fry them with eggs. I never knew what my parents did to feed themselves. Maybe they went out to eat while I was at school."

"Maybe your mother started cooking for them after you had gone to sleep."

"Probably. I slept early because I didn't want to be late for school in the mornings. I enjoyed my school a lot. Life seemed normal there."

"It is a blessing that you made that choice. Some kids from troubled families, sometimes skip school and find some really bad company on the streets."

"Yes. When I look back I know that things could have gone wrong many times. What about you, Nancy? Did you like school?"

"I am much older than you, dear. Things were different back then. I had some classes at the orphanage where I lived, and thanks to that I am not illiterate. But as soon as I was fourteen I went to work for a family. It was hard work, but at least I had a roof over my head. And I went from one house to another until I had a little money saved to pay a couple of months' rent."

"And that is how you went to live in the house you are now, right?"

"Yes. It took me a long time to be able to pay rent and move on my own. I was over forty when it happened. You see, I always had to pay for my clothes, shoes, and medicine. The family only provided the food, and not always a good one."

"Our lives have so many coincidences, Nancy. I think that is why we understand each other so well."

"Today I am sixty-two. And finally, I know what a family feels like, Michelle. I think of you as a daughter. And I love Scott like a grandson."

"And we love you too, Nancy."

BECAUSE HE SAYS SO

Naturally, when Tom was home, everything changed. Michelle had to interrupt her morning studies and do them on the weekends, instead. This was mainly because Tom demanded that she cooked every day for lunch. He ordered very complicated dishes and she just had to find a way to excel at cooking, or else he would complain so much that she always ended having a headache.

One day she saw an ad about cooking classes and since they were near their house, Michelle thought it could be a good idea to take some classes.

"Tom, I am thinking of joining a culinary school. They have a program of three months classes that sound interesting. You choose the course, for example, 'The art of pasta' or 'Spicy food' and after three months you get a certificate."

"Why do you want a certificate? Are you planning on working in a bakery?"

"Of course not, Tom. It is just for the knowledge. This way I can cook meals that you will really enjoy. You can even choose the course because I don´t mind."

Though she noticed the cynicism in his words, she tried to get his agreement. She could pay for the course herself, but he would have to agree with her being out of the house three times a week for two hours a day. The courses happened in the morning, so Tom would have to stay with Scott or have Nancy babysitting on those days. But he was far from agreeing.

"You are a mother now, Michelle. Your place is in the house taking care of your son."

"It is not true nowadays."

"It is true because I say so."

"That is unfair, Tom. Many mothers work and still take care of their children."

"But those are capable women and you know that."

These words should not hurt her since she knew he said them just to put her down. But it was so hard to take these offenses from him. Michelle had chosen Tom to share her life, not to mention that he was the father of her son. She was not asking him to love her, since it is not possible to force feelings to happen. But she longed for his respect and he refused to give her that.

When he was home, Michelle didn´t work at the restaurant only to be available to go out with him. She went dancing even when she had a headache and she went to his favorite restaurants, never even once being asked for her preference. Michelle took care of his clothes, she cleaned the apartment and he never thanked her or made a simple compliment.

Sometimes she imagined if he thought of her as his personal maid because she didn't feel like a cherished wife. The talk of marriage seemed to anger him, so she had dropped it long ago.

One day Tom gave her a password for an online culinary course that he had paid in full for her to learn to cook international food. She thought it was his way of saying he was sorry, then she thanked him.

"It is a nice course. Thank you for thinking about my request, Tom."

"I don't see why I should have to eat trash. Either your mother was lazy to teach you how to cook or you were lazy to learn."

If Tom's intention was to strike where it hurt more, he was successful with his comment. And he seemed to know it. Michelle couldn't hold some silent tears and then she turned around to leave the room, but he grabbed her wrist. She looked at him feeling very confused because it was as if he wanted to watch her suffer. Then he kissed all her face very slowly. He started to undress her right there in the living room, not bothering to take her to their bedroom.

"Sorry, Tom. It is almost time to pick up Scott. And I am not in the mood anyway."

"Michelle…"

"What?"

"Shut up."

Michelle felt so used and so confused that she indeed was beyond words. What could she say to a man that acted like an animal?

Later, on the way to pick up Scott, all she could think of was that she needed to organize herself and leave Tom. In a way, it was funny to think that she wouldn't even need a divorce for the simple reason that they had never married.

Chapter 12 – End of stress, beginning of sorrows

Past:

It is strange how Tom seemed to sense a change in Michelle. She continued to do all her usual chores and she never complained or treated him in any different manner. But her heart was not on it anymore. It was as if she had stopped believing that they had a future together. She was even more quiet and thoughtful than usual.

Tom only saw life in her eyes when she was playing with Scott. Even her lovemaking was sort of automatic and at those moments it was like she had not only shut up as he preferred, but also shut off. Her mind appeared to be somewhere else and Tom was not a fool, so he concluded that she was out of his reach.

His mean words didn´t affect her anymore and she just nodded to him when he mistreated her or asked her to do extenuating chores, like cleaning the bathroom after midnight or ironing all of his shirts first thing in the morning for no reason at all.

It was as if Tom was testing Michelle and after a few weeks, he changed too. He was very thoughtful with her needs, bringing her flowers and candies. He bought expensive toys for Scott and offered to pick him up at school after work, so Michelle could have some more time for herself.

He didn´t know that she used that time to illustrate children´s books. Michelle saw it as the means for an independent life with her son. She was also checking on small houses or apartments to rent.

But one day, Tom sat by her side on the sofa and hugged her tenderly. She was surprised to hear him talking to her as if he was addressing a child because he was extremely kind.

"You know, sugar. I booked a hotel lounge for our wedding party in six months."

"What?"

"You heard me right, sweetheart. We are getting married. I was being silly wishing for two hundred guests. Let´s keep it very simple. Thirty or forty people at the most. Are you okay with that?"

"I don´t know Tom. I have wanted it for so long. Scott is three years old now. I thought we would get married when I was pregnant. Maybe it is too late now."

"I see what you mean, pumpkin. But life is not that simple. And since you mentioned Scott, we should do it for his sake too. Children could be mean to him or even bully him if they know that his parents are not married."

That caught Michelle´s attention.

"Do you think it is possible?"

"It happened to me."

"Oh!" Michelle had never heard him mention his childhood or any fact about himself really. "I am sorry, Tom."

"It hurts me bad. I prefer not to talk about it."

"But that is one of our problems, Tom. We never talk."

"I promise you that we will. After we get married we will cuddle and talk all night long if you wish."

He saw hope in her eyes.

"I always wanted for Scott to have a normal family."

"Me too, sugar. Me too. So, will you marry me?"

"Yes. I will."

He kissed her passionately and when they parted he said,

"I know I should get you a ring now. But I want you to choose the best one at the store tomorrow. Your opinion matters to me, and I will use the rest of my life to convince you of that."

These words made Michelle take the initiative and kiss all his face. He was laughing happily and only stopped when she gave him a long kiss on the mouth. Tom carried Michelle to their bedroom and kept her busy there for hours.

The next morning, Tom brought her breakfast in bed and told her to go back to sleep after eating. She smiled at him and asked what time he wanted to go to the jewelry.

"We can take Scott to the kindergarten and stop at your favorite store on our way home. Later I want to take you to a romantic dinner and after that, we can repeat last night. I will never get tired of you."

"It sounds great. I will sleep a couple of hours and then take a shower and get ready."

"Take your time, sugar. I will take Scott to the park now."

"Thanks, Tom. I am so happy."

"Me too, pumpkin. Me too."

Michelle had sweet dreams and woke up feeling very relaxed. Tom, in turn, had taken Scott to the park and allowed the toddler to play with water. He saw his son go to the fountain, fill his plastic bucket with water and come back to sit on the grass and pour the water over his own head. The little boy would laugh hard and his father encouraged him to do it again. At this age, they never tire of a fun activity, so Scott repeated that many times.

A woman that was nearby watching them, put her baby in a trolley and came to talk to Tom.

"Oh, excuse me. Maybe it is a fun thing to do, but the boy could get sick being wet for so long. Look, he is trembling a little."

"Mind your own business."

"How rude."

"Are you hitting on me? Do you want to go somewhere and I will
see to your needs?"
"How dare you…" And by saying that, the woman rushed away
from Scott, considering him crazy. She felt sorry for his boy.
Tom had a cynical smile on his face and then he proceeded to dry
Scott and change his clothes. He had a towel and some dry clothes
with him because it was his idea to get the boy wet in the first place.

JUST THE FLU

When father and son entered the apartment, they saw that Michelle
looked radiant. A big smile was on her face and she kissed both of
them loudly on their cheeks.
"You smell so good, sugar."
"Thanks, Tom." Michelle felt that she certainly could get used to his
nice words. Tom was so charming when he wanted to be. That was
the man she had wanted to marry from the beginning of their
relationship.
"You know, sugar. I think Scott has the flu or something. Maybe you
could give him some Vitamin C or something before we take him to
his school."
Michelle felt the boy's temperature touching his forehead and was
surprised to find it so high. She checked again using a thermometer
this time.
"Tom, he has a high temperature. I don't think it is wise to send him
to school today."
"Whatever you say, sugar. I trust your decision."
Michelle watched Scott and tried to make him rest after she had
given him some medicine for his fever. Since Tom hadn't slept much
the previous night, he napped on the sofa all afternoon and told
Michelle that she could call him at any moment if she decided to
take the boy to the pediatrician.
He sounded worried and she was thankful that he had taken the day
off, even if the reason for that was for buying an engagement ring.
Fortunately, the boy was feeling much better and very talkative
during dinner. Tom and Michelle had canceled their night out and
she was delighted to see that there was not even an ounce of
selfishness in him.

He suggested that Mrs. Chairtall should come to the house anyway because they could use her opinion and knowledge of babies. Michelle watched Nancy explain to an attentive Tom that these three days viruses were very common for children this age.

Scott slept well that night and Michelle could rest too since Tom decided to cuddle that night.

It was so good to be looked after, for a change. Tom brought the breakfast to her in bed again, the next morning.

"This way you will just spoil me."

"It is all that I want."

"I will check on Scott before eating."

"I just checked on him. He is sleeping soundly. I have the baby monitor here with me."

"And the fever?"

"No fever. I checked."

"You are a wonderful man. Do you know that?"

"Not really."

She felt very guilty because he was telling the truth. She had not been nice to him in the recent past. But she was in favor of second chances. So she invited him to share the breakfast with her. And she fed him on the mouth as he did to her. And they exchanged little kisses and tender words. Then Michelle took the initiative to undress him. He loved that. When he asked her to stand and let him look while she undressed herself, she was glad to do it.

They made love sweetly and took a shower together.

After lunch, Tom had to go to work but not without promising to take the next day off.

Michelle agreed with his plans and thought that life could be so great when two people understood and cared for each other.

The next day, after the park, Scott felt sick again. This time, Tom insisted that they should take him to the doctor. Fortunately, it was just the flu.

"Michelle, the time has a way of passing so quickly. I hope you don't mind if I tell you that I asked a work friend to recommend a caterer for the wedding. And a nice place to print the invitations."

"Of course, I don't mind. It makes me happy that you want so much to marry me. I am sorry if I couldn't stick to our plans. It is just that I worry about Scott."

"You did the right thing. You are a good mother, Michelle."

"Thank you, Tom. It means a lot to me hearing you say that."

"I want to prove that I am committed to you. And that is why I opened a joint bank account for us."

"A joint account?"

"Yes, this way, you can draw money anytime you want. Or you can use our credit card. I put one hundred thousand dollars in the account."

Michelle was moved when she signed the papers for the opening of the joint account and saw the value.

"I feel relieved now. If the baby gets sick when I am traveling on business, you can use the money."

Michelle laughs at him and teases him a little.

"With this money, I can buy a hospital."

He looks a little embarrassed.

"I know I am being silly, Michelle. And I plan on taking you and Scott with me on my next business trip anyway. This account is just to be on the safe side. And to give you some sense of independence."

"Oh, honey. Thank you so much."

"You deserve it, Michelle. So, can we go tomorrow to buy that ring?"

She hugged him so tight that Tom just whispered, "I will take it as a yes."

But Scott had a bad fever the next day. Many children get worse during the night because it is chilly and all, but this boy got worse in the mornings, after spending a couple of hours alone with his dad. It was a mystery.

"Michelle, I have some more papers for you to sign."

"Can't it wait, Tom? Scott is throwing up nonstop."

"It is nothing important. Just sign it to get rid of it."

"What is it about?"

"Bank papers. In case we need a loan."

She didn't think they would ever need a loan, but Tom had a stern face and she was so busy with Scott, that she only made sure the title read 'loan proposal' and signed it without further talk or delay.

Two things happened after that. Scott recovered his health completely. And Tom left in a week. For good.

Chapter 13 - Indebted

This time Michelle knew that Tom had gone away for good because he had left her a note that said 'More than naive, you are a fool. Goodbye!!!'

He had not said a word about Scott. And the goodbye was pretty emphatic. She decided to keep the note, in case he changed his mind and asked for the boy's custody. So she could prove that he had abandoned his son.

Anyway, she didn't believe that Tom would want to have his son with him because he had proved his distaste for responsibilities.

Another indication of his intentions of never coming back was that he had taken all his belongings with him. Moreover, the joint bank account showed a withdrawal of all its amount except for three dollars.

But it was not the first time that he had left zero provisions for Michelle and Scott, so she didn't feel helpless.

One thing surprised Michelle though. She was not as devastated as she thought she would be. Her dreams of a wedding had evaporated together with the father of her son and still, she didn't shed a tear.

Could it be that she was cold? She concluded that she was not as fool as Tom had believed since she was sure that he was no catch.

Michelle was a practical person, then she dove into her work while deciding that she didn't need to live in such an expensive place. Also, she knew that she couldn't afford the school that Scott attended at the moment, so she started to look for a smaller house and a simpler school. Fortunately, Scott's tuition was already paid for another semester and she would have some time to make the new arrangements.

There was no way for her to request the child's support because she had no idea of Tom's whereabouts. Maybe it was better this way. If Tom helped financially, maybe he would request shared custody and it gave her a chill just the thought of leaving the boy with an unbalanced man like Tom.

It is funny how a person that thought the world about himself, left the impression of being a lunatic.

By now Michelle had almost twenty thousand dollars in her saving account and she decided that she would only have to take one day at a time.

This decision held good until the next day arrived. The doorbell rang and there were two men dressed in dark suits who wanted to talk to

Tom. It was about the apartment rent. Michelle asked them in and decided to say that Tom was traveling. It was not a complete lie, but she felt she should learn more about the matter before opening up to these strangers.

"I thought the apartment was always paid in advance for one year."

"It certainly worked that way for the first two years, madam. But right now, the rent is already late by three months."

"But how did you allow such a thing to happen?"

They were surprised by her question. Usually, tenants made a lot of excuses for the delay. But they never questioned their business strategies.

"Mr. White asked for some time. We agreed to it."

"How much does he owe?"

"As you must know, the monthly rent is six thousand dollars. He owes us eighteen thousand for the three previous months and this one will be due in a week. The total of twenty-four thousand must be paid by next Friday. Otherwise, we start to apply the fines for the delay. We will also take it to court. The contract is in the name of Michelle Clarkson. I am assuming that is you, madam."

She went pale now. Michelle had completely forgotten that Tom had made the contract in her name long ago. It dawned on her that Tom had had some bad intentions from the beginning.

"Can I pay in installments?"

"Maybe. In that case, we will have to work out some interest fee."

"Also, I think I should leave this place right away since I can't afford the rent."

"I am afraid it is not possible. Even if you leave, your contract states that you have to pay for twelve months. If there is a breach in contract, the fine is thirty thousand dollars. You agreed to it when you signed the contract."

She felt lost and confused. Hadn't she read what she was signing? How could Tom have done it to her?

"Well, gentleman, I will think of a solution and get back to you. Is it okay?"

"Certainly. We will talk to you soon."

TALKING THINGS OVER

That night Nancy learned about her friend's situation and she was astounded by the news.

"How can a man be such a lowlife?"

"Oh, Nancy, I don't know. Maybe he was right by calling me a fool. I let this happen."

"Dear, we have to trust somebody at some point in our lives. You just chose the wrong man."

"I can't afford this lifestyle. I don't know what to do."

"Dear, if I can be of any help to you it will make me happy. I could never save much because there were always so many bills to pay. Bills from the dentist, the doctor, the car insurance. Even an old model car like mine consumes money. But I have saved eleven thousand dollars for an emergency. I want to give it to you now."

"My sweet friend. You touch my heart. But I would never drag you into this situation. And as you put it so well, this money is for some emergency. I can't accept it."

"Please, dear. Think of the boy. I need to help."

"I don't want to worry you more than I already did, Nancy. But I can't take your money. See, it wouldn't solve the problem anyway. By the end of the next week, I will have to pay twenty-four thousand dollars. And six thousand every month after that."

"Wow. It's unbelievable. I pay eight hundred dollars for rent."

"Yes, I know it is crazy. Tom insisted on having the best of everything. I just wish he had paid for it."

"Me too, dear. Me too."

Because there was no way around it, Michelle paid twelve thousand dollars and negotiated installments for the rest of the amount overdue. She decided to tell them the truth about Tom's abandoning her. It was the right thing to do because they felt sorry for her and did not charge fines or interest. She felt humiliated as if she was a beggar because they gave her pitiful looks.

But at least she was facing her problems and Michelle was confident that things would improve much for the next year.

Nancy had moved in with her. This way she could watch Tom every night while Michelle went to work as a waitress. The eight hundred dollars that Nancy used to pay for rent was now going to her savings account. It allowed her to quit babysitting for the two other families that used her freelance services. She assured Michelle that it was good for her to take a rest from work. Scott was no work at all, she repeatedly said to her concerned friend.

"In a way, it is as if I was expecting something like this to happen. I am certainly glad that I have stocked food for almost one year."

"You are right. One less worry is always welcome."

"The publishing companies agreed to double my workload. In a way, when all of this mess stays in the past, I will have found a way to make six thousand dollars a month. Think on the bright side, Nancy. We can move to a small house with a rent of one thousand and a half tops. Then we can spend the rest in nice clothes and fine restaurants."

"We sure can't afford any of those now."

"I am glad that the restaurant offers a uniform," Michelle said this jokingly because she didn't want her friend to be burdened by her problems, being of old age and all. But she had to share some things with Nancy otherwise she would go crazy keeping all the worries to herself. Michelle had started to have nightmares and she knew that they were caused by all the insecurity in her life.

"I want to give you a dress for your birthday, dear."

"Ah, sweet Nancy. I was not fishing for presents, my friend. I have dozens of dresses and shoes in my closet. It was only a joke to make you laugh."

Since Nancy was not so convinced of that, Michelle had to take her friend to look at her clothes in her bedroom.

For the second payment that also consisted of ten thousand dollars, Michelle sold the rest of the jewels that Tom had given her.

"Nancy, things are under control which is a relief. I can still sell my car to help with the payments. And in the worst case, I can try for a bank loan."

"You are so smart, dear. I am proud of you."

"I couldn't do it without your help, Nancy."

And just as they were holding hands in the kitchen, feeling hopeful for their future, the doorbell rang.

Again, there were men in suits asking to talk to Tom. She had no idea who they could be and this time Nancy was by her side when she told them to come in and take a seat.

"I am afraid Tom is traveling. Can I help you?"

"Are you Michelle Clarkson?"

"Yes, I am."

"Then you can certainly help us. We are from the 'Global Bank of the World' and it concerns your loan."

Michelle looked confused but Nancy was smiling when she told the men.

"What a coincidence. Michelle was just telling me that she was thinking of making a loan."

"Another one?" Now the man showed confusion and looked from one woman to the other questioningly.

"What do you mean, another one, sir? I never made a loan in my life."

"According to these papers you did. They are signed by you and Tom White requesting a loan of seven hundred thousand dollars."

"Did you lend this money?"

"Yes. The whole amount was deposited in your joint account a couple of months ago. And it was withdrawal a few days later."

Michelle was speechless and very pale. Nancy had silent tears running down her face. A lot of them.

Chapter 14 - The loan and the banker

The main building of the Global Bank of the World was an impressive skyscraper. The facade had the capital letters, GBW, detached in a golden sign.

There was no other way but to face the redoubles Tom had caused her. And in order to do that, Michelle needed to understand her situation in detail. The men that had visited her home were not the ones that had lent the money to Tom. They were simply the employees in charge of collecting the delayed installments.

When she told them that she preferred to visit the bank personally, there was no argument against it. That is why she was here staring at the building and gathering her last drop of courage to go in and face her predicament.

Michelle was surprised to be ushered into the banker's office. She thought she was going to deal with a manager or an assistant, but Stanley Worthgold himself was shaking her hand and offering a seat in front of his enormous mahogany desk.

"How can I help you, Ms. Clarkson?"

"Well, Mr. Wrothgold. First of all, I want to say that I am not just a little intimidated, on the contrary, I am very nervous. I never imagined I would be talking to the owner of the bank."

"That is still my father, Christopher Worthgold. He is the president of this bank. I am only one of the directors."

"Still. I have seen a lot of news about you, over the years. You happen to be his only heir."

"That is accurate. But it is nothing to worry about at present. My father is a very healthy man."

"Of course. I am glad to hear that."

Stanley was starting to feel intrigued by this woman. She was very polite and gentle. The folders in his hands indicated that he would be dealing with cunning people who had decided to escape the payment of debts. This description didn't seem to fit the woman before him.

"Then, Ms. Clarkson, what has brought you here?"

"I had a visit from some of your employees concerning a loan. I was informed that the lack of payment can lead me to spend some years in jail."

"It is true. The law guarantees it."

"Mr. Worthgold, why did you lend the money to Tom? And such a large amount?"

"It is simple, really. We have a new line of credit to benefit new companies. The goal is to create more job opportunities. I am responsible for this project in our bank and I am proud of it. After this line of credit is tested here in the headquarters of GBW, it will spread to all of our branches. We have provided funds for entrepreneurs to start private schools, computer shops, and clothes stores. Tom White came to talk to me and provided an excellent business plan to open a restaurant."

"But Mr. Worthgold… How did you give him such a huge amount without collateral?"

"It is a new way of doing business. The loan was insured, so we can't lose a dollar. The insurance was paid by the money discounted from the loan. The contract explains it in detail."

"Can I have a copy? I never read it."

"That is an unusual request, but of course you can have a new copy of it. Not that I am judging you, but people don't sing just anything without reading nowadays."

She looked so depressed when he said it, that Stanley immediately tried to correct his statement.

"Of course when you trust someone, things are different. Is Tom White your husband?"

"No. We never married."

The woman had become red by now. Stanley wanted to bite his tongue. What was the matter with him today? He didn't seem to be able to open his mouth without offending this delicate woman. He could read the hurt in her eyes.

"Shouldn't he be here with you to negotiate your options?"

"I will be straight with you, Mr. Worthgold. Tom left me and our son. He took all the money and disappeared."

"I see."

"I am alone in the world. Any way out of this mess will have to come from me."

"If you don't make the agreed payments Ms. Clarkson, and remember that the first installment was due last week, I am afraid I won't be able to help you. Because in the lack of payment, you will owe the money to the insurance company."

"Does it mean that you transfer the debt?"

"Yes. They will start searching for Tom White and believe me that they will be able to find him. They will also ensure that you do your time in prison."

Michelle became thoughtful. He gave her time to understand all this new information. It was also as if a magnet was drawing him to her. Michelle was a beautiful woman and he was admiring her brave behavior. She had not cried or begged.

"As soon as I am out of here, you get reimbursed by the insurance company. And I am not your problem anymore." It was as if Michelle was thinking aloud.

"That is a way to put it."

"But I am still here."

"Indeed you are."

She attempted a shy smile. He rang his secretary and asked her to bring them some coffee. When Michelle asked to see the business plan for the restaurant, Stanley took a chair by her side and explained each detail to her.

She looked into his green eyes with such confidence that he subconsciously became protective of her.

TELLING NANCY

"The only way out of the problem is to go ahead and open the restaurant, Nancy."
"But how will you do it without any money, dear?"
"It is a bank, Nancy. They have money by the billions."
"Why would they give it to you, dear?"
There was not a simple explanation for that because even Michelle wasn´t sure of the reason for Mr. Worthgold to give her that chance. She guessed that he didn´t want to see a baby´s mother sent to jail, after all.
"Well, Nancy… I suppose it is for the same reason that they lent it to Tom. They can´t lose anything since it is insured."
"I was not aware of that. Maybe I should go there and get myself some thousands too."
"Let´s not press our luck, Nancy. Come on. We must celebrate."
And so they took Tom for ice cream and felt happy that destiny was finally dealing them a nice card. These two women were not afraid of hard work. The threats of prison, on the other hand, had scared them to death.

A BUSY MAN

Everybody complained about Stanley Worthgold´s lack of time. The man was the director of a bank that had hundreds of branches all over the world. He also had investments in many industries, mining companies, and petrol enterprises that demanded his attention and consumed his time.
Even his closest friends didn´t see him enough.
But whenever Michelle Clarkson wanted to talk to him or meet him, Stanley was free.
His assistant John and his secretary Susan already knew that Michelle was his top priority. They were surprised by this, but too discreet to comment.
Michelle was in his office for the second time this week.
"Thanks for receiving me on such short notice, Mr. Worthgold."
"You are always welcome here, Ms. Clarkson."

"It is just that I visited some locations for the restaurant and it came down to two choices. Would you mind looking at these pictures and telling me what you think?"

"Of course. I would love to help you choose."

It was hard for Stanley to take his eyes from her to look at the real estate pictures. Michelle really knew how to dress and she had chosen a blue outfit that had the same color as her eyes. Her hair was done in a high bun and it made him urge to undo it and watch the soft curls surround her perfect face and reach her shoulders like waterfall drops.

Stanley was a powerful and handsome man. Being still single, it was natural for him to be surrounded by beautiful women, even models and actresses. They were outgoing females that demanded his attention as well as expensive gifts and exotic trips. He enjoyed all of that and had no complaints about this jet-set lifestyle but there was an emptiness to it that he only realized when he had started to dive into Michelle´s eyes.

In the few time since they had met, Stanley had already witnessed a world of feelings there. At first, he saw the hurt caused by Tom´s treason, and next, her fear of facing prison. Then Stanley perceived that she admired his business skills and he was startled to discover that she trusted him. This realization made him feel so manly that he immediately offered to help her start her business.

Stanley knew it was a stupid thing to do because he didn´t have time to spare. But there was no escaping his new reality, the fact was that Stanley longed to see her.

He watched the hope appear in her eyes as they discussed the possibilities of success for her restaurant.

Michelle confided in him about this being an old dream for her. And she seemed to be thirsty for his opinions and ideas. She hung on every word Stanley said and even took notes and made intelligent questions to him.

The first time Stanley paid Michelle a simple compliment on her good taste and decision-making capacity, she was very touched. It took her a while to recover her control and he noticed that she had to fight not to allow some tears to run down her face.

He excused himself saying he had to sign some documents because more than the need to give her some privacy, Stanley had to put some distance between them otherwise he would just hug her tight.

What had that lowlife Tom White done to the self-esteem of this wonderful woman?

When Stanley confessed to himself that he hated Tom, he also had to admit that he had feelings for Michelle.

He wondered if she could ever return his feelings. Maybe Tom had caused too much damage to her spirit which was a pity.

Stanley decided to be patient and become her friend not only because he wanted to know her better but also because he didn´t dare to scare her away.

Michelle´s eyes were always shining when she talked about the restaurant and it indicated that she was able to face challenges. But Stanley noticed that when she mentioned her son, a sparkle of pure joy appeared in her eyes. He saw all her capacity of loving someone and decided to be worthy of her love someday.

A DATE

When Stanley gave Michelle back the pictures and told her which building he liked the best, she said,

"Thank you, Mr. Worthgold."

"You can call me Stanley."

"Why?"

"It would be strange if you kept calling me Mr. Worthgold when I take you to dinner."

"Then should I take that as an invitation for a date?"

"That is right."

"In that case, you should call me Michelle."

"Can I take that as a yes for my invitation?"

"It is a yes."

"Good." His smile was so charming. It lightened his features and transmitted his warmth.

"Stanley. I can´t make promises to you."

"I know Michelle. I just want to know you better. Can´t we be friends?"

"I would like that. I only have one friend, Nancy."

"Now you have two."

And Michelle knew that he meant it.

Chapter 15 – Desert nights by the fire

Now:

Besides singing, another form of entertainment of Bedouin people had been storytelling, for centuries.

In the same way that some people have the gift of singing, dancing, or painting, there were those that could create realistic images in your head through the way they told stories. And there were many topics to be explored, such as treasure hunting, revenge on wrongs, impossible loves to conquer among others.

Bethany noticed that the people in her caravan felt great enthusiasm when someone started telling these great tales of their land. Every three or four days, they would sit by the fire and hear legends from the past, as well as jokes and anecdotes. It made the long trips more bearable.

"Don´t you want to join them to hear some stories, Adjia?"

"No madam, thank you. I prefer to stay with you. Just in case the baby wakes up."

Ben was reacting well to all the changes in his life. He hadn´t lost his appetite and continued to sleep well. Bethany was very careful and attentive to his needs all the same. Still, it was clear that her baby was as sweet as he had always been.

He moved his little hands and tried to grab every object in sight. His smiles were adorable and Bethany noticed that Adjia was already charmed by the little angel.

"This man that you will marry in the south village, Adjia… How is he?"

"I have never met him. But we have word that he is a hardworking and honest man. He is in trade."

"Yes, I know. My brother told me that he has a fabric shop. Why will you marry him? I thought the arranged marriages were an old custom."

"Nowadays it is not obligatory. Both parts must agree."

"And you have agreed?"

"Yes. You see, my father became sick and couldn´t work as hard as before. By marrying Haroun Mustahraf, I ensure jobs for both my brothers, selling clothes and fabrics in his shop. He also promised that my family can live in some rooms he has behind the shop."

"I understand. You are doing it for your family. That is so nice of you. But it makes me a little sad because girls your age should not have huge responsibilities. At nineteen you should be talking to young men and dancing every night."

"Do girls do it in your country?"

"All the time."

"It sounds nice. But my family couldn't afford to buy clothes for me to go to parties. Even this trip is being paid by Haroun."

"Aren't you curious to know how he looks like?"

"I have his picture. Do you want to see it?"

"Sure."

Adjia went to get Haroun's picture that was in her bag inside the cart. When she returned and handed it to Bethany, there was an expectant look on her face. The man was kind of fat and disheveled. He appeared to be forty or fifty. It was hard to tell. That image was a symbol of the enormous sacrifice Adjia was doing for her family. She was a pretty girl with a nice voice and good manners. Despite being only nineteen she was used to working hard and was able to speak English and French besides her own language. She would make a great wife to any man who was lucky enough to have her. And Bethany was sure that Haroun was very aware of that. She couldn't tell Adjia how repulsive she thought that Haroun was. So she said kind words.

"He sure looks respectable. And you said he is hardworking which is a good sign."

"Yes. My mother's cousin works as a cleaner for his family. She suggested the match when she knew he was looking for a wife. Haroun is a widow with three kids."

Of course, he had to be. Bethany could only imagine the hardships Adjia was going to face in her future.

If only Bethany was still in the palace, she would have the power to help this girl. But again, in that case, she would never have met this young girl.

Who knows. Maybe Adjia would find happiness despite everything. Life was full of surprises, as Bethany knew so well.

SEARCHERS TO THE EAST

The first group that left the palace, headed to the east. Khaleb was leading them and he wouldn't allow many stops or much rest. It was as if he was driven by some lunatic thought.

The men admired him for this demonstration of loyalty to his cousin, the sheik.

After a few days of riding t full speed, they could see signs of a caravan camping near some rocks.

The people were startled to see these armed men approaching them, so they ran inside the tents.

Haroun dismounted his horse and proceeded to tear down the tents with his sharp sword. There were screams of terror as he violently grabbed small children and pulled them away from their crying mothers. Following this barbarian example, other soldiers did the same around the camping. It made some of the caravan men react with indignity and there was an exchange of shots.

When Kahleb finally spotted a woman holding a baby, he grabbed her hair with all his strength and it was a miracle that he didn´t break her neck. He didn´t care. He just took the baby from her and when he noticed it was a little girl and not the prince, he just dropped the baby to the floor. It is true what people say about the strength of a desperate mother because the poor woman jumped to catch her child in mid-air, avoiding the fall to death.

The poor people were defeated and just sat there crying their losses and their dead relations while watching a furious Kahleb confer with some soldiers.

"There is no baby and nowhere to hide, sir. From here onward it is only rocks. These people came to this exchange point for supplies and plan on going north from here."

"These stupid people made us waste precious time following their tracks."

"Should we burn their belongings?"

"No. My cousin would become enraged if we harmed them. We have more important matters to attend to. Let´s just head south."

For the travelers, it was a relief to see the soldiers leave. They couldn´t even understand the reason for the attack because they didn´t take anything from their victims. It was not a simple robbery, but they couldn´t grasp exactly what their intentions had been. They kept saying something about a baby. They felt sorry for the people who would be in their way.

And the reason is that, if the soldiers had visited a poor camping site, they for sure had left a miserable one behind them.

A WISE COUNSELOR

Sheik Omar was listening to his uncle's advice on the matter of Bethany's escape.

"It is a dishonor. You must punish her severely for damaging our family image like that."

"First I would have to find her, uncle."

"There are search parties, right?"

"I must go personally. I leave in the morning."

"No. you can't. It is beneath you. Let others handle the rebel woman. You are royalty, Omar."

"And so is my son. I must find Ben."

"Your cousin is on the task. He is a very capable soldier as you know so well."

"Of course, uncle. Your son is my trusted advisor. And a very capable man. But this is one case where I must act. Otherwise, I would go crazy only waiting for the results."

"You have to think of your responsibilities to the country and the people, Omar. There are some investors arriving this week and they expect you to sign new agreements and trade contracts."

Sheik Omar gave a cold and long look to his uncle. Even being family and one of his advisors, uncle Malouf had just gone too far, accusing him of negligence.

Every cell of his body emitted authority and he didn't even need to utter a word. His silence spoke louder than any word ever could.

"I am sorry, Sheik Omar." The old goat was wise enough to start using the nephew's title again. The sheik himself permitted the casual talk when he was alone with the family members. But Malouf knew it was necessary to show respect and deference. "You have to forgive me. I am an old man and the disappearance of the young prince has made me fearful for the country.

"Then you should go and rest, uncle."

"But…"

Another look from the sheik made the old man rush from the room. It was an order. Who dared not to follow the sheik's orders would be risking the loss of titles, properties, or even their lives, depending on the gravity of the matter.

Sheik Omar was far from being a sanguinary man. He ruled his people with justice, competence, dedication, and generosity. He was loved and respected by his people. But he was also known for his absolute authority.

As the sheik watched his uncle leave the room he thought that maybe it was time for the man to retire. It was not only a matter of his prejudices and outdated ways anymore. Malouf was showing signs of greed in his actions. And greed was a destructive feeling.

After Omar found Bethany and Ben, he would have to deal with that matter.

Chapter 16 – The bachelor

Past:
SWEET TALKS, SWEET DATES

Stanley took Michelle out for dinner at least once a week, sometimes twice. And they talked about everything, arts, politics, sports… They enjoyed sharing facts about their lives, their dreams. She often mentioned how much she was relieved for not having to go to jail.

"At least some good came out of all this stress, Stanley."

"What do you mean?"

"Well, according to the conditions of my loan, and again, thank you so much for that… In six years, I will have paid all my debts and become the proud owner of a nice restaurant. I can finally have my own business which has always been my dream."

"And you made a new friend."

"Yes, Stanley. You are the cherry on top of my cake."

"Sweet silly girl."

"I am not so young anymore. I am already 26."

"Tell that to a guy who is 38 and you will make him feel ancient."

"You don't look ancient to me, Stanley. You look your own handsome self."

"And again, maybe you are just being kind to an old fool like myself."

"I hope always to be kind. But you are neither old nor fool and you know that."

"Maybe I needed to hear it from you, Michelle."

"Now you have my opinion, my friend."

When she called him friend, Stanley knew that she was kind of letting him know what stage their relationship was in. And he gave her time to know him better, no forcing Michelle to have a romance with him. Stanley hoped that she would spontaneously yearn for his company. The truth is that he didn´t want only a night in some hotel from this woman. He wanted to share his life with her. Because by now he had admitted to himself that he loved Michelle.

The following week, when they went to see an art exposition and Michelle was telling Stanley about the marketing campaign that she was preparing for her restaurant, Stanley noticed that she was looking forward to starting that business.

"I am so excited about the possibility of finally being independent."

"I am proud of you, Michelle."

"Thank you. I owe it to you. Now I will have to be extremely organized otherwise I will have zero time for my son."

"Maybe you should just get married and dedicate yourself to raising Scott. You seem to love being a mom."

"Indeed I love being a mom. It makes me happy in a way that not even ten lottery prizes could. But as to getting married, I don´t think Tom is coming back."

"I don´t mean Tom."

When she heard that comment, Michelle knew that she would have to make a decision very soon. It was not fair to keep Stanley in expectation after all the help he had offered her. Also, it was not the way to treat a friend and she wanted to be fair. So, she asked him,

"Will you allow me to cook for you? I want you to come to my apartment next Saturday night, so you can meet Scott and Nancy."

"I will be honored, Michelle."

When they resumed their walking in front of the many paintings showing in the gallery, they did it arm in arm.

MEETING THE FAMILY

Michelle had told Nancy that she found Stanley Worthgold to be a great friend. And from his first visit to the apartment, Nancy could witness that it was true. He took an interest in Michelle´s life and showed appreciation for her son. After he had taken her to some nice restaurants around town, Michelle had finally invited him to dine at her home. She enjoyed cooking for him and he was generous in his praise of her talents. He was also very cordial toward Nancy and Michelle could see that he was relaxed around her little family.

"I think Scott will be an athlete someday, Michelle. He is big for his age. And look at that appetite. He is a healthy boy, right Champ?"

Scott giggled and made a mess with his pasta. Nancy hurried to clean his little hands, but it was pointless. There was tomato sauce all over him.

"Don't worry, Nancy. I will give him a bath before bedtime. Stanley is right about his appetite. He ate most of it, so I don't mind a little mess. Would you like a second helping, Stanley?"

"Don't mind me if I do. You have to tell me the secret for this sauce."

These were the right words because they made Michelle feel valued and proud of her talents.

"That I can not do. All the recipes for the food that I intend to serve in my restaurant will remain secret."

They are smiling broadly at each other and Nancy finds an excuse to take Scott to his room and stays there with him playing with some toys, in order to give the couple some privacy.

When they are alone, Stanley holds her hand and says what is on his mind.

"Michelle, I wish you would give up on the restaurant idea."

"Why?"

"I want you to cook exclusively for me."

It takes her by surprise.

"But Stanley, I have a debt to pay."

"Please, allow me to take care of it."

"I just can't. It is too much money."

"Michelle, I don't want to sound arrogant but for me, it is a trifling amount. I have one motorcycle that is more expensive than that. And then I have cars, yachts, and jet planes. I am willing to share all of that with you then I can't allow some small change to get in the way of our happiness."

"Oh, Stanley. I don't know what to say."

"Say yes. Marry me."

"Can I answer you in a couple of days?"

"Sure, Michelle. I know you have to be careful because your son's wellbeing depends on your decision. If I could erase the hurt from your heart, I would. Unfortunately, I can´t. But I promise you that I will never intentionally hurt you as Tom White did.”

After he left, Michelle told Nancy about his proposal.

“Oh dear, should I congratulate you?”

“Not yet, Nancy. I asked him for a couple of days to think before I give him an answer.”

“That is wise.”

“You know, I feel that my biggest challenge in this situation is not to surrender to pessimist thoughts or prejudiced ones.”

“What do you mean?”

“I will try to explain to you how I feel. Some people say that all doctors are bad because one doctor prescribed them the wrong drug. Other people say that all shops work with overprice because they bought something expensive in one place and found it half priced elsewhere.”

“It is true.”

“Also some men say that all women cheat because they suffered one woman´s betrayal.”

“It happened to my neighbor.”

“Right. Now some women hate all men because they experienced violence or betrayal from one guy. They shut themselves to new experiences. They don´t give a second chance to themselves.”

“I see what you mean. By your reaction to Tom´s abuse of your confidence, you could either be rid of his influence or permit his outlaw acts to inflict you fear for the rest of your life.”

“Exactly. I will not allow Tom to have any more say in my life. My decision about marrying Stanley has to be based on the man Stanley is and on what I feel about him.”

“He is handsome, dear. He likes children. And he gives you adoring looks.”

“Yes. He is very handsome. And I love the way he and Scott interact.”

“Also, he is a billionaire. It is just a reality. If an unemployed man had proposed to you we would be talking about it. So, it is natural to discuss the perspective of a life with much money.”

“It is true. There is no need to be a hypocrite. His money is welcome in our lives.”

“And then what is left to ponder is how you feel about him.”

"Yes. But before I can honestly answer this question I have to confess to you that something about Stanley intrigues me."

"What is that, dear."

"Well, he is so handsome and rich. He has a good taste in clothes and he has a sense of humor. Stanley is 38 years old. Why has he never married?"

"Michelle, there is only one way to find out. You have to ask him, dear. The key to a relationship is communication."

"Yes, Nancy. I know."

Michelle couldn't help herself but wonder how Stanley would react to that question. Tom had always hated to talk about himself and she feared that Stanley could accuse her of prying. And that is why she decided to do it fast before it became a trauma for her. She phoned Stanley the next day and he agreed to take a walk in the park in front of her apartment because Michelle needed to talk.

QUESTIONING HIM

When Michelle met Stanley at the park, the first thing she noticed was that he looked great in jeans. Normally he wore a suit when he was at the bank. And when he took her out, Stanley usually dressed formally too.

After they greeted each other and sat down on a bench, she asked without thinking much,

"Do you work out?"

Stanley was surprised by her question and he laughed while he answered that.

"Yes, sweet Michelle, I work out. Is that what has been worrying you? My health?"

"Stop teasing me. I don't know why I said that. It is just that you look great in jeans."

She was so embarrassed trying to explain herself that Stanley found it cute. He took her hand.

"Thank you. I find you beautiful too."

They stared into each other's eyes and there was a communication between their souls that didn't need the aid of words. Stanley approached her face and her eyes shone even more. He then took her lips and started to explore her sweetness in their first kiss. Michelle was surprised to realize how much she had wanted this kiss to happen. Her arms went around his shoulders and her fingers touched the back of his neck encouraging him to kiss her deeper.

Stanley felt her delicate touch and he inhaled her scent while kissing her in a possessive way, almost desperate to make her agree to be his wife. He loved her, he needed her, and now that she allowed him to come closer, Stanley knew for sure that they were meant to be.

When their lips parted, Michelle was breathless but her arms were still hugging him and this made Stanley kiss all her face in an exploration that caused her to take his lips this time. They were devouring each other's mouths and Stanley embraced her waist and with one single movement had Michelle sitting on his lap.

"Oh, Stanley…"

"Yes, my love."

"We look like teenagers, here in the park."

"Yes, I know. It feels great."

They said it between kisses.

"Stanley, there are people walking by."

"Do you want to stop?"

"I can't." She touched his face and caressed his hair. "I was afraid you wouldn't like the audience."

"I don't care. There are other couples dating here. I don't think people mind. But we can leave, if you are uncomfortable."

"I am not. I feel that I belong with you."

"Good. Because you do."

Stanley kisses her neck and her earlobes. It is as if he is drawing a map of her as if he needs to memorize every part of Michelle. She sighs and brings his mouth to hers again.

"Oh, Stanley, I never knew I could feel like this. I love you."

"I love you too, my angel. So, will you marry me?"

"I will Stanley. I will."

"I am the happiest man on Earth."

He squeezes her before they stand up and walk to the apartment to tell Nancy the good news. She congratulates them and goes to fetch some glasses because they want to make a toast to the couple's happiness.

Later, when Michelle and Stanley are snuggling on the sofa, she remembers that she wanted to ask him something.

"Stanley, why haven't you ever gotten married?"

He looked thoughtful.

"I proposed to someone once. I was very young then. Barely nineteen."

"What happened?"

"She said yes. Ann was a friend of my family and I knew her since our childhood. We both knew it was expected from us, and then we decided to do it soon. The families wanted to unite the fortunes. She was sweet and as young as me. Maybe she was in love with me, I don´t know. For me, marriage was one more obligation but I didn´t dislike Ann."

"But you didn´t marry her."

"No, I didn´t. Soon after we got engaged, Ann started a battle against cancer. It was all very sad and painful. I sat by her side for many hours and I watched the life leaving her. There was nothing I could do. Neither of us could, but I always felt kind of responsible for her."

"Stanley, Ann was lucky to have you."

"But I was so useless."

"No, darling. You were by her side all the time. I am sure that it gave her comfort."

"Thanks for saying that, Michelle. After that, I never thought much about marriage. I mean, I dated a lot. And I had my share of models and actresses because my money attracts women who want to enjoy international trips and expensive gifts. I am no saint, Michelle."

"You are a good man. It is all I expect from you. But from now on, I want you to be my man. I can´t stand the thought of you with all those models…"

"Oh, my angel, don´t be jealous. There is no one as pretty as you. I am your man. You know that, don´t you?"

"The only thing I know is that I love you, Stanley."

"Good. Because I love you too."

Chapter 17 - Finally married

Life is full of surprises and it had shifted in Michelle´s favor. Not only had she married within few months of the proposal but also she found herself completely in love with her husband.

Stanley had taken her to Paris for a wonderful honeymoon. You can't get more romantic than dinners at candlelight and romantic walks to explore old monuments. During these walks, they often told each other about their love and made many plans for the future.

Stanley also insisted that they visited the most exclusive clothes stores and he showered her with gifts. Clothes, shoes, hats, gloves… Nothing was missed. Not to mention jewelry, makeup, or perfumes.

It was really like a dream. For both of them. It was curious how Stanley got the same amount of excitement in buying these gifts as Michelle felt by receiving them.

When Michelle told him of her concerns about him spending too much on her, the answer was that a man is lucky if he is not reduced to buy only stock shares or real state properties. He assured her that it was a pleasure to make her happy.

"Stanley, I am happy because I have you!"

She said it with simplicity and because it was true, Stanley loved her even more. And he bought her diamond bracelets and watches made of pure gold.

When the time arrived to return home, Paris had already become extra special for both of them and they decided to return every year at that time, to celebrate their love.

MY HOME, OUR HOME

Stanley's house was one of those huge classic mansions. It had spacious rooms spread through the four floors that made it look as impressive as a small castle.

"I was born here and I don't intend on moving. I hope you can be happy here, my angel."

"It is a beautiful house, Stanley. I am sure we will be happy here."

"I plan on buying a beach house for us. Or a country house to spend vacations. You choose. But for our home, I would like it to be in this place."

"I agree with you, Stanley. It is where your memories are. Your roots."

"I knew you would understand, Michelle."

And as they walked hand in hand into the beautiful house, Michelle felt as if she was marching towards happiness.

MY ENEMY-IN-LAW

When Michelle had first met Christopher Worthgold, Stanley's father, she hadn't been able to form an opinion about his personality. He had stayed quiet during the meal and addressed mostly Stanley, to talk about things she didn't understand at all, like foreign trade or the growth of undeveloped countries. The dinner was soon over and Michelle understood that it was more a matter of formality before her wedding ceremony than a way to make a new friend.

But now that they shared the same house, Michelle couldn't avoid noticing the looks of despise that her father-in-law sent her way.

During breakfast, when she tried to contribute to the conversation, the old man would frown at her and stop speaking completely.

Christopher also ignored Scott on every occasion. The boy was a little over four by now and he was in that cute phase that brought many smiles to Michelle's and Stanley's faces. But to the old man, he was invisible.

Stanley didn't seem to perceive anything wrong with his father's attitude, then Michelle decided not to create unnecessary problems. It was his father, after all. Maybe in time, Christopher would warm up to her.

There was so much happiness in her life right now, that Michelle decided not to allow one grumpy person to spoil things. Michelle only stayed extra quiet when he was around and moved on with her life.

Nancy had moved in with her because as Michelle had explained to Stanley, she was not a simple maid. Nancy was family. He didn't oppose taking Nancy to live with them. In fact, Stanly insisted on it, "The more the merrier."

But Nancy insisted on sleeping and eating her meals at the maids' quarters. She didn't say anything to Michelle but the truth was that Christopher scared her. He made her feel inferior and unworthy of his presence.

"Nancy. This is nonsense. You can take a bedroom near Scott's. Stanley agreed with this."

"I know, dear. And I am very thankful for that. But, you see, it is good for me to be near people of my age. We share stories and exchange recipes."

"That sounds nice." Michelle still missed not having many friends. And she felt happy for Nancy because she had found people who appreciated her. "But you are not to do any house chores. I won´t allow that."

"Don´t worry about it, dear. I get busy enough running around Scott all the time. He loves the gardens and the pool. I am glad that he has had swimming lessons otherwise, I would go crazy every time he jumps in the pool."

"Yes, I agree. One thing that makes me relieved is to be able to keep him at his school. It is great how they encourage sports, music, and arts. Scott swims better than me."

"I know. Our little boy is amazing, isn´t he?"

"Oh, Nancy. You are amazing too."

Michelle had talked to Stanley about buying something special for Nancy´s birthday. He agreed that Nancy was like a grandmother to Scott, so he promised to go present hunting with Michelle. They were together a lot, no matter how simple the errand could be, Michelle was amazed at her husband´s wiliness to share with her and accompany her everywhere. Many times, she forgot that he was an important banker and businessman. Above all, he was the love of her life.

Christopher, on the other hand, was showing to be unpleasant by the hour.

One afternoon, Michelle was reading at the library and she heard perfectly what he said to Nancy, "Keep that little brat away from me."

"Yes, sir."

Michelle went to the door just in time to see Nancy taking Scott to the garden. Christopher acknowledged her presence with a smile. It sent a chill to her bones because it was a mean smile. She never knew that those existed. But there it was, on her father-in-law´s face, the meanest smiled she had ever seen.

That night she talked to Stanley.

"You know, my love, I never saw myself living in a place as big as this."

"You deserve it, my angel. And more."

She tried another approach.

"Stanley, what I mean is, if we moved to a smaller house or apartment, it could be our love nest."

He looked thoughtful for a moment and then tightened their embrace.

"Ah, Michelle, I know what it is all about."

"Do you?" There was relief in her voice.

"Of course I do, sweetheart. You know, you can talk to me openly. You can ask me anything, Michelle."

"It is just that I was a little embarrassed. I didn´t want to sound ungrateful."

"You didn´t. Tomorrow we go looking for a beach house."

"A beach house?"

"Yes. Like I promised to you. I am glad that you reminded me of that."

And he looked so happy, almost childish, that Michelle decided not to mention for now that his father was creeping her out.

VISITORS FOR COCKTAILS

Michelle had noticed that Christopher had a way to declare some facts that would put Stanley in an inferior position. It was as if he had pleasure in making it clear that he was more capable of doing business than his son. Many times, during meals, he would say to Stanley, "The work that I do in one day, you can´t do in one year. Remember that."

"Sure, father. I will remember."

Later, in their bedroom, she asked her husband if it was true.

"It is true, Michelle."

"Is the work so hard? What skill does your father excel at? Is it math?"

"Not so much the math. It is not a matter of calculating. It is the skill of negotiation, that my father has developed like nobody else."

"I understand. But does he need to show off like that?"

"It is all he has. His business is his life. I, on the other hand, have you to make me happy and proud."

"Thank you, my love."

Since it didn´t seem to bother Stanley, Michelle decided to ignore the old man´s arrogant talks too. And she was successful until one night when they were offering a cocktail to some important clients of the bank. Christopher spoke in a sarcastic tone, loud and clear, "The work I do in one day, Stanley can´t do in one year."

Even Stanley who was such a calm person and made an effort to always maintain peace could hide his embarrassment. And Michelle couldn´t help herself and made her opinion known to anyone who was listening,

"Maybe it is true. Maybe. But then, again… Why the hurry?"

Everybody laughed hard. Now it was Christopher´s turn to feel embarrassed. And more than that, he felt humiliated in his own house. In a way, he had been called a liar. Michelle had shown that she despised the same skills that Christopher was so proud of.

It was the first time that Michelle saw hatred in his eyes. And she was the recipient of that.

Stanley took Michelle away from the guests and while he prepared a new drink for her and repeated that she looked beautiful, she kept the feeling that she had not won the argument, only stepped on dangerous grounds and gained an enemy for life.

When they joined the group again, the place seemed to be as cold as Antarctic ice. Christopher sent Michelle all the glacial looks he was capable of.

Stanley chewed his canapes like a child in the lap of his mother. He talked about sports and arts as always. He didn´t have any concerns. In fact, Stanley was living the best days of his life because he was married to the woman he loved.

Chapter 18 – Baby Bethany

It turned out that the beach house was a great acquisition and Michelle enjoyed being there with Stanley and Scott. She made sure to bring Nancy along because when Stanley went to exercise at the beach or locked himself in his office to take care of some businesses, Nancy kept her company.

Scott was a smart and healthy five years old boy. He made friends with the neighbors´ kids and they took turns playing their games in each other´s houses.

One afternoon, while they were sunbathing by the pool, Nancy told her friend,

"I never thought this could happen to me."

"What do you mean, Nancy?"

"Well, living in a mansion with you and Scott who I love dearly, and spending most weekends and all the vacation months in this magnificent beach house. Maids come here to serve us ice tea, imagine that. A luxurious life like this was not even part of my dreams since I considered it impossible to happen."

"I see what you mean Nancy. In my case, I dreamt of studying and working hard to achieve success one day. But God permitted that I skipped those steps and went straight to the money part."

"Yes. We must thank God that you found yourself a good husband, dear."

"I told Stanley that I would like to start a business, to test my business capacities, you know…"

"I think it is a great idea. You are so talented."

"Thanks, Nancy."

"What did Stanley say?"

"He said that I am so capable that I could even start five or ten businesses."

"That is sweet. And encouraging. Will you do it, then?"

"I want to. But Stanley asked me to wait a couple of years before I get so busy. He wants to take me to Italy, Spain, and Greece. He can't believe that I never visited these countries. Also, when Scott is a little older, Stanley plans on taking him on a Safari trip."

"Oh, dear. Isn't that dangerous?"

"I certainly hope it is safe. We will find out because you and I are Stanley's permanent VIP guests."

"Imagine that…"

And they kept talking and enjoying themselves until it was time for Nancy to pick up Scott from his friend's house. Michelle joined Stanley for a long walk along the beach.

The next morning, Michelle was a little dizzy and she told Nancy that she would avoid the sun for a couple of days because she thought it had an effect on her. But when she threw up after lunch, it made Stanley look worried but it brought big smiles to the women's faces.

Nancy ran to the nearest drugstore and when she came back, Michelle took the little package from her hands and went to the bathroom. Nancy took Scott to play ball in the sand, in a way to give the couple some privacy.

Stanley was sitting on the bed and saw that Michelle looked radiant when she came from the bathroom holding a positive pregnancy test.

"Stanley, you will soon become a dad."

"Are you sure, my love?"

She just nodded yes and waited for his reaction.

And Stanley acted like a man who had won the lottery. He screamed, "Yes!" Then he took Michelle in his arms and kissed her intently. When they broke the kiss, both were out of breath. Stanley picked Michelle up and spun her around the room. Then he got worried and made her sit on the bed.

She was laughing and enjoying seeing him so happy.

Later, they decided to tell Scott together. And the little boy was happy with the news. He held their necks in a cozy group hug and then went to tell Nancy that he was going to be the best big brother in the world.

PREGNANCY

If it is possible, Michelle felt even more connected with Stanley. It was common for them to finish each other's sentences. By one look, they knew what the other was thinking. They spent much time together and Stanley talked to her belly assuring the baby of his love. When they snuggled on the sofa, Michelle would sing lullabies for the baby and watch Stanley relax into a peaceful nap that she would soon join.

The proud dad went to all the doctor's appointments with her and after they heard that they would have a baby girl, he kept the same enthusiasm and went with Michelle to buy the pink baby furniture.

He bought the first gift for his girl and it was an enormous house located in the mountains. Michelle was amazed by that. Stanley told her that real estate was always a good investment. But it was only the beginning. Stanley bought the most expensive jewels for his girl. Every month of the pregnancy was a reason for a new celebration. He bought farms, houses, and even an island for his daughter.

And when the day arrived to welcome Bethany Worthgold into this world, Stanley had arranged for a show of fireworks that lasted for one hour. He sat on the hospital bed beside Michelle and while she held Bethany, they watched the beautiful fireworks of all colors through the huge glass windows of the hospital.

After a week in the hospital, they went home and Stanley was holding Bethany when they met Christopher in the living room.

"Let me see her."

Stanley gave the baby to his father. Christopher looked at Bethany with adoring eyes.

"Stanley, you did well. This is my only heir. Bethany Worthgold."

This caused such a surprise that Michelle couldn´t avoid questioning him.

"Aren´t you disappointed that the baby is a girl?"

"Why should I? She is a Worthgold and that is all that matters."

"She looks like you, father."

"Thank you, Stanley. I agree with you."

"I thought you wanted a male heir to take care of your business."

"You are wrong as always, Michelle. The world has had many strong female leaders."

"Name one, please."

"Cleopatra. For starts. And now is your turn, Bethany Worthgold. I will give you the world."

"That is so nice. But now, I need to give her some milk. Please, hand her to me."

When Christopher didn´t move, Michelle thought she would have a problem from the start. But it was a relief when Stanley started to laugh and took the baby in his arms. Michelle followed him upstairs.

"Stanley, have you just been disinherited?"

"In a way, yes. But I don´t mind. Bethany is my heir too."

"What do you mean?"

"Well, I have a fortune in my name that came from my mother´s family. I never depended on my father´s money."

"I am surprised to hear that."

"I never knew my mother since she died from childbirth, but I know she had great taste because she left me original art pieces, all her jewelry including diamond tiaras and emerald necklaces. They are in a safe, but of course, Bethany can use them whenever she feels like it. To tell you the truth, they are already hers because I won´t sell or use a tiara."

He was laughing softly while he said that.

"Stanley, I am so sorry that you never met your mother."

"Yes. I always felt that loss. Anyway, my mother left me stocks and bonds, which I invested again. That amount today puts us in the top hundred richest families in the world."
"In the world?"
"Yes, my angel. Unbelievable, right? And if you add father's money, Bethany is the richest baby in the world."
Michelle was glad that Stanley had already put off the lights. She didn't want him to see her face because she felt scared. It was too much pressure for a tiny baby girl.
This was the opinion of a caring mother.

Chapter 19 – A loving dad

From the day Bethany was born, Stanley started to shine. He took the baby on his lap and danced cheek to cheek with her.
Stanley sang to her, talked to her, and bought her many clothes and toys.
He was generous to buy them for Scott too. The truth is that Stanley enjoyed being a father. Many of his appointments were canceled because he would rather go to the park with Michelle and the children.
They spent weeks at the beach house and he explained to Bethany about the ocean, and the sky, the trees, and nature in general. She couldn't even speak but she seemed to be paying attention to her dad and she followed his hand as he showed her around.
Scott also loved Bethany with all his heart and he called her 'little sister'. He often gave her his toys and offered her ice cream or chocolate. Michelle explained to him that the baby only drank milk for now, but it was very kind and generous of him to offer. He was proud to be a big brother.
When they returned home, Christopher would show that he had missed Bethany by taking her to his office and showing her albums and albums with pictures of her Worthgold ancestors. She stayed quiet in his lap and seemed to pay attention. She never touched the albums, which was curious because when grandpa finished with those and started to show pictures in world atlas and drawings of African or Brazilian animals, Bethany would giggle and touch the pages.

All the while, Stanley would be seated at a nearby armchair reading the newspaper and staring at his daughter adoringly. When Bethany finally dozed off he would take her to her bedroom and watch over her sleep for a while.

The first word that Bethany spoke was 'dad'.

It gave Stanley such pleasure that he ordered a buffet of children's food to prepare thousands of candies, ice creams, and snacks, then he threw Bethany a party. It gave an opportunity for Christopher to invite some of the prominent families with babies to the house.

Michelle was suspicious that he was choosing a husband for Bethany. Scott's friends were invited too and the day was very joyful and noisy.

At night, Stanley was boasting to his wife.

"Did you hear, my angel? Bethany said: dad."

"Yes, my love, I heard her. And she keeps repeating it. She is calling you."

"She is so sweet. I should have recorded that."

"You recorded her a lot at the party."

"But not the first word."

"It is the only word she says, Stanley."

"That's true. When she is bigger, I will just have to explain to her exactly how it was when she said 'dad' for the first time."

"I am sure she will love that." Michelle was not jealous because the baby had not said mom for her first word. It was not in her nature to envy other people's happiness. Quite the opposite, she was amazed to watch how much love Stanley felt for their baby girl. Every day he had something special to tell about Bethany. How she liked or disliked some foods. Her interest in birds and little animals. How smart she was. How nice she smelled.

And Stanley could never stay long away from the baby. Michelle was always happy to watch them together.

"I love you, Michelle. I want to ask you something."

"Anything, my love."

"Give me another baby. I mean, many more… We never talked about it, but I feel like having a big family."

"How big?"

"Besides our two children… At least three or four more."

"Stanley, I feel the same. There is nothing I love more than being your wife and a mother."

"Oh, Michelle. You are everything to me."

She felt lucky that Stanley included Scott in his plans of fatherhood. She could feel his sincerity and all the love he gave the children. Now that Stanley had mentioned it, Michelle noticed that she was looking forward to having more babies with him.

ARRANGEMENTS

Stanley was a powerful man. His money could obtain anything he wanted. He was also very intelligent and capable, no matter if his father sometimes said otherwise, out of insecurity or simply to be mean.

And right now, Stanley wanted information.

He felt like the luckiest man on earth because he loved his wife more than he loved himself. And he accepted her boy as his responsibility. But recently, since his daughter was born, Stanley had discovered a different kind of love. One that would make you sacrifice for the person you loved. He knew he would do anything for Bethany. And he felt very protective, there was an instinct inside him that made Stanley wake up at late hours and go check on his daughter. She always slept peacefully. Bethany was healthy and happy, which contributed to Stanley's wellbeing.

But he felt a threat. And it came from Tom White. After all, that man was Scott's father and if he ever came back with any kind of demands, he would put a shadow over his happy family. They trusted him and Stanley knew that he couldn't let them down.

When he had paid Tom and Michelle's debts, the insurance company had closed the matter and stopped trying to find Tom's whereabouts. Stanley decided to hire some private detectives since he wanted to know exactly where Tom White was and what he was up to.

It took only a couple of months for Stanley to receive the first reports about the man. He was traveling around Europe, applying dishonest schemes and frauds, from country to country. He was a small player, taking amounts like thirty or forty thousand dollars from widows who found him charming, forging some signatures to get elderly people's pensions, or getting amounts of five or ten thousand from some naive businessman who believed his tales of great investments. After getting around a hundred thousand dollars, he moved to another country. People seldomly thought about going after him because it would be more expensive to pay the travel expenses to find him than to accept their losses. The emotional loss usually was crueler than the financial one.

It seemed that the biggest amount Tom had ever gotten was that one he took from Michelle, but then, he had years to plan that scam.

Stanley hired his own con man and attracted Tom to a country that didn´t exactly follow step by step on human rights. When they threw somebody in jail, they sometimes would just forget the person there.

Tom took the bait because it was in the amount of one million dollars. He was glowing when he shook hands with his partner, and after he was red like beet when the police cars surrounded him.

He was committed to fifty years in jail. Because Tom thought the world about himself, he couldn´t believe that he had been caught. It didn´t make sense to him. Also, there was no way to understand why many prisoners entered his cell that night and beat him unconscious. Later he grasped that they were marking the territory, mainly because he was a foreigner. Tom woke up in the prison´s infirmary with some broken bones.

He was taken back to his cell and after one or two days, Tom remembered that he had a friend who was a lawyer and asked to make a call to him. It was worth a try.

When he made the request for a phone call, Tom was surprised to receive a visit from the warden in person.

The man looked at Tom in silence and then handed him a note.

It read, 'More than naive, you are a fool. Goodbye!!!'

The note was written in his own handwriting. When he had left Michelle, she used the note to prove that she was not his partner in crime, but a victim as well. Stanley had kept the note until now when he decided that it was time the message returned to its sender.

Tom drank from that glass of revenge. He was smart enough to give up on the phone call to the lawyer.

Chapter 20 – Tragic News

Michelle was in such a happy phase of her life that it amazed her that they had already celebrated Bethany´s third birthday. Time seemed to speed. The birthday party had been mentioned by every paparazzi in town. Hundreds of guests who belonged to top society came to wish the best to the toddler. They brought bracelets, necklaces, and earrings made of gold. She also received the best clothes and toys as presents.

And Bethany had a smile for everyone. People were drawn to her and she welcomed them all. Of course, her favorites were daddy, mommy, and Scott which was expected because they also loved her much. Bethany liked grandpa too but she saw little of him because the billionaire man traveled a lot on business.

Life was so perfect that Michelle was not ready for the tragedy that came her way. One afternoon, while Bethany was taking a nap and Scott was busy at school, she noticed that Stanley was already late to get home. He was supposed to be getting ready since they were going to have an early dinner at a friend's house and later the group was going to an art exhibition in town. It was not in Stanley's nature to make people wait and Michelle started to wonder what could have kept him in his office at the bank.

Then the doorbell rang and some police officers were there to tell her about an accident involving Stanley's car and a truck. Just like that Michelle became a widow.

The days that followed were like a blur of sadness. Giving the sad news to Christopher and realizing how old he was when his strength left him and he had to be carried from the floor to his bedroom.

Getting the children ready for the saddest funeral of their beloved dad and stepfather. Everybody was devastated because Stanley was one of those people who had no enemy. He had had the gift of sharing his life and it built friendships.

For a couple of weeks, Michelle couldn't eat and she soon became a shadow of herself. Her dreams were full of nightmares and if it was not for Nancy she would have gotten pretty sick. Nancy made her eat a little and sat by her side until she fell asleep. Like only a mother would do.

But for the sake of her children, Michelle didn't surrender to depression and after a month of mourning, she was able to resume some simple tasks regarding the children.

By then, Christopher was feeling stronger too. But instead of connecting with her at such a difficult time, he directed all his bad energies and emotions at Michelle.

At the table, during their first dinner together after Stanley's death, Christopher called her a gold digger and made sure to accuse her of

Stanley's death. It was such an injustice since Michelle was not even present at the time of the accident that she just sat there, waiting for her father-in-law to take back the accusation.

But he didn't. Christopher didn't see the need to hide his hatred for her anymore. He called her the worst names ever invented by men to vilify a woman.

After cursing all he wanted and watching the silent tears running down her face, Christopher was not yet satisfied and then he started screaming in anger and punching the table.

The commotion brought some maids to the dining room and a very scared Nancy who used all the courage left in her system to grab Michelle's arm and take her to her bedroom.

The next morning Michelle was told to leave the house and since it belonged to Christopher, there was nothing she could do.

The butler told her to take only one bag since time was of the essence according to his boss. The rest would be packed and sent to her later.

She agreed to this. All Michelle wanted were her children and her friend Nancy anyway.

And here is where her nightmare came to life. Bethany couldn't be found in the house and the butler told her that Mr. Worthgold had taken her with him.

Michelle went to the bank and emptied her lungs screaming there. The security guards who had known Stanley for years took her to his old office and a manager came to talk to her.

"I know it must be terrible for you to be away from your daughter for a while. But she has brought new life to Mr. Worthgold at a time like this. He took her on a short trip to India and Japan. They must be aboard his jet plane as we speak."

If Michelle had not fainted when she heard the news about Stanley's death, now she did.

VISITATION RIGHTS

Stanley had left a huge amount of money to Michelle when he died. The beach house was also in her name as she soon found out. There was a fund to put Scott through the best schools including any college of his choice.

But the heir of his fortune was his daughter Bethany Worthgold. She was to receive billions of dollars when she completed eighteen years of age. And all the belongings that Stanley had accumulated over the years, like islands, farms, and commercial buildings around the world. And Michelle was glad for that because she hadn´t married Stanley because of his money despite what her father-in-law believed in.

But with the money her late husband left her, Michelle bought an apartment of three bedrooms and moved in with Nancy and Scott.

And she used some of it to enter a judicial battle for Bethany´s custody that had already dragged for some years.

If she didn´t have the means to pay a good lawyer, Michelle was sure that she would never have seen her child again because it was what Cristopher desired. Fortunately, he was not the decision-maker. But he had many lawyers working for him and making it difficult to have access to Bethany. At first, Michelle couldn´t take her out of the mansion. It was a struggle to take Scott with her to spend time with the sister he loved so much because the old man said that the brat boy broke his furniture.

It was a blunt lie. Michelle dealt with this by going to the bank and causing a scene. Since the image and appearances meant everything to Cristopher Worthgold, he would go back on his decision and accept Scott and Nancy to visit his house along with Michelle.

Scott had a bond of love with his sister that not even the mean man could ever destroy. He brought her the little gifts that he had made at school, like portraits of her and puzzle toys. They were both extremely intelligent and they spent hours entertaining each other, telling stories, and playing games. Michelle loved to sit near them and listen to the stories that Scott told his little sister called 'The man that loved you the most.'

"He would kill a dragon for you. He adored you and threw many parties for you. He took you everywhere and declared to everybody that you were his pride and joy."

"And that was my father…"

"That was your father, Stanley Worthgold. He loved you with all his heart."

"And he loved you too, Scott."

"How do you know?"

"People who love much, also love many…"

"That is a funny way to put it. Okay, today your title will be Funny Head."

"No…" She was already giggling.

"Okay. Princess Funny Head then."

"Then your title will be Loser in the Pool."

And after saying that she would run to the pool and jump in with her brother right behind her. Michelle enjoyed listening to this game that they had invented of giving each other titles. They were always surprising and funny titles. They teased each other all the time although they were never afraid to say how much they loved each other. Michelle was proud of her children.

And then by one of these turns of destiny, when Bethany was eleven years old, her grandfather suffered a heart attack and died in the hospital after a few hours that he was admitted there.

His will confirmed that Bethany Worthgold was his only heir. His fortune would be available to her, from the moment she turned twenty-one. Until that day arrived, a team of lawyers was at her disposal to see to her every need and wish. An allowance was provided every month for expenses and new purchases. All she had to do was ask.

The first thing she asked was for her mother and brother to move in with her. Of course, Nancy was welcomed back too.

There were capable business people employed to administrate Bethany's inheritance until she was ready to do it herself. And these people reported to Michelle, the sole guardian of Bethany.

Nobody ever had a problem with that because Michelle was polite, intelligent, and extremely dedicated to Bethany.

After only one man had stopped breathing, many others could breathe easily now. The opposition was finally buried.

Chapter 21 – Teenage years

Michelle had made up her mind to provide happy memories for her children because she had experienced pain and strong battles when she least expected. She was thankful for this peaceful period with her beloved children and being so full of energy, Michelle decided to take them to visit the world.

All the effort she had dedicated in negotiating debts she had not made due to Tom's dishonesty and the hours she had consumed in tribunals because of her father-in-law's injustice, Michelle would use now to plan wonderful trips for her family.

She started with amusement parks and children's museums around the world. Bethany owned a bank, so money was not of consequence here.

When they went to the first amusement park, they stayed in a luxurious hotel and dined with characters from the movies they loved. Bethany would be dressed as a princess and Scott would usually dress like the prince charming or some other themed character, only to please her. He was eighteen years old and in no hurry to start college. Bethany also went to school very little because her mother hired excellent tutors. The main goal at the moment was to spend the most time together and enjoy themselves.

Michelle was amused to see her children buying every kind of gift the park had to offer. They purchased swards, arrows and bows, spaceships, wooden horses, crowns, treasure boxes, and any other toy that caught their interest. Back home, Michelle made a large room available for them to deposit these things and it was common for friends to visit them and be taken there to enjoy this world of imagination.

They went to a Water Park in France and when they were back, Michelle agreed with Scott that they could have a miniature one made in their backyard. It was a sensation among the teenager's friends.

The science parks in Africa showed discoveries from ancient times that inspired Bethany to make beautiful drawings and to write poems and songs about nature.

The jet plane never stopped much since it had to take the little family to many countries in Europe. In the passing of the years, they added the famous tourist destinations and visited Egypt, India, Japan, Australia, and China.

The Amazon Rain Forest. The Pyramids of Egypt or The Great Wall of China were such delightful routes that they visited more than once.

When they were home, Michelle took them to the beach house that Stanley had bought for her years ago. That place was where she remembered having been the happiest because Stanley was still alive.

Bethany and Scott also loved the place and they made many friends there. In fact, Scott met his first girlfriend there. Her name was Kate and her family owned a magazine stand by the shore. They fell in love and went everywhere together while it lasted. It was a six-months time romance.

Then he met Alice who was an interior decorator and stayed with her for almost eight weeks. She broke up to go study abroad and Scott found consolation in Rita´s arms.

"Scott, I worry about the velocity it takes you to break up with a girl."

"Mom, don´t worry. I am not looking for anything serious."

"Please, don´t play with their feelings."

"My overprotective mother. Sometimes they break up with me, you know."

"Oh, Scott."

He always dismissed her worries with jokes, smiles, and hugs. But it was impossible for him not to date. He was young, handsome, and rich. He had a great sense of humor and girls soon found out that he was generous.

After a couple of months and a dozen more girls, Michelle tried again to advise Scott.

"Son, if one of these girls gets pregnant, you will be stuck with the one you don´t love."

"Mom, let´s worry when the situation arrives, okay?"

And how could she contradict him? Nobody was pregnant or complaining and Michelle preferred to meet the girls than to have him hiding his relationships, which he never did. But again, Michelle wouldn´t insist on the subject, only let her son know her thoughts.

When he was little, Scott had asked about his father. Michelle didn´t want him to develop resentments or hate for Tom, so she had told the little boy,

"You see, Scott, your father loves you very much. But he wants to get rich, so he is trying his luck around the world. He wants to throw us parties for two hundred guests."

"I don´t care for parties."

"Neither do I son. But it is important for your father. And he works very hard to become rich. People are different, that is all. But it doesn´t mean that he doesn´t think about you. Here, let me show you something."

Michelle got the postcards that Tom had sent her and gave them to the boy. It was common for him to sit with a world map on his lap and highlight with a marker, the countries he saw on the postcards´ stamps.

Michelle would sit by his side and they would talk about the beautiful things Tom must have seen there. He carried a box full of these postcards almost everywhere.

Then Stanley had appeared in their lives and he left the box inside a drawer. More than a father figure, Stanley had been a presence in his life that fulfilled the boy´s need for a father. Stanley was there at his school to watch him play soccer and to applaud his musical presentations on father´s day. The truth is that the boy was thirsty for the love of a father and Stanley had loved him.

Tom´s name only came up again when Scott was already eighteen. Stanley had already passed away for eight years and there were two months that Christopher had died.

Scott sat in front of his mother at the library and asked to talk.

"Sure, Scott. Tell me what is in your mind."

"Well, mom, I have been thinking. My father left when I was little because he went in search of richness."

"It is true, son."

"But now we have a fortune. We could hire someone to find him and then he could come back to live with us."

"Do you miss him so much, son?"

"I don´t miss him at all, mom. I don´t even remember Tom White. I miss my stepdad, Stanley."

"Oh, son. Then why did you make this suggestion?"

"Because I worry about you. I don´t want you to be lonely."

"I don´t feel lonely. Thanks to God I have you and Bethany. And the best of friends: Nancy."

"But a woman needs a man."

"Son, I never felt lonelier in my life than when I lived with Tom White."

There was a pause when she said that. Scott stood up and hugged his mother.

"I suspected that there was more to the story than what you told me when I was a boy."

As Michelle watched her son go back to his share and look at her with tenderness, she knew he deserved to know the truth.

"You know, son… I thought it was useless to hurt your feelings by saying bad things about your father. It wouldn´t solve anything and probably you would feel abandoned and confused. So I told you some truths since indeed your father was very ambitious and a treasure hunter. But I didn´t say the negative things I found in his character. Even now, you have the right to maintain only the good memories.

"Mom, you succeeded because I never felt abandoned or helpless. I even dreamt of becoming rich and traveling to space with you and my mysterious father."

"I am glad to hear that. It is good for a boy to have hopes and dreams."

"Thank you, mom. You provided that. But I am an adult now and I want to understand my past."

"Scott. You can always put down to a resentful mind of an abandoned woman, the bad things I will say about your father, now. Promise me to keep two things in mind: first that it is my point of view, only. Maybe Tom would tell the story differently. Second, it was me whom he abandoned and never you."

"Okay, I promise." He held her hand when he said that because he knew that some of those memories would be painful for his mother.

And Michelle told him everything. From the day she met Tom White to the last time that she saw him. There were moments of tears and Scott interrupted her twice to make her drink some water and hug her again.

When she finished, Scott went to his room to get the postcards box. Michelle was surprised that he had kept it for so long.

The fireplace was not lighted but as soon as Scott threw the box there, Michelle got some matches and they both lightened some and threw at the box. It quickly caught fire and Michelle was embraced by her son as they both watched the box being consumed to ashes.

It brought them the necessary closure.

Chapter 22 – Preparing to lead an empire

Bethany had decided to study business administration because she wanted to follow in Stanley´s footsteps and that was what he had majored in.

She decided on living at home and attending a nearby college because she felt that she had been apart from Michelle long enough and the going to college experience didn´t attract her as much as being with her mom.

Scott had gone to college in another town and lived in a fraternity with friends as eager as him to enjoy their youth. They went from party to party and practiced many sports like wrestling and judo, mainly to impress girls. Somehow, he had managed to graduate in computer science. He had a position at GWB, the Global Bank of the World, but being already twenty-six, Scott traveled a lot on his own and people could rarely find him behind his desk. Though he had enjoyed traveling with his mom and little sister, it was time he went on some adventures with his buddies. They went to search for polar bears, crocodiles, and whales. It was an exciting life he led and who could blame him?

As for Bethany, she had developed a sense of responsibility to lead the empire that was going to be left for her. The years she spent with Christopher Worthgold had allowed him to explain to her the main purpose of their conglomerate. The objective was to keep an enormous flow of money through the family bank and expand through high technology companies and investments in sources of energy.

Many of the business dinners that Christopher held at the mansion intended to make the tycoons familiar with his successor, Bethany. She was his pride and joy and often he would tell her about the family history and the way their fortune had started.

Bethany´s love for her grandpa soon influenced her to love the family business too. It was not spending money that made her passionate, although it was pleasant. It was the process of making money that drove her.

The things that Bethany learned in college were soon put to test at her companies and at the bank. She dedicated herself to the studies but also spent many hours at Stanley´s office at the bank, which was now hers.

She participated in most board meetings and sent Michelle to those she couldn´t attend.

"But sweetheart, I never finished my studies."

"Mother, Mozart played the piano at the Queen's palace when he was only five. No school taught him or anybody, as a matter of fact, to be a genius."

"But there are certain capacities that you need to develop to work with finance."

"I agree. But you can hire people to teach you what you need to know. My grandpa majored in philosophy. It had nothing to do with his actual work. I guess he just studied anything to please his family. But he was always more interested in trading, investing, and starting businesses than he was in books."

"I didn't know that."

"Dad thought you were capable. Scott told me he planned on investing in a store or a restaurant for you to manage."

"But I think Stanley saw it more as a pastime for me. He never asked me to work in the family business."

"Well, you are family and I am asking it. Let's give it a try. You can stop whenever you want if you don't like it."

But the thing is that Michelle loved her new responsibilities. She hired the top advisors to help her understand global matters. At night, she and Bethany would sit at the library and explore many possibilities. Michelle read all her school books and helped Bethany study for her tests.

They implemented production systems from the most developed multinational industries. And Bethany started to leave her mark as a just leader because she promoted people by merit and gave equal rights for men and women. All her buildings were adjusted to have daycare for employees' babies and children.

"The paparazzi started calling you 'the feminist CEO', sweetheart."

"And to think that I am still a director. Another two years before I become the CEO and sit on Christopher Worthgold's chair."

"That is just a formality, Bethany. One more legal step to overcome. Everybody knows that you are the owner of the Worthgold dynasty. And they jump at your smallest wish."

"Then I will keep wishing for things. This way they stay in shape."

"You silly thing. You are a powerful woman, Bethany, but for me, you are still my sweet baby. I can't help to think how proud your father would be to see the great person you have become. Never in

my life, I saw somebody love a baby with the intensity your dad loved you, Bethany. It always amazed me."
"I wish he could be in our lives for longer, mom."
"Me too, Bethany. Stanley was one of those persons that made the world a better place."
"That is the kind of person that I want to be, mom."
"You already are, sweetheart."
And it was true. Bethany examined things and thought in ways of improving the mechanisms as well as the people involved with them. The world saw her as a feminist and for now, she accepted it, but her dream was to be seen as a humanist someday. It meant for her that all humans deserved equal rights and should be respected. But she was a realist and knew that the process of change took time. She was just trying to do her part to build a better planet.

BALLROOM DANCES AND SUITORS

Michelle accepted all the invitations for parties and balls and took Bethany to mingle with the young people of high society.
Exactly the contrary of Scott's personality, Bethany had had few dates and showed no interest in going steady with anybody.
She danced at the balls and talked to the guys, laughing at their jokes. Bethany even agreed to go to the movies with a school friend, John Emeralrock.
"Your grandfather would rejoice, Bethany, if he could witness you going out with John. Emeralrock is a prominent family whose fortune was made through cattle farms. They were his close friends."
"Grandpa was nice to me, mom."
"I know, sweetheart. And I am not against John as a suitor for you. He is a nice young man."
"I am sorry to disappoint you, mom. I find him immature. John is always babbling about his stamps collection."
"Maybe it is a sign that he is passionate."
"Then I will print a stamp with my face and send it to him."
"Bethany!"
"Sorry, mom. I didn't mean to sound disrespectful."
"You weren't. You just surprised me, that is all."

Michelle came to the conclusion that she shouldn´t interfere with her daughter´s matters of the heart just as she had decided to do with Scott. They were old enough to make their own choices.

AN INTERNATIONAL VISITOR

Then, one night, Scott brought a client from the bank to have dinner at the house. It was usual for them to do that or even offer cocktail parties or barbecues for some of the VIP clients. The housemaids were used to getting things ready on short notice.
But this young man was not part of a group, he had come alone. First, he made an appointment with Scott at the GBW bank and after they discussed opportunities for investments, Scott heard about his visits to the Worthgold´s house when he was a child.
"My father used to be in business with Christopher Worthgold before our country faced a civil war."
"Well, then you must accompany me to the house for dinner and tell me if you find it very changed. Later we can join some of my friends and go to a nightclub." Scott made friends easily because he was always warm and included people in the activities he had scheduled for himself.
When Bethany saw Omar al Malik, he was very relaxed, sitting on an armchair and talking to her brother. Something happened to her heart when their eyes locked. It was as if they had been separated for a century and at the same time, she felt as if they had parted only yesterday. She felt something like a mixture of pain and relief when she looked at him. Then he smiled. And Scott started with the introductions.
"This is my sister, Bethany Worthgold. And this is Omar…"
"al Malik." She finished his sentence without realizing it.
"The little girl from the garden," Omar said that as he took her hand in his.
"Oh, so you know each other."
"We met in our childhood," Bethany explained as she took a seat by her brother´s side on the couch. "But I don´t expect sheik Omar to remember that."
"I am still a prince since my father is still the sheik. I could not forget you, Bethany."

"Wow. I didn´t know you were royalty. I am glad I gave you the VIP treatment though. The amounts we discussed demanded that." Scott was light-hearted about the whole thing and he couldn´t suspect the turmoil his sister was feeling right now.

"These are nice words and I thank you, prince. But you never contacted me and I believed you had forgotten all about me. Because I forgot you."

A small silence followed her statement. She hated herself by saying that because it made her sound weak and spiteful. Fortunately, Michelle entered the room and the conversation regained a normal rhythm.

Nancy rarely joined them for dinner anymore. Due to her old age, she used to have an early supper and to retire early to watch some tv shows before sleep.

At the dinner table, Scott told his mother that Omar and Bethany were old friends.

"Oh, how nice. So, you thought to check on your friend?"

"Yes. I thought it would be nice to visit the little one."

"I am not so little anymore."

"But you are just as pretty."

There was such tension between them that anyone could sense just by looking at the couple. They didn´t even try to hide it. So, it was not a surprise when Omar declined the invitation to go to the nightclub with Scott and told him he would stay to chat with the ladies.

Bethany was very silent and Michelle talked to the guest about international politics for a while and then decided to excuse herself to give the young couple some time alone.

When she left, Omar respected Bethany´s need for silence and just looked into her eyes, drinking all her beauty. Then she asked him abruptly,

"Why did you come?"

"I came for a kiss."

"Don´t be arrogant, prince."

"Call me Omar, as you did before."

"You left for a long time."

"I am here now."

"And does that solve everything?"

"I hope so. I came to marry you."

"Marry me? Are you out of your mind? I am still at school."
"So am I. It will be perfect. This way we will have time to enjoy your country before we go to my country for good."
"For good? What do you mean?"
"I mean that one day my people expect me to be their leader. And I will have you by my side as my wife, then."
"You are out of your mind, prince Omar."
She was walking from side to side of the room and he was sitting on his armchair admiring her all the while. But now he stood up and she saw all the strength of his body that matched the decided look on his face.
"Come here, Bethany." It was a command by no mistake. But his voice was hoarse and he spoke in a tone that sounded like a caress for her. Bethany stopped in front of him like one helpless prey in front of a hunter.
Omar took her in his arms and kissed her passionately. It was the kiss from a man starved for the woman he loved. His arm in her back pressed her body to him and his other hand went to the back of her head and his fingers were buried in the softness of her hair.
Bethany didn´t need much encouragement because she longed for him. Her hand embraced around his neck and she opened her mouth to taste all the sweetness he was offering her.
It was more than the warmth from their bodies and the perfection of their scents to each other´s senses. There was a feeling of belonging and a notion of finally achieving some long-lost dream.
When their lips parted and Omar made a way of kisses down her neck, Bethany brought his mouth back to hers and it was her time to demand. He had a smile that disappeared as she savored his lips and caused him to give small bites in her lower lip. Then they were completely out of breath and Bethany walked to the bar to drink some water. He watched her trying to regain her composure. She stood her arm to him offering the glass of water and he took her hand and pulled her toward him. Their bodies were intertwined again and he was kissing her mouth before the glass hit the carpet.
It took them some minutes to be able to speak.
"My sweet. My love."
"Don´t say that, Omar."
"I must say what I feel. Tomorrow I will take you out to dinner."
"No. I can´t."

"Why?"

"I have a boyfriend."

He was so surprised by that information that he let her take some steps away from him.

"You didn´t kiss me like someone who is in a serious relationship."

"But I am."

"I don´t believe you, Bethany."

"You took me by surprise, that is all."

"That is all?"

"Yes. Please, try to understand. I am already spoken for."

"We will see to that."

And by saying that Omar left. That night, Bethany stayed awake for a long time wondering why she had lied to him. The truth is that she was scared of her own feelings.

Chapter 23 – The competitor

Bethany had kissed other men before. But it had been an encounter of lips, not an encounter of souls, as was the case when she kissed Omar.

She woke up thinking about him. His dark hair which was so soft to touch, his bright eyes that weren´t afraid to transmit to her what he was feeling, and his mouth. It felt so right to kiss him and she wished the kiss would never end.

But all these feelings upset her. What was she? A powerful tycoon woman that could change and impact people´s lives or a very silly young girl who was in love with a prince?

For a moment she chose the second option, only to be able to kiss Omar again.

But then she took the decision of not indulging in these daydreams.

The nerve of the man. He had kept away for many years without any contact with her to finally show up demanding kisses? Unacceptable.

And what was all that talk about marriage? As if she had been sitting around idly waiting for his decision about her future.

Bethany had a life! And a good one, indeed.

Now, all she had to do was to avoid Omar and return to her usual activities. But who was she lying to? She knew that he could not be stopped or avoided. He made his intentions very clear the previous night.

If only she had a boyfriend to protect her from his advances. And why shouldn't she? Was she ugly or something? Well, she said to Omar that she had a boyfriend and now she would prove to him that she did. Maybe she could turn the lie into truth. And she would do it this afternoon, at college.

JOHN EMERALROCK

Bethany found John in his usual spot, sitting on a bench, under a walnut tree located in the nice lawns of their college. He had his stamp album on his lap and was adding new ones to his collection.

"Hello, boyfriend."

When Bethany greeted him with those words, John looked around to find the person she was talking to.

"Can I sit with you, John?"

"Sure you can, Bethany. I thought you were talking to somebody else."

"Don't be silly, John. Who else is my boyfriend?"

"I am?"

"Of course you are."

"Wow." He became thoughtful. "It is not that I am complaining, Bethany. It is just that I don't recall asking you, even having meant to all the time. And if I remember well, you never asked me too."

"But that is it exactly, John. Because you are so intelligent, I understood that you wanted to ask me. And the answer is yes."

"Bethany! My girlfriend!" John looked a little euphoric.

"So, John… Do you want to go for a walk? Or to the movies?" She thought they should celebrate or something.

"I have a better idea. Since you are my girlfriend, you will be the first to see the new stamps of my collection."

"How interesting."

"Brace yourself, Bethany. You are in for a treat."

She was in, all right. She was in to face boredom. John went on and on about the characteristics of his beloved stamps and Bethany thought it was a deserved punishment for her for being a coward.

Later, when Bethany arrived home, hundreds of roses were waiting for her. The card said, "Love, Omar."

SUITORS MEET

The next weekend, Bethany brought John for his first dinner with her family. Scott had invited Omar because both had become friends very quickly. Michelle made the introductions,
"Omar, I want to introduce you to Bethany's new boyfriend. This is John Emeralrock."
"Nice to meet you, Omar."
"Nice to meet you too, John. New boyfriend, she said?"
"Yes."
"Not really," Bethany was quick to interrupt. "We have been going out for a while now. It is just that we kept it to ourselves."
"Isn't that marvelous?" Michelle was happy for her daughter. John was a nice and quiet young man.
"Indeed. It is amazing how good she is at keeping secrets." Omar said that and watched Bethany become very red and uncomfortable. She blushed for two reasons… First, because it was clear to her that Omar was referring to their kisses. Second and most important, because she thought Omar would call on her bluff any moment now. But he didn't. Omar seemed to be enjoying her game.

THE STAMPS

During dinner, John made sure to share the details of his last acquisition: a very rare stamp from Italy.
"I have stamps from Italy… I have stamps from France… I have stamps from Mexico…"
His voice was so monotonous that Michelle was forced to hide a yawn.
"I have stamps from Spain…"
"Did you say Yemen?"
"No, Scott, he said Spain."
"Oh, Spain. I see. I don't understand this passion that both of you have for stamps."
Bethany couldn't believe her years. How could Scott think that she shared John's interest in stamps? He knew her so well! But then, when she looked at her brother he blinked one eye at her and she understood that he was teasing her. So she teased him back.

"Well, Scott, some of us can't help being intellectuals, that's all."
"Oh, I see, your royal intellectual. May I count on your wisdom to decide among the potatoes or the tomatoes that are being served in your honor tonight?"
"You should eat both, your royal vegetable eater!"
"I don't want to stuff myself. I am thinking about eating a dictionary for dessert. This way I can rise in knowledge high enough to kiss your feet."
"How rude! Why are you mocking me?" And after he said that, John rose from the table and went to the other room to sulk.
Everybody was so surprised that nobody moved at first. Then Bethany went after him followed by Michelle. They did their best to explain to him that it was only a joke, a kind of game that Bethany and Scott played since childhood.
At the table, Scott told Omar about it.
"No need to explain, my friend. I guess some people lack a sense of humor."
"I am afraid you are right, Omar."
When the other three came back, John continued with his dramatic scene, making sure to shake hands with Scott.
"No hard feelings, Scott."
"Of course not, John. After all, we are to become brothers-in-law, someday."
When she heard that, Bethany couldn't avoid reacting with a shiver. Fortunately, nobody noticed, least of all the easily offended boyfriend. Nobody, except Omar, who as always didn't take his eyes from her.

A TOAST

It was kind of silly and really an exaggeration, but after dinner, Michelle proposed to make a toast to the happy couple. Bethany thought it was better to accept the situation, so she could get rid of the embarrassment soon enough.
They went to the next room and while the maid brought the champagne and the glasses, Michelle went to get Nancy from her room.
Scott invited John and Omar to the library to check on some old stamps and make sure they weren't valuable or rare.

Bethany took the opportunity and stepped outside for a moment. Maybe the garden would relax her a little and the fresh air would inspire her next actions. Because she thought that things were going too far in what related to John. Brother-in-law. Indeed. For two people who had never even kissed.

"Congratulations are in order." She was startled by Omar's voice. She turned to him and answered his comment.

"It is okay. There is no need for that."

"Are you afraid?"

"Of you?"

"Yes."

"Don't be so full of yourself, Omar."

"Then, let me wish you happiness. I will kiss you now."

He approached Bethany and his strong arms surrounded her shoulders. She held her breath, but his lips moved to her ear and Bethany heard him whisper, "You are so beautiful."

Her breathing accelerated while he moved back to face her. She opened her lips, expecting his kiss. He smiled slowly and broadly while he ran his lips through her face and planted his lips on her other ear, speaking in a tone that only Bethany could hear, "Congratulations."

She couldn't take it anymore. She grabbed his face with both hands and brought his mouth to hers. She kissed him deeply and felt complete when his tongue moved inside her mouth asking for her surrender. She gave herself to him and hugged him tightly. Then the noise of someone popping a bottle of champagne alarmed her and she pushed him away.

"That is how it is done."

"Oh yes, Bethany. It is."

He was laughing in delight and Bethany tried to hide a smile as she ran inside offering an explanation for her actions.

"The congratulations, I mean."

"Of course. I believe you."

He was in no hurry to follow her inside. Instead, he walked a while around the garden, thinking about how much he enjoyed having Bethany in his life. He could see right through her and he sure liked what he saw.

Chapter 24 – Business expansion

It was kind of a relief when the weekend was over and Bethany could go back to the familiar environment of GBW bank. From that building, many decisions were made regarding the conglomerate to which Bethany was the sole heir. The truth was that the Worthgolds had always used the top floors of the bank building as a sort of headquarters to hold meetings with their directors, suppliers as well as partners and clients.

And Bethany had continued with that tradition since the bank was near her house. She loved that place because grandpa had taken her there since she could walk. She spent hours drawing at her little desk or making her homework from school, waiting for grandpa to finish some meetings. When Christopher was over with his compromise he would immediately go to the adjoining room and check on Bethany. Every time he complimented her childish drawings and even hang some on the walls. Her babysitter Lucy was then told to get a cab back home. Christopher paraded Bethany to his employees and people nodded and smiled at her a lot. The tour finished with both of them going across the street for ice creams and cakes.

It was all coming back to her, as Bethany walked the long corridor and entered the large business meetings room. As she looked around the table the faces of the directors showed their approval of her.

She was dressing in a label suit and high heels. Her long hair was pinned to the top of her head, giving her a look of efficiency. Bethany wore light makeup and French perfume. She was not a woman who could walk around unnoticed.

"Miss Worthgold, we are pleased to join you in this presentation." The chairman of the board of directors welcomed her very politely. There were eight directors there and three of them were women hired by Bethany.

"Thanks, Mr. Zeroly. Have our guests arrived yet?"

"Yes. They are having some refreshments with our public relations team and should join us any minute now. Besides the three potential investors, two engineers are accompanying them."

"That is odd."

"They were brought by the main investor. We didn´t think we should refuse their presence."

"Of course, not." Bethany took her place at the head of the table and Mr. Zeroly took the seat by her right.

She had been working hard on her expansion project that comprised the purchase of some communication companies in South America.

It was as if she was testing herself before she took her grandfather's place in six months.

The board of directors expected her presentation to be perfect but instead of making her nervous, it challenged Bethany to achieve a level of excellence.

In this meeting, the reason for the investors to be invited was to give them a chance of having their doubts cleared by no other than the person in charge of the project, Bethany herself.

As they were ushered into the room, Bethany was startled to see Omar al Malik leading the group.

While he shook hands with some people at the entrance of the room, she asked Zeroly.

"Wasn't our main investor the Japanese tycoon, Mr. Stee Ling?"

"Mr. Ling gave up on the last minute. But before we could worry, Mr. Maliq took his place. He was referred to us by your brother, so we thought it would be okay."

She would have a word with Scott later. This project was the apple of her eyes and he knew it. Any changes should be brought to her at once. Even if it was good news as the replacement of an undecided investor.

But since she needed to focus on her presentation, Bethany decided to forget about it for now. Omar finally was greeting her.

"What a surprise to see you, prince Omar."

"It is always a pleasure to be with you."

"So, besides petroleum and building sector, you have now developed an interest in telecommunication…"

"When Scott told me about your interest in expanding to the South of the globe I found it innovative."

"Thank you. I take this project very seriously."

"Great. Because I thought to myself: I take Miss Worthgold very seriously. Why not make some millions of dollars together?"

Everybody in the room relaxed and laughed at what they thought was a joke. But Bethany knew that he didn't intend to be funny.

And the meeting became a nightmare for her. Every fact Bethany presented, even the smallest one, had to be explained in detail to a doubting Omar. She said those were growing markets and he wanted to know if it was a growth of population or a growth of income. She explained the technical measures that were necessary to be implemented and the engineers Omar had brought to the meeting contradicted her step by step.

The people in the room were astonished by this turn of events. They were proud of Bethany because she didn't even blink at the opposition, she continued to present her ideas and to prove the viability of the project with excellent graphics and researches. Her assistant would produce new documents at her request and Bethany showed all her enthusiasm. Omar, on the other hand, almost ridiculed her work. The other investors followed his lead because he was one of the richest men in the world and they valued his opinion. Although the Spanish and the Austrian investors didn't speak much, their faces showed that they were reluctant.

"Prince Omar, allow me to hand you this piece of paper with accurate information."

"Thanks, Miss Worthgold. Oh, but this is the number of the population in those countries."

"Exactly. Since you had some problem with everything I had to say today, I was wondering if you have anything negative to say about this too. Or about their weather or the color of their roofs."

"Calm down, Miss Worthgold. I am trying to be professional here."

"While you try, sir, I am being the professional one."

There was an awkward silence in the room. These two tycoons had crashed and none of them seemed to be thinking of taking a step back. There was an aura of authority surrounding these two people and the others could almost touch it.

"You are aware that we are not discussing a bingo night. Millions of dollars are at risk here."

"I don't gamble, Omar Sahid al Maliq."

Omar felt so happy that Bethany had remembered his middle name that it was impossible for a smile not to form on his lips and he looked at her almost as if caressing her. Both of them seemed to have forgotten the other people in the room and as they addressed each other, there was an intimacy only completely understood by the couple. Their eyes were very bright, their voices contained all their determination and vivacity.

"Neither do I, Bethany Worthgold."

"Then, what is your decision about this investment?"

"I will have to analyze it carefully and obtain extra data. Maybe next trimester we can meet again here and I will have an answer for you."

"That won't do, Omar." Subconsciously she had dropped the formality of using his title. It brought another smile to his face. He seemed to be obtaining other satisfactions from this meeting beyond the monetary gains. "In three months, the competitors might be able to make new offers and we lose our advantages. I need an answer this week."

"If that is the case, I will answer you now."

"Even better."

"I will have to pass on this opportunity."

"Is that so?"

"Yes."

"And what about you, gentlemen?"

They tried to be polite about it but the answer was also no.

"Well, I have to thank you for your time and your interest in our company."

They said some polite words that she decided to ignore. Bethany rose to her feet and looked straight into Omar's eyes.

"Because you made a major contribution to this presentation, prince Omar, I would like to give you and information, before the media does."

"And what is that, Bethany Worthgold." He was looking at a lioness. He admired this strong woman more by the minute and if he hadn't already decided to marry her, he would be sure of it now.

"I am investing in this project myself. We are expanding to South America starting this week."

"With your own money?"

"Naturally. I have enough to do it ten times. My interest in partners had to do more with sharing technologies, supporting each other based on successful past experiences. And as you said o well yourself, sir, why not make some millions out of it?"

"I admire your leadership."

"Thanks. Now if you will excuse me, I have matters to put into action. Have another coffee. Our PR team will be glad to take you on a tour of our building."

"Can I have one more minute of your time, Bethany?"

"Certainly."

"Because you are inexperienced and the world of business is aware of that fact, I had to be sure that this project was not only a hobby or a pastime for a spoiled rich girl."

"It is not." Bethany was so angry now that she could even punch Omar and he knew it.

"Yes. You have proved how serious and committed you are to this project if you are willing to risk your own money to make it happen."

"It is a very controlled risk."

"I know. And that is why I will invest sixty percent of my money to become your partner."

Some jaws dropped on hearing that. Except for Bethany´s. She just gave him an intent long look and they were locked in that private world of emotions while the others kept busy getting the contracts to be signed. After Omar´s decision, the other two men invested twenty percent each.

Later in her office, Mr. Zeroly congratulated her effusively.

"Congratulations. You deserve the name Worthgold alright. Your first project passed and your company didn´t have to invest one cent on it. We are so proud of you, Miss Worthgold. That man seemed to be made of ice."

Bethany thanked him and thought about his words. Maybe to the outside world, Omar could seem cold but he had her blood burning through her veins.

Chapter 25 – A reason to celebrate

On the way to the underground garage, Bethany kept replaying the events of the day. She looked at the enormous mirror inside the private lift and was surprised to see that her face didn´t show how much stress she had felt.

She had wanted to scream at Omar each time he challenged her. But every time she had controlled herself in order to guarantee a high-level presentation of her project.

Why had he made her day so difficult? Was it revenge because she had invented a false boyfriend? But it couldn´t be it, not only because Omar seemed to be amazed by that game, but also because he was extremely serious about business decisions. The newspapers always talked about him as the surgeon-negotiator. She could understand what they meant now.

She felt exhausted and still victorious because even if he had taken her to explore limits and capacities she didn´t even know she had, in the end, she had proved that she was a businesswoman from the Worthgold lineage.

She had a smile on her face when she approached her Ferrari Roma and was not the least surprised to see Omar leaning on her car with his arms crossed and a relaxed posture as if he had all the time in the world to wait for her.

Her smile disappeared and she made it clear that she didn´t want to talk to him.

"Leave me alone, Omar."

"You don´t mean that." He didn´t allow her to enter the car, no matter how hard she tried and after some unsuccessful attempts, he just took the keys from her hand. "Come on, my love, talk to me. What is upsetting you?"

"You, Omar Sahid. You are upsetting me. How dare you call me love, when you acted as if you despised me or even hated me at that meeting?"

"Come on, Bethany. I was only helping you. In the competitive world of business, you will always find people to confront you and your ideas. You proved that you can be sharp under attack. I savored every minute of watching you fight for your beliefs."

"But then you would invest anyway? That´s condescending."

"No. I was ready to invest only if you convinced me. And you did, my beauty. So let´s kiss and make up."

"In your dreams, Omar. In your dreams."

"And in your dreams too, Bethany, I am sure."

She blushed intently because he was saying the truth. Lately, she had dreamt of him almost every night. He thought her embarrassment was cute but decided to change the subject because they had had enough friction for one day.

"So you lake Ferraris? I have a Lamborghini and a limo myself."

"Also a great car. The Ferrari accommodates my needs to beat the traffic to go to work or school. Now give me my keys back."

"Only if you give me a ride. I let my chauffeur go just before you stepped out of the lift."

"All right. I am too tired to argue."

"Or better yet. Let me drive. I want to take you to a nice restaurant and celebrate our first business partnership."

"I would have to change for that."

"Nonsense. You look beautiful. People will take you for a top model."

"You can be so charming when you want, Omar."

He opened the passenger's door for her and took his seat behind the wheel. Before he started the car, Bethany placed her hand on top of his to get his attention.

"What?"

"Next time, Omar, let someone else be the opponent."

"Why is that Bethany?"

"Because I want you to always be on my side, Omar."

"You got it, my love. You got it!"

As the powerful car rode along the roads, Bethany sat back and closed her eyes, enjoying the company of the man that populated her dreams.

THE TALK

Omar took her to a very nice restaurant and the host had them seated at the best table of the house. While they waited for their order and savored some delicious ice mint juices that made them feel refreshed, the couple started to talk.

"Bethany, why do you need a fake boyfriend to defend you from me? Do you really believe that I could harm you in any way?"

"No, Omar. That is not it. It is just that you appeared so suddenly and I was caught by surprise."

"But then, for you, it was a bad surprise…"

"Not at all. I had missed you for many years until I finally understood that it was going to be just a childhood memory between us."

"I remember clearly all our talks, Bethany. And I was hoping to take you out on dates, then we could know each other better and I could show you that my love is sincere. But you brought Emeralrock to the equation."

"Sorry, Omar. I remember our talks too. But we were so young and innocent. We knew nothing of the world."

"And what do you know now that puts you on guard."

"I know for instance, that our customs and cultures are so different. That your father's word is the law and yours will also have to be obeyed someday."

"And is that such a bad thing? My father is not ordering people to jump from bridges. He rules our country with authority to guarantee order. But the people love him because he dedicates his life to create jobs and improve life for all. My father is very fond of high technologies that help to improve people's lives. He has invested in hospitals and nurseries. I could talk during a month and not even begin to describe all the things he does for others."

"I remember your father and I respect him very much. My grandpa thought highly of him."

"Thank you."

"But there are other matters too. You talk about marriage, but I am afraid that one day you will be interested in having a harem. Your law permits it."

"A man will have a harem only if he chooses to. I chose you."

"You say that now, but what if you change your mind later?"

"Tell me one thing, Bethany. Don't married men in your country ever change their minds?"

"Of course they do. Many people get divorced."

"I think you answered your own question. I guess everybody dreams of a life together forever. But it is necessary a leap of faith. If you love me, you will have faith in us."

"Omar, since we are opening up to one another, there is another point I would like to discuss."

"What is it, Bethany?"

"It is about the clothes. Even if we moved there, I don't see myself dressing the djellaba, your traditional tunic, or the niqab, the veil that covers women's faces…"

"You wouldn't have to wear them every day. Occidental clothes are allowed in informal situations. I would only ask you to compromise with official events. But I guess it also happens here. I have received some invitations that mention black tie as obligatory garments…"

"It is true. Oh, Omar. I am afraid that because of ignorance I have been so unjust with you. I sound pedant and prejudiced."

"It is normal to feel insecure towards the unknown. When I first started coming here everything was so different and complex that my fears almost froze me. Fortunately, my father was there to explain to me that men are just men. And that everybody is trying their best to achieve happiness.”

“That is wise.”

“In my personal case, I concluded that you are essential for my future happiness Bethany. I will consider myself lucky if you one day correspond my feelings. That is why I ask you, Bethany, will you think about the things we talked tonight?”

“I will. I promise you, Omar.”

Chapter 26 – John's birthday

After that dinner with Omar, Bethany really thought about her feelings. Deep down she knew that he was the other part of herself and she longed to be with him. In a way, she had known it since childhood. These feelings were too precious and rare to be mistaken by anything else. She loved Omar, she belonged to him, and as soon as they started their lives together the better. She felt the same urges as he did.

But there were also her fears. Bethany knew that this marriage would bring an enormous change to her life. And she didn't know if she was ready for it. One thing was for sure, she knew that she could count on Omar to help her adjust at every step of the way. They would do it together. Their love would be their source of strength and happiness. Bethany took the decision to say yes to Omar because she had zero inclination of allowing her fears to have the last word in the matter.

And then there was John Emeralrock. Oh, how she wished that she hadn't brought this complication to her own life. Now she would have to break up with him, which was a pretty simple act. But the timing was the problem. John's birthday party would happen in two weeks and he made a big deal to his family about his girlfriend's participation. When Bethany had met John's family they acted as if it was a miracle for him to finally introduce a girlfriend to the family. They kept offering her food and drinks. His mother offered her extra cushions to be more comfortable on the sofa and a stool for her feet. They pampered her so much that when she left their presence, she felt a terrible headache.

Bethany didn´t have the heart to break up with John and humiliate him a few days before his party. He was her classmate, so their age was the same, John was turning twenty-one and it was a big occasion for him.

When the day finally arrived Bethany saw herself on the ballroom dance floor, waltzing with John to give a start to the festivities. Two hundred guests were spread around sipping wine and champagne, eating canapes and candies. John was happy to be the center of attention. Earlier he had introduced Bethany to his twin cousins, Dottie and Bernie.

"It is short for Dorothea…"

"And short for Bernadette…"

They gave this information while they giggled and took turns touching Bethany´s hands. John was proud to tell something else about Dottie,

"This one here collects butterflies." He squeezed Dottie in a one-arm hug as he said that.

"I help her… I help her…"

"I know you help her, Bernie. But Dottie is the mind of the operation. We could even say she is the 'scientist' in our family."

Dottie was so touched by his comment that Bethany was uncertain if there were tears in the girl´s eyes. She felt she had to congratulate her since they were making such a big deal out of it.

"Congratulations, Dottie. I don´t know how you do it."

"I know. I amaze myself."

Now, during the dance, Bethany felt Dottie´s eyes following John´s every movement and he seemed to be showing off to her. Bethany felt better to think that John would find someone to comfort him after their breakup.

After two dances, Bethany sat in some chairs positioned along the wall with the excuse to rest but keeping in mind that John should have a chance to dance with his cousins.

And that is when Omar approached her. He had received an invitation to the party, as well as three others of Scott´s best friends. John was making an effort to please his future brother-in-law' as he had gotten used to calling Scott.

"Hello, Bethany. You look beautiful tonight."

"Thank you, Omar. I saw your entrance with my brother´s noisy group. I hope you are not all already drunk."

"That is something you will have to ask Scott. As for me, I don´t drink alcoholic beverages."
"Oh, I didn´t know about that."
"Don´t blame yourself. You have a boyfriend to dedicate your thoughts to. It would be unnatural if you took an interest in me."
"Please, Omar, try to understand. How could I break up with him so near to the party?"
"I see what you mean. So, tonight, after the party, you break up with him."
"Omar, you can´t tell me what to do."
"Why not?"
"Because I like to make my own decisions. Stop being a male chauvinist."
Omar kneels at her feet and when she least expects he takes her shoe off.
"What is that about, Omar? Give me back my shoe."
She stands from the chair and he stops in front of her hiding her shoe behind his back.
"No way. I won´t give it back to you, beautiful Bethany."
"Isn´t that just the opposite of Cinderella? She was supposed to lose the shoe, not to have it taken from her foot."
"That was her destiny there and this here is yours."
"And what do you intend to obtain by that?"
"Now that you only have one shoe, you won´t be able to dance with John anymore."
"That´s outrageous. He is my boyfriend, you know."
"You keep saying that."
"And you have to accept it, Omar. Here. I just took off the other shoe. Now I will be able to dance all I want."
"Clever move. Maybe it will cause scandal to the prude John."
She laughs a little because it is really a possibility.
"Bethany, listen to me. If I find a way to put the shoe back in your foot, do you promise to dance only with me for the rest of the night?"
"I don´t need that shoe anymore. I can dance barefoot."
"Does it mean that you won´t take the dare?"
"Is it a dare?"
"Let´s call it that."
"I accept, then."

"Good. Give me your foot, Bethany."

"No. It is cheating."

"It was worth a try."

"I am not your vassal, you know."

"And I don´t want you to be."

"What is it you want from me, Omar?"

"I told you, Bethany. I want you to be my wife."

"So, behave yourself and maybe I will be convinced that it is a good idea."

She walks away from him and he notices that because she is wearing a very long silver dress, few people would notice that she not wearing shoes.

Omar bends down and grabs the other shoe that Bethany had abandoned there. Then he joins her at the punch table where Bethany is talking to John and some giggling twin girls.

"Congratulations, John, on your birthday."

"Thank you, Omar. I am glad you could come."

"My pleasure. And I am glad I came because then I can save you from the germs."

"Germs?"

"Yes. Bethany had lost her shoes. But I searched every inch of this dusty floor until I found them."

Bethany didn´t know whether to scream or laugh. John´s reaction was that of a man facing a contagious disease and an agonizing death threat.

"My God! How did this happen? What can be done now?"

"With your permission, and if the lady agrees, I will put the shoes back on her feet."

"Oh, yes. Hurry. Why wouldn´t she agree? What a relief!"

Bethany holds on to Omar´s shoulder for balance while he puts her shoes on and can´t avoid a cynical comment, "I don´t see any dust. The floor is pretty shining."

"That is the danger of germs. They are invisible! Do you know the difference between virus and bacteria, Dottie?"

"Sure. I will explain it to you…"

"Excuse us…" Omar takes Bethany to the dance floor and the others hardly notice them because they dove into a scientific conversation that was the most enjoyable to their tastes.

EQUAL RIGHTS

It feels perfect to be in Omar's arms. Bethany has to control herself not to kiss his sensual mouth right there and then. She feels so warm inside his arms and even though they had never danced before, their rhythm is perfect. Everything is right except that Omar is so quiet now. Bethany sees in his eyes that he is hurt.
"I am right where you wanted, Omar. And I confess that it is what I wanted too. So, what is the matter?"
"You have accused me of being male chauvinist and old-fashioned. But the way I see it, you have started your own harem, Bethany."
"What do you mean?"
"You are here in my arms. But you got yourself a boyfriend. Do you think of me when you are kissing John?"
"No. It is not like that. He never kissed me."
"Are you telling the truth?"
"Yes."
"What is wrong with him?"
"I don't know. And I don't care. Please, take me to the garden and I will show to you that I long only for your kisses."
These were the right words because Bethany saw the hurt leaving his eyes and an enormous passion for her took its place. Omar did as she asked and took the love of his life to a corner of the garden with its shadows and perfume of roses that became the perfect nest for them to whisper love words to each other between passionate kisses.

Chapter 27 – Young and impatient

The morning after the birthday party, Bethany called John and asked him to join her for lunch in a quiet restaurant near her house because she needed to talk to him about something important.
When she arrived, John was seated by the window, with Dottie and Bernie by each side of him on a large table that could fit ten people.
"Bethany, I am glad that you arrived to hear the best news ever."
She was a little confused since she was supposed to tell the news not John. And it concerned her intention to break up with him. But he

was kind of euphoric, so she just took a seat facing the trio and waited for him to speak.

"My grandparents are coming from the farms. They arrive in two days."

"And it is an honor because they never leave the farms."

"That is right, Bernie. But this time they are coming all the way from the south just to meet Bethany."

"Oh, you are so lucky." Dotty seemed sad when she issued this opinion.

"Maybe they expect to hear the announcement of John's wedding."

"Oh, Bernie. How can you say that?" And with this anguished complaint, Dottie burst out in tears and ran from the restaurant.

John immediately ran after her.

"You must forgive my sister. She is very upset."

"And why is that, Bernie?"

"Well, she is kind of in love with John. And since we are distant cousins, there is not really a reason for them not to stay together. Except for you, I mean."

"I see."

"Of course Dottie doesn't have anything against you. It is just that John had taken her to the movies and to the museum a couple of times. It made her hopes of ever dating him rise. But then he told the family that you were his girlfriend and we knew that Dottie didn't stand a chance."

"Why not?"

"She is not as beautiful or as rich as you."

"But it shouldn't matter. Love should be the only factor."

"Then you love John."

There was a short silence after this question because they both already knew the answer.

"Sorry, Bethany. I didn't intend to be rude. It is only that I feel so upset to see my sister heartbroken."

They were interrupted by John's return to the table. He didn't even sit down and Bethany saw his face frowning.

"Dottie is so upset that I decided to take her back home. I can't stand not seeing her sweet smile. Do you want to join us or do you prefer to have lunch and take a cab later, Bernie?"

Bernie jumped to her feet saying that she would go home since she had lost her appetite. She acted as if she had been called to some emergency room to tend to a dying person, moving fast between the tables, pushing some waiters from her way, and apologizing to strangers on the other tables.

John gave Bethany an accusing look and followed his cousin after he said very gravely to Bethany,

"I will expect you for dinner in my home in two days. Dress formally, if you like because my grandparents are a little old-fashioned. Now excuse me. Enjoy your lunch."

Bethany saw him leave without giving her the chance to say anything. As she sat there alone, all she could think about was: 'who are these people?'

DISAPPOINTMENT

When Bethany arrived in her office at the bank that same afternoon, she was told that Omar was waiting for her. She was torn between her desire to see him and the fear of his reaction to what she was going to tell him.

And as he sat there listening to her story about grandparents and twin cousins, Omar didn't look like a patient person. He would shut his eyes a little and stare at Bethany with still more intensity and it was making her feel uneasy.

"The breakup didn't go as I planned."

"Breakup? Was there a breakup?"

"Not really. As I told you, I didn't have the chance. Please, Omar, try to understand."

"What I understand is that you still have a boyfriend. And it is not me."

"But I am pretty sure that John is in love with his cousin Dottie."

"One more reason for you to end the relationship."

"I want to. But now I need to wait just a little longer. I will do it after I meet his grandparents."

"I can't accept any more of your excuses, Bethany. This game has gone too far."

"Please, Omar, be patient."

"First it was his birthday, now it is some grandparents... Then, maybe later you will get engaged to him because it is good for his image. And before you know it, you will be sending out your wedding invitations and becoming Mrs. Emeralrock."

"No, Omar. I could never marry him. It is you that I want."

"Then prove it to me, Bethany. Break up with him tonight."
She didn't answer because it was very hard for her to hurt people intentionally. Moreover, if they were elderly people. But Omar had a limit to his control over his emotions. He felt very possessive of her and this situation was making him jealous since it seemed that Bethany was more concerned about hurting John than him. So he decided to go and stood up.
"You know, Bethany, I expected more from you. But maybe I was wrong and you are too immature to be with me.
"We are almost the same age. You are only one year older than me."
"Yes, I know. But the one-year difference seems to be a mountain separating us."
"I don't think that is the reason for our problems."
"Well, Bethany, in a way you win. Because I won't insist anymore. I won't try to separate you from John since you don't make the least effort to do it yourself. It is bitter to recognize that I have been a fool, but I will just do it once and for all. I will leave you alone."
"Please, Omar, don't say that."
"Goodbye Bethany. Maybe within five or ten years, you will be mature enough to know what you want. If we meet and we are both single, we will talk then."
"Omar..."
He strides away from her in such a decided manner that Omar doesn't see the tears in Bethany's eyes.

THE EMERALROCK GRANDPARENTS

There was no way of telling who was feeling more miserable during the dinner with the grandparents if Bethany or Dottie.
During the introductions, the old lady had not even looked Bethany in the eyes. She looked bored and bitter. The grandfather had said something like, 'so, this is John's lottery ticket' and ignored her for the rest of the night. He complained about the weather, the noise, the government, the pollution, the ozone layer destruction.
The food was not to his taste and the lights annoyed him. People went on agreeing with all his remarks and adjusting the lights, the chairs, changing the dishes that were served trying in vain to please the man.

John had contributed very little to the conversation, and after telling his grandparents about an Egyptian stamp that he had recently purchased he said nothing else.

Dottie took every possible opportunity to sigh loudly and send resentful looks in Bethany's way.

When they all left the dinner table and headed to the living room, Bethany took Dottie's arm and dragged her to the nearest toilet.

"What is it you want from me, Bethanie?"

"Can you keep a secret, Dottie?"

"It depends. Why should I?"

"Because it is in John's interest. This way he will not be embarrassed. And also to protect the grandparents from unnecessary stress."

"Now I am curious. All right, Bethany. I will keep your secret."

"Well. I intend to break up with John."

Dottie was not expecting that and all her surprise showed on her face.

"But why are you telling me?"

"I couldn't take it anymore watching you suffer like that."

"So you will sacrifice yourself because of me?"

"It is not a sacrifice. I am in love with someone else. And I am sure that John is in love with you."

"Are you certain of that?"

"Pretty much."

"Oh, this is the best day of my life. When will you tell, John?"

"In a couple of days, at the latest."

"I will be prepared to help him overcome the suffering of the breakup."

"Dottie, I am sure there will be no suffering for him. Maybe a little scratch of the ego. But we never even kissed. It has been more like a friendship than a romance between us. I think you deserve to know this."

"Oh, thanks for telling me. John kissed me when we went to the museum. And more than once if modesty allows me to say."

"See? He loves you. I told you, Dottie."

"He even kissed my mouth today. But it is not that he was trying to betray you. John likes the danger, that's all."

Bethany didn't even want to try to understand these people anymore.

"Well, Dottie. Let's now return to the living room and try to be discreet about the whole situation."

"Of course, dear."

And Dottie was everything except discreet, she started to say dear Bethany must sit in the best chair, dear Bethany must try this delicious drink, dear Bethany this, dear Bethany that… It was such an enormous change of behavior that it caught everybody's attention. Bernie was suspicious of some gossip happening without her being able to access it and then she started to ask John if he didn't think that Dottie was being extra generous with his girlfriend, or if Dottie hadn't done an extra wonderful job with her makeup and hair, and extra this and extra that.

John looked to be upset by Dottie's high spirits. It was as if he needed her to suffer for him and worship their impossible love. Bethany wondered if he planned to have extramarital relationships in his future since he liked danger so much. She was glad to realize that it was none of her business if he did because she didn't plan on keeping in touch with John after their breakup.

Suddenly, grandpa's voice rose and they could all hear his request, "Won't the lovebirds kiss for us to applaud?"

Dottie shouted something like 'aarghhh' and ran upstairs with a handkerchief drying imaginary tears. John immediately went to her rescue and Bethany found it the perfect excuse to say goodbye and leave the house.

Her Ferrari Roma proved its name when Bethany reached the speed of 120 mph in few seconds. She wasn't sure about what she was trying to escape, but she hurried all the same.

THE EMBASSY PARTY

When Scott told Bethany that the Arabian Embassy was throwing an elegant party to honor Omar al Maliq for his generous contributions to many humanitarian causes, she saw it as the perfect opportunity to make things right with him.

There was the small matter of Bethany having not broken up with John yet. The morning after she had met the grandparents, she had phoned John only to find out that he was on some exotic trip with his twin cousins hunting for stamps, or butterflies or whatever.

But she knew that Omar would give her another chance. He had to because Bethany missed him so much that she had lost her appetite and couldn't sleep well anymore.

So Bethany gladly told her brother that she would accompany him to the event at the Embassy and she was looking forward to seeing Omar again since he had kept his promise and stayed away from her for almost a month now.

Chapter 28 – Princess Liyah

When Scott and Bethany arrived at the Arabian Embassy, the place was already full. There was a mixture of guests using Arabian outfits and occidental clothes. Scott had chosen a dark blue suit and as soon as they entered the place he got many admiring looks from girls. Bethany was dressing a light-yellow dress that floated around her softly. Her black high heel shoes made her look almost as tall as her brother.

The place had many chandeliers that gave it the elegance and importance that the occasion requested. There were flowers everywhere and most of the furniture was even golden or had golden details in it.

"Here is a place I won't mind coming back to, Bethany."

"Me neither, Scott. It looks like a movie set."

"Let's see if we can find Omar since he is the only one we know here. Maybe he can introduce me to some of these beautiful girls."

"I am sure he can." As Bethany said that she felt a pang of jealousy. The idea of Omar knowing so many gorgeous women made her uncomfortable.

Scott pointed to Bethany that he had found Omar surrounded by some authorities and they approached the group to greet him.

He was wearing Arabian white traditional clothes and Bethany noticed that the keffiyeh over his hair had a plaid design in red and white that was kept in place by an elegant black thick kind of rope or better saying, hoop, called iqal.

He looked like the king he was destined to be. People talked to Omar respectfully and many bowed to him. He was attentive and polite to everyone. Bethany was holding her breath until he acknowledged her presence.

He hugged Scott and accepted his congratulations, then he turned to Bethany and she saw warmth in his eyes. Omar took her hand in his and kissed it in a very charming manner. That was the moment chosen by a group of four or five girls to approach Omar. They were all wearing tunics, shawls, and soft scarfs of different colors. It seemed that Scott's wish to meet some pretty girls was about to come true.

As Omar let Bethany's hand go, she gave a step back and watched the girls admire him and dispute a place by his side. The winner, of course, was Liyah, a princess from a country that was neighbor to his. She was wearing bracelets, rings, and necklaces which prices if summoned would be enough to buy a small island. But she probably already had that.

Bethany saw the adoring way that Liyah looked at Omar and was sure that the princess had plans for the future that included him.

Omar's presence was requested by the main table to receive some certificates and medals. Then everybody was invited to take their seats because a delicious dinner was about to be served. It was not a surprise to see that Liyah took a seat beside Omar at the main table.

"I am glad for Omar that he found a beautiful woman to help him rule his country."

"Yes, Scott. You are right. He deserves it."

"And she is nothing less than a princess. Imagine that. He must feel fortunate."

Bethany thought that destiny had a funny way of solving things. John had his cousin Dottie, Omar had his princess Liyah and Bethany had a broken heart. Well, in all fairness, she had been offered a chance to be with Omar, but she blew it.

A little later, Bethany watched Omar and Liyah having the first dance of the night and people applauded the couple with enthusiasm. She thought it was a moment as good as any other to tell Scott that she had a migraine and leave the event.

"I am sorry to hear that, Bethany. I will go with you."

"Nonsense. It is a great party and you should enjoy yourself. Who knows, maybe you will find a princess for yourself."

"I wouldn't mind that. If you are sure that you don't need my company, little sister…"

"I am sure, Scott. I will have the chauffeur take me home and then I will send him back to wait for you."

"Thank you. I hope you feel better tomorrow."
Bethany watched Omar and Liyah giving new twirls around the dance floor. She left feeling desolated.

LONELINESS

When Michelle passed in front of the living room she saw the light under the door and thought that a maid had forgotten some lamp on. She was surprised to see Bethany laying on the big sofa with her long dress all around her legs and her head resting on the soft pillows. She looked as if she was posing for a portrait by one of the great Renaissance masters. When Michelle approached her daughter she saw that Bethany looked sad and tired.
"Hello, sweetheart. Isn´t it early to be back already? Didn´t you enjoy the party?"
"No, mom." Bethany pulled her legs under her body and gestured for her mother to sit by her side. "I felt very lonely and defeated."
"Dear girl. All that only because John is away for some days?"
"On the contrary. That is a relief. In fact, I am waiting for his return to break up with him."
"I see. But then, why are you so sad?"
Then Bethany told Michelle everything about her feelings for Omar. About their few encounters in childhood followed by a separation of many years and his sudden return.
"Well, Bethany, I am sure you will work things out. I will be glad to see you together. John goes beyond anybody´s understanding."
"I am sorry I brought him to this house. I was lying to you but the worst of all is that I lied to myself. Now that I lost Omar, I feel helpless."
"Cheer up, Bethany. There was no harm done in bringing John here for some meals. And I am sure that things are not so bad between you and Omar."
"He called me immature. And now he is dating an Arabian princess."
And then Michelle heard everything about the event at the embassy and how everybody seemed to believe that Liyah was going to be the future wife of Omar al Maliq. And Bethany couldn´t avoid crying in her mother´s arms while she told her these facts.

"Oh, mom. I acted like a fool. Now I know how Omar felt hurt to watch me dancing with John weeks ago. It served me right to see another woman in his arms tonight. It hurt me physically to see her touching him and smiling so close to his face. Then I couldn´t take it anymore and I left like a coward."
"Come on, Bethany. Calm yourself. Things will look better in the morning. They always do. I will ask the maid to bring us some tea."
"Thanks, mom." After Michelle rings for the maid she tells her daughter,
"You know, Bethany, a little competition never hurt a relationship. It is the same for you and for Omar. You will not take the other´s feelings for granted if you witness the interest of a third party."
"If I could do things differently I would not drive Omar away from me. And hand him to some horrible beautiful princess. I hate her."
And she hugged her mother again, sobbing and crying on her shoulder. The truth is that she was feeling that it was too late to have Omar back now.

NOT MUCH SLEEP

After taking Bethany upstairs to her room and waited for her to calm down, Michelle went to Nancy´s bedroom to check on her friend´s condition. There was a nurse who stayed nights with her to give her medicine and help her if she needed anything. Because of her old age, Nancy had developed some illnesses that demanded attention. Mostly in her kidneys and lungs.
Michelle sat by the bed and told the nurse to take a break. The thankful woman went to fetch some fresh coffee and Michelle held Nancy´s hand.
"Don´t you feel sleepy, Nancy?"
"Not really, dear. But I don´t want to disturb you."
"You never disturb me, Nancy. You are my family. I don´t know if I make that clear enough."
"Of course you do, dear. You have always been kind to me. And your kids gave me more joy than I thought it would be possible for an old spinster like me to have."
"You are not old, Nancy. In fact, I want you to get well so we can go out dancing. We must find ourselves some handsome men to marry us."

"Wouldn´t that be nice?"

"Yes, Nancy."

"But maybe in a few days, I will see myself meeting an old friend. A very handsome guy, indeed. And I will have to update him on everything about you, and Bethany, and Scott. I bet Mr. Stanley will feel proud of his family. I sure do."

"Oh, Nancy."

"Don´t cry, dear. It has been a good life I´ve lived. At least since the day that I met you. I love you like a daughter, Michelle, my dear."

"I love you too, Nancy. Now, don´t tire yourself talking nonsense about death. We still have places to go and things to do."

"That will be nice, dear."

"Try to rest, sweetheart."

Michelle leaves the bedroom as the nurse returns and she feels glad that money can buy some services and medicines to help her friend become a little more comfortable in her last days on Earth.

Chapter 29 – A tender goodbye

And within a couple of days, Nancy passed away peacefully in her bed, holding Michelle´s hand in a tender goodbye. It is funny how some people have such a huge heart that the simple fact that they are present bring happiness. That was the case with Nancy. She was a second mother to Scott, there was no doubt about it. Love was natural between them. When Scott returned from some trip, he always had equal presents to Michelle and Nancy. If he chose to give a purse, two identical purses it was. The same for expensive chocolate. Or perfumes. He always bought the same for both of them, but for his sister, Scott had something different, like a bracelet or a cell phone.

It never made Michelle jealous of her son´s love, it showed to her that he had a great heart and valued true love. Nancy had helped Michelle raise him and she supported her younger friend when she faced the hardest challenges of her life.

Bethany didn´t live with Nancy for as long as Scott but she thought of Nancy as a grandmother too. The loving woman never raised her voice, never offended anybody and even when life treated her with cruelty as an orphan child, Nancy saw no reason to be rude to others because of her personal problems.

Some people are so rude and abusive making sure to use the sentence 'ah, you don´t know what I suffered' as an excuse for their mean acts. That is their way of spreading suffering and hatred.

Nancy was the opposite of that. She offered people her friendship and her smile.

For those reasons, many people attended her funeral. Michelle had Scott by her side all the time, and one was offering his strength to the other. Bethany wanted to take her mother´s other side, but she couldn´t since John had suddenly appeared from his trip and stood by her side as if posing for the photographers.

And it caused her an extra weight of pain because she had been feeling lonely in the last days and now that she needed comfort and warmth, John´s presence forced her to disconnect a little from reality and she felt totally isolated.

It was exactly as if some cold shadow surrounded Bethany and when Scott went ahead to say some words of goodbye to Nancy, following the priest´s blessed words, John made everything worse by saying, "I don´t know why all this fuss for just a maid."

Bethany shrank as if he had hit her. She looked at her mother to see if Michelle had heard those rotten words, but she was concentrated on Scott´s words that sounded like a prayer.

And then Bethany felt a strong arm surrounding her shoulders and she heard Omar say, "Okay. Time to end this charade."

He walked with Bethany a little farther, in order for the others not to hear them. "Follow us, Emeralrock." This was the only thing he whispered to John.

Then, still holding Bethany in his arms, Omar asked Bethany in a patient and hoarse voice, "Tell him, Bethany."

She understood exactly what he meant. There was a communication that came from their deep connection.

"John, it is over. I am breaking up with you."

"Why would you say that?"

"Because it is true. It didn´t work out between us. Sorry."

"No. I am the one breaking up with you. It is Dottie whom I like."

"No problem with me. Goodbye, John."

Since he just stood there looking confused and a little offended, Omar added,

"Now get lost, Emeralrock. Before I kick you."

That put John on the move. As Bethany saw John walk away from her, the relief was enormous. She felt almost as if someone had lifted a rock weighing a ton from her breast.

She nested even deeper into Omar's arm and allowed him to walk her back to the (awake) ceremony, placing her between himself and Michelle.

She looked into his eyes with gratitude only to see his love for her there.

HIS ARMS

Later, when they were at the Worthgold residence after Michelle and Scott had excused themselves and gone to their rooms, Bethany was snuggling with Omar on the same sofa that had received her tears a while ago.

"I don't mind if it makes me seem weak, Omar. I need your arms."

"Are appearances so important to you, my love?"

"I thought they were. But you taught me differently. I love you, Omar."

"Bethany, you can't imagine how much I urged to hear these sweet words from your mouth. My love, you've made me so happy."

He caresses her face and kisses her mouth possessively. And they talk about themselves and their feelings.

"Since I was very little, my grandfather demanded that I was strong because I carried the family's name and he wanted me to be worthy of it."

"But you are worthy of it, Bethany."

"I hope so… Grandpa was very nice to me. But his demands were enormous. I had to have straight As at school and behave perfectly at social gatherings. In a way, it was like a military lifestyle."

"What was your mother's opinion about it?"

"He kept me away from mom. She had to fight fiercely at court only to be allowed to see me three or four times in a year."

"My love. This is so hard for a child. It pains me that you had to be forced away from Michelle. And I pity her too, poor woman."

"I loved my grandfather very much. I still do. But today I understand that he was very cruel. And I don't understand why he did those things."

"It is in the past now. Some things will remain a mystery. It is just how the world is, unfortunately."

"I guess you are right. It wasn´t a matter of money. He had enough to feed and dress a whole city for centuries. Why not welcome my brother and my mother in our lives? He chose to hate them. But you are right, it is in the past."

"Your future is with me now, Bethany. And I will do everything in my power for you not to cry even one tear anymore."

"I believe you. Because I feel the same. I want to make you the happiest man who ever lived. I love you!"

"Say that again…"

"I love you, Omar Sahid al Maliq."

"And I love you, Bethany Worthgold."

"I ache for your kisses, Omar."

"Here, my sweet, let me help you."

And he kissed her as if it was their first time. There was no hurry to end it and his lips searched for her treasures while his tongue asked and received the delights Bethany had reserved only for this man.

"Bethany, my Bethany. I can´t live without you, my love."

"Me too, Omar. I thought I would die when I saw you with princess Liyah."

"I was not with her, my love. She is just the daughter of the man that was honoring me."

"Really?"

"Yes. In fact, I was looking forward to getting rid of all the social obligations and dance with you. When you left I felt very disappointed. Then I asked your brother if you had broken up with Emeralrock and the answer was no."

"John traveled without notice."

"I finally understood that you are the sweetest person in the world and it would be hard for you to inflict pain even in an idiot like Emeralrock. I saw how you rejected his presence at the funeral, but you endured him all the same. When he offended Nancy´s memory and caused you even more sadness I couldn´t take it anymore. I had to step in."

"I am glad you did. I enjoyed having you taking charge, controlling the situation. I know that it was my mess, but I was glad to accept your help. Thank you, my love."

"You are welcome. I will always protect you and help you."

"Omar, there is one thing that makes me wonder if you don´t mind my curiosity."
"You can ask me anything, Bethany."
"Why did it take ten years for you to come back and see me?"
"Bethany, my love, I had all the intention of coming more often and even stay for some years... But when I returned to my country, a revolution was starting. Tribes went against tribes for a dispute of power and land. My father immediately started to defend our people from the rebel tribes because they didn´t spare women, children, or elderly people. Their vicious attacks lasted many years. My father decided not to send me to the war zone since I was too young to fight. Instead, he left me in charge of many business decisions. Being a warrior, my father joined the soldiers on the battlefield. My work at the offices for many years made me famous in the world of finance. My decisions proved to be right and profitable. I gained experience investing huge amounts of money and multiplying them quickly because the war consumed much of our country´s reserves. Before my father left to fight he signed documents that guaranteed that my word and my signature were the law during his absence. He ensured that because there was the possibility of his death while fighting. I am glad to tell you that my father wasn´t disappointed in me when he came back to our palace."
"I understand now. There was a reason why you forgot all about me."
"No Bethany. You don´t understand. I never forgot about you. I thought about you and I planned a future with you. One day, when I was around fifteen I could ask my father because he often returned to the palace, I said 'Dad, I want to visit my friend Bethany', and since he never refused my wishes he tried to contact Christopher Worthgold to set a visit for me. Naturally, I would travel with many bodyguards because those were very dangerous times for my family. Unfortunately, your grandfather had passed away. My father decided to cancel the trip because it was very risky to send me anyway and without a person that he trusted to wait for me, he wouldn´t feel at ease. By the way, I never said to you Bethany: I am sorry about you grandfather."
"Thank you, Omar. I was very young when he died."
"I know that, my sweet. Anyway, the war finished, a couple of years ago, and we won. It was thanks to my father´s strategies and to the

soldier's loyalty that we were the winners. That war cost the lives of many of our people. And we had a period of rebuilding the country which is an ongoing process even as we speak. But when things were a little bit more under control and I felt that my father didn't need me so much by his side, I told my jet pilot to fly me here because I ached to be with you."
"Oh my love, I am glad you came back to me."
"I am all yours, Bethany."
"And I am yours, my prince."

Chapter 30 – Dating a prince

Omar and Bethany spent all of their free time together. They were discovering the world through each other's eyes. People threw parties for them, not only because they were the most influential couple in the world but also because their company was the most enjoyable.
They had an excellent taste for clothes, food, drinks, and art. They visited museums in France and art galleries in the south of Spain. They took Michelle to Italy for her birthday and she enjoyed the musicians hired to sing songs that were made inspired by her name.
Scott had already been Omar's friend from the beginning but now they felt closer because their devotion for Bethany created a new bond between them. The three of them flew together to Australia for an unforgettable adventure trip.
And then there were the royal compromises due to Omar's status as a prince and the future sheik of his country. Bethany surprised him the first time she had dressed in Arabian clothes for one of those occasions. She chose a delicate robe with a soft golden color and she wore sophisticated jewels. The paparazzi went crazy when she appeared at the exclusive party. They crowded the entrance door trying to take pictures of the beautiful billionaire woman that was about to become a real princess. It went beyond any girl's dreams.
Bethany loved to buy gifts for Omar and she gave him the most expensive watches, pens, and electronics that money could buy. And he showered her with diamond necklaces, emerald bracelets, and ruby rings.

Then, on her twenty-first birthday, at her party, he proposed. In front of family and friends, Omar went down on one knee and asked Bethany to marry him.

When she happily screamed yes, Omar put a 20-carat diamond ring on her finger. It was an unforgettable day.

And the preparations started because there would be a wedding here and another in his country.

They also set a date for Omar to take Bethany, Scott, and Michelle to meet his father, the Sheik Mohamed al Maliq.

Life felt pretty perfect for the happy couple by then.

SCOTT´S DECISION

One Sunday, after lunch, Scott told them about his decision.

"You know when we visit Omar´s country in a few weeks… After you guys come back, I intend to stay there for a while."

"How long, son?"

"I don´t know, mom. Maybe six months or one year."

"Wow. That long?"

"You will be very welcome as a guest in my palace, Scott."

"Thank you, Omar, but I don´t intend on staying for long at the palace. The thing is, after Nancy died, many childhood memories came back to me. I didn´t always lead a life of luxury."

"Oh, son. I am so sad if I made you suffer."

"On the contrary, mom. I remember being so happy under your care and Nancy´s. The thing is, money is nice but not essential for me. So I would like to take this opportunity to discover who I am. I want to cross the desert with the nomads."

"But must you go to the desert to be in touch with your inner self, son?"

"I think it will build my character."

"Scott, I say this not because you are my brother but because it is true. Your character should inspire other people."

"Thank you, little sister. But there is always room for improvement."

"If you have made up your mind I will assist you in any manner that I can."

"Thank you, Omar. I knew that I could count on you."

"And you must promise to come back for my wedding, Scott."

"I wouldn´t miss it for the world, little sister."

"Son, if you have a chance to contact me, you must call me or send
me letters. But never ever send me postcards, please."
"I know mom. I promise you."

THE TRIP

Even if their stay was going to last only two weeks, Bethany and
Michelle took extra care of what to take in their luggage because
they had never stayed in a palace before. Bethany´s assistant had
gathered valuable information about the country´s main customs.
"Mom, what do you think of coming with me to purchase some
djellabas and bournous for you?"
"And what are those, if I may ask?"
"They are typical clothes from Omar´s country. The djellaba is a
traditional tunic made of silk or some other fluttering fabric. There
are many colors and designs to choose from. And the bournous is a
long cloak perfect for cold days or nights."
"Are you buying some more for you?"
"Yes. Just for the first days there. After that, we can always go
shopping for the original pieces there."
"You have just talked me into it, Bethany. I think it could be exciting
to change my look and check on the result."
"I am sure you will look great, mom."
A schedule of the planned activities had also been provided and
there were two gala dinners to be held there during their stay.
Bethany noticed how much Omar had missed his father by the way
he talked about him. There was more than respect and gratitude, it
was the love of a son for a just and caring father that she sensed in
Omar.
"Bethany, there is the matter of a present that we should take for the
sheik. But for a man that has everything, what could we choose for
him?"
"Well, mom, Omar told me that his father loves horses. He has some
great ones in his stables."
"Are you thinking of buying him a horse, Bethany?"
"No, mom. But it inspired me to buy a painting of horses made by a
renowned artist."
"Won´t a painting be too simple for a sheik?"
"I guess not since it costs three hundred thousand dollars."

"Wow, sweetheart. Now I am impressed."

"I hope it impresses the sheik too, mom."

"I see what you mean. He will soon become your father-in-law. Are you nervous to meet him?"

"I met him when I was a child. And I remember that there was nothing to fear about him. He was very polite and treated me with smiles and compliments."

"Let´s hope he keeps that attitude."

"By the nice things Omar says about him, I am sure we will get along."

Michelle didn´t want to influence her daughter. And it was always better to keep an optimistic view of things and people. It is only that by Michelle´s experience, Stanley had spoken highly of his father and, all the same, her father-in-law had been extremely cruel in his treatment of her.

Well, they would soon find out what destiny had prepared for Bethany. Michelle sure hoped for the best.

AIR VIEW

When the airplane approached the city, Bethany was holding Omar´s hand and looking out the window with interest because this was the place that she would live as his wife. Their future was going to be there and their family would belong to this place.

Omar was watching her first reaction to his country and he was glad to see on her face the admiration for this wonderful landscape.

Bethany fell in love with the place. The city was modern and well taken care of. The tall buildings formed drawings against the skyline and the constructions made of glass and steel showed progress and prosperity.

She was delighted and started to ask Omar about the different details that appeared before her eyes. He sat closer to her and when Bethany learned about the different sights and monuments, she was face to face with Omar.

It was a happy start.

Chapter 31 – The royal family

If Omar had missed his father, the same could be said about the sheik Mohamed al Maliq. For the benefit of his people and thinking of the modernization of his country, he had sent his only son to study abroad and prepare himself to be an accomplished leader. But he missed him so much that he didn´t even wait for Omar and his guests to arrive at the palace. He went to greet them at the airport.

And from that moment, Bethany started to understand the importance and power of the royal family. Everybody bowed or saluted them. Many bodyguards and assistants surrounded them at all times. A line of eight limousines made the short trip from the airport to the palace.

As Bethany sat very close to Omar inside their limo, he whispered in her ear.

"Don´t worry. It won´t be always like that. It is only because my father is with us that everything becomes so formal."

"Won´t I have ten limos driving me to buy a pencil?"

"Only if you want, my love. Only if you want."

The sheik Mohamed had a banquet waiting for them in the palace. While they ate the delicious foods from the Arabian culinary, Omar answered his father´s questions about his studies and his last investments. The sheik was delighted to know that Bethany shared their interest in technologies. Omar encouraged her to tell his father about her South American investments in telecommunication because he wanted his father to see her shining. Bethany was very passionate about her work and Omar felt proud of her when his father showed his appreciation.

A little while later they were taken to their accommodations to freshen up and rest. Michelle and Bethany were given adjoining rooms and they were exchanging first impressions.

"Mom, everything is so different. The palace is so big, I could get lost in here."

"I think I will buy a compass for you, sweetheart."

"Oh, mom. Be serious. I feel so strange. Even if our host speaks English, I heard the foreign language all around us. In the airport, in the driver´s talk while they took care of our luggage…"

"Maybe I will buy you a dictionary."

"Mom! You are impossible."

"Bethany, I know you. Tell me what is really bothering you. And I know it is not the size of this place since the Worthgold residence is

pretty huge too. And it is not also a problem with the local language because I am sure that most people speak English and you can always hire people to translate for you.”
“I know.”
“So, what is it?”
“I don´t know, mom. I think I am afraid to disappoint Omar. I was not raised to be a princess or a shaikhah.”
“That is like a queen, right?”
“Exactly. It is the wife of the sheik. In the West, we have kings and queens. Here in the Arabian countries sheiks rule the kingdoms and the shaikhahs have many responsibilities.”
“Well, Bethany, you will just have to prepare for that. There is still time since Omar´s father is in good health. It will not be easy but Omar will help you. Are you sure that you love him?”
“With all my heart.”
“Then, love will be your fuel to face any task that presents to you.”
And Michelle was right about that. When Bethany was with Omar everything assumed a different perspective. The two hundred rooms palace did not seem so scary after he took her on a tour and showed her the room where he played as a child, the one where he had his lessons and the swimming pool complex where he spent time with his mother and she personally taught him how to swim.
“My mom broke all the protocols just to be with me. She sent nannies away to exchange my diapers herself and insisted that my father should teach me to ride my bike. I remember the three of us laughing in the palace gardens, involved in many games that she invented.”
“What happened to her?”
“She died when I was eight. It was the only time I saw my father cry. He was heartbroken and so was I. We bonded even more, after that.”
“And he never married again?”
“No. you see, he could have a harem. But he always only wanted love. My mother was the love of his life.”
“Was your mother a foreigner? I ask you this because you said that she often broke the protocol.”
“No. She was from here. But my father and my mother always had a modern way of doing things. She broke the protocol because she could. She used her power to create happiness for our family. The only voice stronger than hers was my father´s. What he says is the

law. But because he loved her so much, he always told people to do as she said."
"I am so sorry for your loss. I wish I had met your mother."
"She would have loved you."
From these talks with Omar, Bethany started to feel more confident about their future as rulers of his country. She understood that as a member of the royal family, she could fulfill her obligations without losing her personality. Omar didn´t expect her to be only a pretty person on display. He really wanted her to share his life and raise a family destined for power but mostly for happiness.

KEEPING HIS PROMISE

On their visit to the stables, Omar gave Bethany a magnificent thoroughbred horse. It was all white and very imponent. Michelle was with them and gave her opinion.
"You will look great riding together. Bethany on the white horse and Omar on the black stallion."
"Yes. But first I will teach Bethany how to ride as I promised her when we were children."
Bethany was delighted.
"Do you remember that, Omar?"
"I remember everything, my love. Now, because you are a beginner, you will be riding this mare. She is as docile as a sheep."
And they had riding classes every morning.

RELATIVES

The opportunity for Bethany to meet Omar's relatives presented itself at the gala dinner later that first week. Among the tens of guests were Omar's uncle Malouf and his son Khaleb. Also his aunt Iasmin and her two daughters.
They greeted Bethany with enthusiasm and welcomed her to the family. She felt sincerity and warmth from Iasmin and her daughters.
"My sister would be so proud to see the wonderful person that Omar has become. And she would delight in his choice of you to be his wife."
"How kind of you to say that, princess Iasmin."

"You can call me aunt, dear. And these are my daughters Amal and Nadia. They both speak English well."

"How nice! I hope we become friends."

"We would love it, princess Bethany."

"Oh, please call me Bethany. I am not a princess yet. Only after the wedding takes place."

"It is just a formality. In our hearts, you are already part of the family. I watch my nephew and see how happy you have made him."

"Omar makes me happy too."

And as if it was his cue to appear by her side, she feels Omar's strong arm around her waist.

"I see that you have met my mother's sister. How do you like my fiancée, aunt Iasmin?"

"I completely approve of her. I was just telling Bethany that your mother would be proud of your choice."

Omar kisses his aunt's cheek in a gesture of thanks for her kind words. Then his uncle approaches the group.

"And this here, Bethany, is Iasmin's brother, my uncle Malouf."

"We were introduced earlier. And I must say I am charmed by this young woman."

"Thank you, sir. I thought you were the sheik's brother."

"No. Just like Omar, his father is an only child. I am the brother of the sheik's late wife."

"I see."

"Uncle Malouf is also one of my father's trusted counselors. That is why you will see him seated at the main table."

The main table had five chairs to the sheik's left side and five to the right. Omar, of course, sat at his father's right, and from now on, Bethany sat by Omar's right side. The other chairs were for distinguished guests and the sheik's counselors.

All around the spacious room, round tables for six people were positioned facing the sheik.

People were standing and talking while some appetizers were being served. But when dinner started, everyone took their places. Michelle and Scott were seated right in front of Bethany, sharing Iasmin's table, which was an honor. They were being included in the family.

Sheik Mohamed started the dinner with a short speech,

"I want you all to welcome Bethany Worthgold as a part of the al Maliq family. She was chosen by my son Omar to be his wife and future shaikhah."

As he said that, everybody applauded and Bethany felt Omar's hand on her elbow encouraging her to stand and as she did it, Bethany made a delicate gesture of bowing to the applauding group and they became euphoric shouting 'princess Bethany', 'prince Omar', and mixing it with words that wished the couple much happiness.

Everybody looked happy except for Malouf who kept exchanging worried looks with his son Khaleb.

Although there were so many people present, Bethany did not miss that.

Chapter 32 – Royal functions

As the days passed Omar made sure to keep Bethany at his side during all royal functions. And she loved every moment of them. Being with Omar made everything special and there was not a dull moment. They shared the same sense of humor and the prince loved to hear Bethany's remarks while he presented his world to her.

"And that is the minister of commerce from our neighbor country. There is no one in the world more important than him. Of course, it is only in his own opinion."

"Not even his wife's?"

"Oh, Bethany. You are a helpless romantic."

"And who is that guy wearing funny glasses."

"That is Sleepy Abraham. He wears colorful glasses that allow him to doze off during long boring meetings."

"The idea is good. He can hide it behind the glasses. But how did he get the nickname Sleepy, if people weren't supposed to know what he does."

"He almost succeeded if it wasn't for his loud snoring. Therefore, Sleepy Abraham."

They would laugh at these curious facts about the people that surrounded them. Later they would eat the delicious banquet foods and dance all night. But what Omar most cherished were their moments alone when Bethany would sing only for him at his request and his spirit would recognize hers and their love would grow even more.

TALKING TO THE SHEIK

One day, Bethany was invited to have breakfast alone with the sheik. Omar was busy signing some papers about the acquisition of new lands. Michelle had joined Iasmin and her daughters in a visit to the mall. And Scott was exploring the city outside the palace. So Mohamed saw the perfect opportunity to talk to his future daughter-in-law.
"I remember you as a child. Very pretty and smart. You were the apple of the eyes of Christopher Worthgold."
"I know. I loved him very much."
"He was a great businessman."
"Thank you."
"Now you have become a very powerful and rich woman."
"It is true, sheik Mohamed. I was educated to lead an empire and I intend to do so. Omar knows these characteristics of mine."
"I am sure he does. Having already talked to him I know that he doesn't expect a wife who stays home while he goes to work."
"It makes me happy because I know that I couldn't do that."
"I approve of you, Bethany. You don't have to worry about my interfering. I even wonder if my son's inclination for a modern lifestyle didn't start with me. I have always had an interest in new technologies and modern administration processes."
"I am sure you influenced him. Omar admires and loves you so much."
"Thank you. He is not only my heir, my only son but also my pride and joy."
"I know."
"That is why I must advise you. While you both live in your country and finish your studies there will be no problems to face. But once you come to live here, you will notice many differences in our traditions."
"I have started to realize that."
"We from the royal family must sacrifice for our people. We have our duties and we take them seriously. Even if you keep working and

leading your companies, you must accept that here Omar´s word will always be the law.”

“I know that. I love him and have no intention of causing problems.”

“I am sure of that. It is not that you both can´t disagree, but it should happen in private, only between the two of you. It would be disgraceful if you would disrespect him in public.”

“I am aware of that, sheik Mohamed.”

“Good. You know Bethany, I have taken part in some wars. So I speak from my own experience, there is no war worse than the war between a couple in the family´s core.”

“But you didn´t face that one. Omar told me that you loved your wife and she loved you back with the same intensity.”

“I was lucky like that. But take her brother, for instance. Malouf had a violent married life where screams and breaking of objects were a common daily occurrence.”

“How terrible. I didn´t know about that.”

“Few people know it. His wife defied him and he punished her. Sometimes she couldn´t hide her bruises. It was terrible for the boy. My late wife brought him to live with us for a couple of months expecting things to improve but they never did.”

“What did Malouf´s wife demand?”

“She wanted to go out more. She enjoyed dancing all night and riding fast cars which was unacceptable to my brother-in-law. She was much younger than him and I think they didn´t have much in common. Malouf frequently called her a gold-digger in front of others and she called him an old bag. It was shameful.”

“It is terrible for a child to witness this kind of thing.”

“That is exactly my point. After some months with us, Khaleb returned to his house with his father.”

“And the mother?”

“Nobody knows the details of what happened. Malouf declared that she had an accident and died from the terrible fall.”

“What a tragedy!”

“Yes. Every family has its share of happiness but also its share of sadness.”

“Take my word, when I assure you that I intend to make Omar happy.”

“Then you have my blessing, Bethany Worthgold.”

And Bethany saw the sincerity in the sheik's eyes. They enjoyed the rest of the breakfast talking about the improvements he intended to bring to his country.

EVIL LOOKS

Bethany felt Malouf's eyes following her wherever she went. And they were evil looks that came her way. She started to wonder if she had offended him in any manner. She thought about asking him but Malouf didn't give her much of a chance. He simply turned his back and walked away from her. Once he even pretended not to understand English which was absurd since he negotiated with foreigners all the time.

But even if his behavior bothered her, it was not enough to rob her joy. The same couldn't be said by the surprise his son Khaleb had prepared for her. He simply arrived with princess Liyah by his arm at one of the Palace's dances.

He gave Bethany malicious looks and it became obvious that he had no interest in Liyah as he pushed her towards Omar all night.

Bethany was astonished. If she maintained her place at Omar's right when they were seated for dinner, she was surprised to see Liyah taking the seat on his other side because Khaleb insisted on it.

Because this was not a formal event, everybody used the eight places round tables. So, it was Bethany, Omar, Liyah, Khaleb, and kind of facing them, Sheik Mohamed, Michelle, Scott, and Iasmin.

At first, Bethany felt upset and unhappy but when she saw the encouraging look from sheik Mohamed, she changed her attitude. It was as if he was telling her to show who she was and what she had come to do. Then she rose her had and became the adorable hostess she had been raised to be.

She had an intelligent and vibrant conversation with everybody at the table and included Liyah as a common guest instead of a competitor. She knew she had succeeded when Khaleb's face showed how upset he was and he mimicked his dad sending Bethany evil looks.

She remembered what the sheik had told her about him and she started to imagine if he had grown up to be one of those people who had revolted with life. People who acted as if their sufferings gave them the right to make everybody around them miserable.

Then, in the middle of a dance, Khaleb forced them to exchange partners. Omar seemed not to notice his cousin´s bad intentions and acted like a gentleman. He had a polite smile as he danced with Liyah but Bethany could not do the same. As soon as Khaleb took her in his arms on the dance floor, he spilled his poison,
"Now, that is the couple we expect to see ruling this country."
"Why do you say that?"
"Because it is true. I am sorry to disappoint you and interfere with your dreams to become a princess. But we want the real thing and that is Liyah."
"What matters is what Omar thinks."
"As soon as the novelty of a foreign woman passes, Omar will come to his senses."
"Well cousin, the novelty has already passed. I know Omar since childhood and even by then we knew that we were meant to be."
She called him cousin because she knew that it upset him because it meant the seriousness of her alliance with the prince. Her entering the family was exactly what Khaleb disapproved of. She went on making herself very clear, "As to being a foreigner, it is only a matter of geography. Omar and I have residences all around the world, but most importantly, he lives in my heart and I live in his."
"This is romantic nonsense."
"Not only romance but love."
"And you both will live here one day."
"We will live here but we will not be imprisoned. But I don´t expect you to understand that because you don´t have the same means as Omar and myself and it is only natural that your thoughts be as limited as you are."
And because what Bethany said was true, he became very red and escaped her presence as soon as the dance finished.

A MOTHER KNOWS

When Michelle had some time alone with her daughter, she showed her support. She had witnessed how much effort Bethany had to make due to the rudeness of Khaleb. It was confirmed when Bethany told her everything.
"Some challenges seem to be already presenting to you, sweetheart."

"Yes, mom. And the opposition comes from where I least expected. His own family. Go figure."

"It is not a surprise for me at all, dear. Unfortunately, I experienced the same."

"I am sorry, mom. Now I know how you must have felt."

"It is not easy to realize that someone hates you for no reason. Does the sheik feel the same?"

"No. We talked and after offering some advice he gave his blessing to my union with Omar."

"That is a relief. Will you tell Omar about his cousin's little speech?"

"I guess not since we will leave in a couple of days. Omar is so happy to be here and I don't want to make him worry or feel upset. And there is nothing that Khaleb can do to hurt us except throw bitter words my way."

"You are right. But you will be smart if you never confuse him for a friend."

"One thing that was very clear in this situation is that he is not my friend. I will remember that, mom."

Michelle hugged her daughter and deep down she knew that Bethany would have to fight her own battles. There was no way to protect her or avoid it. Because it was life.

Chapter 33 – So long, Scott

Michelle had been watching her son Scott during their visit and she thought that he was very alive. The food and the local customs pleased him. He tried some steps to dance to the exotic music and it made him look manly and powerful. Scott even tried to speak some words in the Arabian dialect and Michelle was sure that he would become fluent very soon. Both her children had the gift of intelligence.

Also, Scott had inherited his father's taste for adventures. When they had traveled the world together, he had always suggested some tours that were not common for tourists. And he had been right because it allowed them to see beautiful sights and explore the music and culture where it was happening, instead of the package offered by the tourism guides.

Scott had already contacted some people about joining a caravan that was headed east through the desert.

"Promise me that you will be extra careful, son."

"I will be careful, mom. You don´t have to worry about me."

As if the worry was not a mother´s job. But she agreed with her son and when he said goodbye to her some days later, she knew that he would be gone for many months. She didn´t cry in front of him since he looked extremely happy, but there was no way to hide her sadness from Bethany.

"Mom, you know that he will be alright."

"Yes, I know. It is just hard for me to miss him so much knowing that he is in the middle of the desert."

"I will miss him too. I guess we will just have to keep very busy until he returns. This way the time will pass quickly."

"You are right, sweetheart. I am glad to have your wedding to organize when we go back home."

"I agree. It will be so nice."

TIME TO GO

Many more people went to the airport to say their goodbyes than those who had gone to greet them at their arrival. Bethany wasn´t sure if they wouldn´t declare it a holiday since it involved an effort. Many of them brought gifts and Bethany lost count of how many times she had hugged each one.

Amal and Nadia couldn´t hide their tears and they pleaded for them to come back soon. Iasmin didn´t let go of Michelle´s arm until the last minute.

Omar and his father kept talking until it was time to board and Bethany saw the pain in the sheik´s eyes, as any father would feel for separating from his son and sending him thousands of miles away. It touched her and she said to the Sheik Mohamed.

"You know, we will be back in a couple of months."

"Really?"

"Yes. I love this place and I intend to open a branch of my bank here. We might as well come back in a few months to make it happen."

It was as if new energy had entered the sheik´s body.

"I will do everything to facilitate the process. We will be expecting you, then."

"Count on that, sheik."

Then Mohamed kissed her on both cheeks and Omar knew that this gesture meant that her father had accepted Bethany as part of the family.

When they were on the jet plane, Omar whispered in her ear, "Although my father loved the painting you gave him, this was his real present, my love."

"I know Omar. I hope this idea pleases you too."

"Very much."

"So I hope we can come to visit your father every two months or so."

"Your kindness always overwhelms me, Bethany."

And he sealed his words with a long kiss. She wondered if he would still consider her kind if he knew how she had put his cousin Khaleb in his place. It was a relief not to see him or Malouf among the goodbye crowd.

BACK HOME

Bethany had assumed her place as the CEO of the Worthgold conglomerate now that she had turned twenty-one. And she continued to implement changes and improve work methods. There were even board meetings held only by women and it guaranteed that the media kept calling Bethany 'the feminist CEO'.

They loved the fact that she was engaged to a future sheik and there were bets about who would influence who.

It bothered her to be passing such a limited view of herself. She wanted to know Omar´s opinion on the matter.

"You are pictured as an arrogant man. And they see me in the whole of a feminist, implying that I use protectionism, which is not true. Does it bother you?"

"Not in the least. You see, my love, the press will always be presenting us to the people in the way they think that will be more profitable for themselves. We should feel lucky that at least they say something about our work and not only about the way we dress or what hobbies we have."

"I guess you are right. But I feel responsible for the image I am passing because it can be seen as a role model for women in fragile situations."

"How would you like to be seen?"

"As a human being with values. A person who will give equal opportunities to workers based on their talents and capacities."

"So you have to say that at press conferences. Talk to the serious journalists and the others will follow the pattern. Forget about the tabloid news with their gossips and scandals. They will have you on the cover as a protectionist boss and a bat that was supposed to be driving a flying saucer. Nobody gives them credit nowadays."

"Will you help me, Omar?"

"Always, my love."

And he brought the attention of his press officers' team to her demands, and they settled interviews for Bethany in the most prestigious TV shows in the country. Her ideas soon became known and appreciated. But her engagement to a prince was just too irresistible to be ignored. Then Bethany talked about Omar in the interviews and since he agreed with it, soon the interviewers were talking to the beautiful couple.

And it was natural for them to start their humanitarian projects together.

EDUCATION, FOOD, HEALTH

Nothing escaped the couple's attention. They cared for the helpless and abandoned people of the world and they had the means to help them.

As it turned out, Bethany and Omar had projects to promote education for children who lived in poor areas. These children should receive good books and musical instruments. Artists were hired to perform theater plays and concerts in these neighborhoods. And private teachers were hired to stay in public libraries reading for the children and helping them with homework.

In the health efforts for improvements, the couple donated millions of vaccines and hospital supplies. They also created scholarship programs for doctors and nurses around the world.

Bethany and Omar sent food to people that were starving after facing wars or tragedies like earthquakes or tornadoes. They also donated thousands of plant seedlings of fruit trees to be planted at public spaces like parks and squares. They had a TV campaign inviting the city mayors to join their efforts and many did. The idea was to facilitate access to food everywhere.

Many serious multinational companies joined these efforts and also donated seeds, plant seedlings, and provided gardeners to take care of public vegetable gardens.

THE WORTHGOLD MANSION

Omar took Bethany to see a gorgeous penthouse apartment located few blocks from the bank. It was modern and spacious.

"Bethany, I would like to live here with you after we marry. What do you think?"

"I love it, Omar. I think it will be perfect for us."

"It will be fun to go shopping for furniture, don't you think?"

"Yes. We can make this place an extension of our personalities."

"That is exactly what I was thinking. It will be our first home."

"I can't wait for that."

"Are you sure that you don't prefer to live in your family's house?"

"I am sure, Omar. My mom can have the house. And Scott."

"Great. Let's tell your mom."

"Will you talk to the realtor about this apartment?"

"I already bought it for us, love. In case you didn't like it, I would just buy you another one. But I couldn't pass the opportunity to purchase this one because the location is so perfect."

"I am glad you did it, Omar."

When they talked to Michelle about their plans the couple found out that she didn't have any attachment to the house. If anything, the place was too big for her to live alone and she chose to move to the beach house that Stanley had bought for her long ago.

"It is near enough for me to visit you frequently. And I made some friends with families from the neighborhood there along the years."

"Oh, mom. I promise that we will visit you a lot too."

"I count on that, sweetheart."

The next time that Scott called his mother, she told him that Bethany was offering him the mansion and was ready to sign the papers to transfer it to him. But Scott declined it. He said that he would also prefer to live in an apartment when he returned.

Then, after giving it some thought, Bethany decided to use the house as an orphanage for children up to twelve years old. They would start with twenty kids and grow from there. Omar agreed and had his best lawyers working to make this dream legal and real.

Michelle was delighted by that and when she told Bethany that her father had once wished to have many children, they decided to call the place 'Stanley Worthgold Orphanage'.

The opening speeches were touching and Bethany knew that she had done the right thing.

Chapter 34 – The wedding

Finally, the wedding day had arrived. And so had the overseas guests. Scott had taken a ride with the Sheik Mohamed entourage. He looked great with his new suntan and a look of wisdom around him. There was also a scar on his face that told of unexpected dangers. And it made him look even more handsome and women kept running after him as if he was a magnet.

"Oh, son. I don´t know if I want to hear the details of the fight that caused this scar."

"I am glad you don´t want to know because I have no intention of telling you, mom."

"Well, I will have an appointment for you with a plastic surgeon."

"He will be very disappointed when I don´t show up."

"Don´t you mind the scar?"

"Not the least. I won this scar and I intend to keep it."

And Michelle dropped the subject since she was proud of Scott for not being vain. And when she got used to his new look she really found him mysterious and a little dangerous She hoped his need for adventure had been satisfied by now. She would be glad to see him choose one among the dozens of girls that flirted with him. But he declared that after the wedding he would return to the desert because there was much more to explore.

Iasmin had also arrived with her daughters Nadia and Amal. The last one followed Scott everywhere and laughed at his smallest jokes and it made Michelle wonder if her two children were destined to marry members of the same royal family.

Scott was charming and always had a smile for Amal. But his favorite girlfriend right now was an Egyptian top model that was sleeping at his new apartment.

Because the Sheik Mohamed had given Omar and Bethany a yacht as a wedding gift, they decided to have the ceremony at the beach.

The guests went to the sea town where Michelle had her beach house and right there on the marina was the impressive yacht with three floors and all the luxury you could imagine in a two hundred million dollars vessel.

For the wedding, Bethany wore a long satin gown made specially to her by a French dress stylist. Omar wore a tuxedo because he had decided to wait for the Arabian wedding to use his hometown´s traditional garments.

The party started at night and went on until they could watch the sunrise. The paparazzi went crazy trying to get shots with their most powerful lenses. Small boats surrounded the yacht all night in an attempt to register the best moments.

The bride and groom were in such a good mood that at a certain point they ushered them in and even posed for some pictures.

When the helicopter landed on the yacht to pick up Omar and Bethany, who were headed for their honeymoon in the Caribbean Islands, the guests applauded and cheered them.

SIBLINGS

Just before the wedding, Bethany had asked her mother and brother to join her at the bank´s office. Omar was also there for this meeting.

"Scott, my life has been better because I have you as a brother."

"Thanks for saying that, little sister. I remember when you were born. Since the moment mom brought you home it was as if light stronger than the sun had come to bathe us. I wish you could have seen the happiness on your dad´s face."

"You always told me stories about my father and I have to thank you for that, too. Because I never felt like an orphan. How could I if you told me of a fatherly love that seemed bigger than death."

"I believe it was, little sis."

"So do I. And that is exactly what I want to discuss."

By now Michelle had some tears in her eyes and Omar handed her a handkerchief. Her children always amazed her and their bond was not only from blood but also a spiritual one.

"What is on your mind, sweet Bethany?"

"Well, I understand that my dad loved you as a son. And he told mom that he would provide for you. Everybody knows that he had no idea that death would come so soon. I mean, he was a healthy man, right mom?"

"That is right. Stanley was healthy and very athletic. It was a fatality that took him from us. And he indeed loved Scott as his own son. From the first day that Stanley saw your brother, he insisted in including him on all our activities. And he would proudly carry Scott on his shoulders on visits to the zoo or the circus."

"I remember. I loved him too. He will always be missed."

"Right. So I have decided that his inheritance must be equally shared among the two of us."

"You must be joking. Those are billions of dollars in real estate and stock."

"It is a huge amount, you are right about that, Scott. So, it should be enough for the both of us."

"Omar, what do you have to say about that?"

"I declare that by sharing her inheritance Bethany made me love her the double of what I already did. I know that Stanley would have preferred it this way."

"But I can't accept. I mean, it's your inheritance and you have a right to enjoy it."

"I agree. And I enjoy sharing it with you."

"Mom, what do you think?"

"I think I have two wonderful children. You both speak directly to my heart. About the money, I think Stanley would have done it just like that. And you don't have to worry about Bethany since she is keeping half of it and also, she has a fortune that came to her from her grandfather. I also would like to think that her husband will be able to provide for her." Michelle and Omar exchanged smiles when she said that.

Scott was very touched and he went to his sister and hugged her tight.

"Bethany, I will accept it then. But I want you to know that to me, it means so much more than the money. You are proving your love for me and I hope someday I can prove to you that I would give my life for you."

"And because you feel like that, Scott, it makes us brothers. Even more than the marriage papers Bethany and I will be signing in a couple of days. Because I also would give my life for Bethany."

Then, after the two men shook hands, they proceeded to sign the papers that put Scott on the top of the list of young bachelor billionaires of the world.

THE CARIBBEAN

Bethany was walking hand in hand along the beach with her husband and the beauty of the ocean reflected on her face.

"This color of the water is really impressive, Omar."

"It is true, my love. This shade of turquoise is frequent in these waters. You can also count on this fresh breeze to make the tropical weather even more pleasant."

"I am glad that you brought me here."

"Our honeymoon has to be unforgettable, Bethany. You deserve it."

"It is always unforgettable when I am with you, Omar."

And it really was. But this place was so special that every moment gave them enjoyment, from the tours to see dolphins to the sunset cruises.

Because the Caribbean Sea has thousands of islands, it is possible to visit several destinations in one trip. That is what the newlywed couple did. They enjoyed the cruises to multiple islands and took part in romantic activities like dinners under the moonlight, walks on white sands, and diving in beautiful reefs.

They stayed in one all-inclusive resort, and the honeymoon suite looked like the set o a love story Hollywood movie.

It was the first place where Bethany heard people calling her Mrs. Al Maliq and she enjoyed the sound of it. Those romantic days passed very quickly and when the time came to go home, Bethany vowed to bring their children there someday.

NEWLYWED

Frequently Omar and Bethany disappeared from the world and locked themselves in their apartment. It had become their love nest, their home.

And there, they had the world of each other to explore. Every cell of their bodies had to be touched and memorized. Every thought had to be explored. They dove into the other's mind and nothing was too small to be ignored. It was a real learning experience of their tastes, their ideas, feelings, and dreams.

There was much in common and it reassured them that they were meant to be together. But also, there were differences that opened a world of beauty and enriched the couple even more.

After these escapades to their private paradise, when they returned to everyday activities, people noticed new skills in their communication. They would finish each other's sentences and say much with only one look.

People admired and got inspired by them.

Chapter 35 – The matter of the water

Omar was always interested in the matter of the water around the world and he shared his knowledge with his wife.

"Did you know, Bethany, that only six percent of all the water on the planet is potable water?"

"Only six percent?"

"Yes. And there are many pieces of research that show that half of that six percent is already polluted."

"It can't be right, Omar."

"I am afraid it is, my love. We consider water like something precious because we are from the desert and we know how hard it is to have it so scarce. But if people keep polluting the potable waters, the rest of the world will soon join us in this hardship."

"Isn't there anything that we can do?"

"We can try. Do you know what is funny? The water is clean and free, to begin with. Then the people pollute it and the cost to clean it again will be around hundreds of millions of dollars for a small quantity of water. If we succeed."

"Maybe we should do an awareness campaign to let people understand what is happening. Maybe they will start to demand the industries to use filters or something when they throw chemicals in the rivers or at the sea."

"I am in favor of educating people, so they can demand protection for what is valuable and indispensable to life."

And they did it. Omar and Bethany had their best professionals creating a handbook that explained the matter of the water in simple words. They started distributing it at schools, churches, clubs, supermarkets. Soon the handbook was everywhere because people with a good conscience made copies of them and passed them around.

They also sponsored TV shows for kids to teach them how to save water instead of wasting it.

IRRIGATION SYSTEM

On her next visit to her father-in-law, Bethany asked Omar to explain to her the sustainable use of the water in the palace. He took her to see the large water tanks that received all the water from the sinks and drains in the palace. This water was then used to wash the cars or the floors outside in a perfect recycling solution.

The city had the same reservoir system implemented by the sheik many years ago.

Omar also showed his wife the intelligent irrigation system they used for the gardens. In order not to waste any drop of the valuable liquid, they had timers that controlled the amount to be used. The same process was used in agriculture all over the country.

At dinner, Bethany shared her impressions with her father-in-law.

"Now I understand your inclination for modern technologies. When they are applied to benefit the population, you can for certain improve the quality of life for everybody."

"I am glad that you see things this way. As the ruler of a country that I love, the way I see it is that my people's wellbeing is my responsibility."

"I wish rulers of all countries could think alike."

"Me too. We have visited countries where the people are abandoned, starving, and sick. In these cases, there is a rise in violence as well because sometimes they will commit crimes in order to survive. It is sad."

"Father offered help many times, only to see the goods he sent being deviated to the fat bellies of some corrupt politicians."

"Really? Did you become enraged, Sheik Mohamed?"

"It is more like, I became sad. I learned a lesson with that: the solutions must start inside and the ideas have to come from local politicians. We need to give our support when necessary, but the initiative must be theirs, otherwise, they will not value our efforts and neither see the process through."

"Wow. Thanks for sharing these experiences with me. The forsaken people touch my heart and I am glad that I found in Omar a partner not only in our private life but also in our actions to make our dream of a better world come true. But from what you have said, I understand that even the charity must be well planned to find legal ways of really helping the poor and not financing the corrupt ones."

"You are a dear girl. I am proud of both of you. I have followed your efforts and can say without a doubt that you have planned for a better future and you are making it happen for the needy. I hope that when you move here you can develop an interest for our people and work in their favor too."

"I have a confession to make. Don't be surprised because I don't even understand it myself, but I already love the people from this country. Maybe because Omar was born here and my love for him is so gigantic that it embraces every single detail about him. Maybe it is because of some maternal instinct that whispers to me that my babies will one day be born here. I don't know. But the fact is that I already love them."

Sheik Mohamed's eyes sparkled when he heard what Bethany said because he knew that she was telling the truth.

"You remind me of my late wife, dear Bethany."

RENOVATION OF THE PALACE

"My love, my father really wants you to feel at home when we move here permanently. For that reason, he has ordered the renovation of some rooms for you."

"My home is where you are, Omar. Tell the sheik that he doesn't need to go to all that trouble. The palace is adorable as it is."

"It is no trouble at all. It pleases him to do something special for you. And to tell you the truth, it pleases me too."

"In that case, I accept gladly."
"There is a tradition here to have the women in separate quarters. They can have their privacy and indulge in female activities."
"Such as?"
"I don't know. Gardening or knitting. Whatever they choose to do."
"It is all in the concept of the harems, right?"
"I guess it started there. But my father never had one and neither did I."
"I know, Omar. I trust you."
"Thank you. Anyway, there is a whole floor that we can renewal to your tastes."
"Omar, it is really a necessity to me to be in the same bedroom as you. In the same bed. I don't know how it affects your traditions but I can't be happy otherwise."
"Bethany, my love, I am so happy to hear that. I promise you it will be as you say. We will just start our own tradition."
And that is what they did. The new plant sent to the engineers contained a very large room overlooking the garden for the couple. The other rooms on that floor were filled with beautiful low tables, very comfortable sofas, colorful curtains, and carpets that were exactly to Bethany's taste as her husband and his father had wished. The place was like a dream. Bethany and Omar's dream.

A REALITY CALL

During this visit, Bethany could really improve her ability to ride horses and she was delighted to join Omar every morning to explore the beautiful sights that surrounded the palace. One day when they returned from their small adventure, uncle Malouf was there to greet them. He couldn't wait to take Omar with him to the office because he wanted him to sign some documents.
Bethany didn't feel like joining them, so, she sat at one of the benches in the garden. To her displeasure, Khaleb found her and sat by her side. He was rude as always and she heard all the disdain in his voice when he said, "So I see that you are back here."
"And so are you."
"I consider myself an essential part of this family."
"At least one person thinks so and that is you."
"I am sure my cousin will promptly agree with me."

"If you say so..."
"We could always ask him. I saved his life once. And it is more than you ever did for him."
"I am sure you have been thanked enough and even rewarded generously."
He became red as a tomato.
"Omar has much money to spare. I am sure he knows that I deserved it because it was risky and I never said that I was a hero."
"I am sure nobody expects noble acts from you. Only payable ones."
"You don´t understand our ways."
"On the contrary, I understand perfectly. Greed is universal."
"Be careful, princess."
"I am always careful. But what is that? A threat?"
"Let´s just say that it would be so much better if you left Omar."
"You are entitled to your opinion."
"Stubborn people get what they deserve."
"Everybody does. Since we understand each other, you must now excuse me."
And after saying that, Bethany entered the palace and decided that it was time for her to tell Omar about his cousin´s attitude.

EXPLANATIONS

"Omar, for some reason that I ignore, your cousin hates me."
"I am sure you are wrong, my love. Nobody could hate you."
"He does. He threatened me saying that I should leave you for my own good."
"I am sure it was not a threat. His English is not so good. The simple explanation for that is that some people, and Khaleb among them, had an expectation about an alliance between the neighboring countries. It would be achieved by my marriage to Princess Liyah."
"I see."
"It would be a manner to avoid disputes. But there is not a concern there because our countries are already allies. Khaleb and his father are very old-fashioned. But they will just have to accept that I chose you and we are already married. You are my princess."
"And you are my prince, my husband, and my love. I would not want to be the cause of problems for you."

"You are the cause of my happiness, I assure you. I will have a talk with Khaleb and make things very clear for him."

"Thank you, Omar. I appreciate that."

Khaleb didn't say another word to her during the rest of the short period of their stay there. But it was so nice to see him leaving the palace. And after a few days, Bethany and Omar were also saying their farewells to Sheik Mohamed and heading home for a busy semester that would be followed by their graduation from college.

Chapter 36 – End of school, beginning of a new life

Omar, being one year older than Bethany, was also her senior at school. However, she wanted to have the graduation party together and it took an extra effort from her because she advanced many courses in order to be able to do it. Her major was business administration with an emphasis in finance and she loved it. All the calculus and comparisons of charts were natural to her. It was like a second language that she had spoken since grandpa Christopher was alive.

Because the couple went to different colleges, they took part in two graduation ceremonies and the next weekend they had a party at the countryside club, eating barbecue and diving at the swimming pool with their school friends all afternoon.

Then, later that night, Michelle was invited to an intimate dinner at their apartment.

"You both did so well that I am sure no challenge will ever be too great for you."

"Thanks, mom. It is a sweet thing to say."

"I second that about you, Bethany. It was amazing that you studied two years of subjects in one."

"It would be selfish of me to keep you here another year only waiting for me to graduate. I know you miss your home."

"It is our home now. Thank you, my love. It means the world to me."

"Then it means that you both will be leaving soon."

"Yes, mom. In a couple of months, we will be having our royal wedding there, as you know. I guess it is simpler if we arrive in advance."

"It will be hard to be away from you, Bethany. But I read only happiness in your face and it is what every mother wishes for her daughter."

"We will visit a lot, mom. And you must come to us, too."

"In fact, at the new quarters at the palace, there are rooms only for you, Michelle. Nobody else will have access to them. You can even change the furniture if you wish."

"Thank you so much, Omar. I am sure they are lovely rooms."

"Also, there is something else I would like to discuss with you, mom."

"What is it, dear child?"

"We know that you like the beach house. But you have compromises that bring you to this city frequently."

"It is true. And since you opened the Stanley Orphanage I can't stay more than a few weeks away from that place. It mesmerizes me how my promise to give Stanley more children has found a way to happen. I care for those orphans."

"I heard you help in the process to select the families that will adopt."

"That is right, Omar. And it keeps me really busy."

"Well, mom, that is one more reason for me to suggest that you use this apartment every time you come to town. This place was our first home and Omar and I would feel sad to know that it just stayed empty after we left."

"What a surprise! I wasn't expecting that."

"It makes sense, Michelle. Why would you stay at hotels when you are family and we have this huge apartment about to be empty? Please take these keys."

"I accept it gladly since you insist."

"We insist. Also, we would be delighted if you came with us right now for the preparations for the wedding. If the orphanage and the bank can spare you for some months."

"I am sure they can. And I miss my new friend Iasmin and her sweet girls. I even miss the Sheik Mohamed. I like his enthusiasm about technologies and life improvement."

They laugh at her sincere description of the sheik.

"It is all settled, then. You will be joining us on our trip home, one week from now. If we are lucky, we can even meet Scott in one of his seldom visits to the palace."

Michelle sure hoped so.

THE LOVE OF THE DESERT

Since the beginning of his adventures with the Bedouins, Scott had traveled many miles and encountered many dangers. But it served his thirst for emotions and he was far from ending this experience.
He joined caravans that traded merchandise from village to distant village. He even made a good profit selling food or clothes. He then donated the whole amount to the needy he encountered at the various destinations. The simple poor people started to see him as some kind of hero. They called him Sadiq min masafa which means the Friend from afar because his looks were different and they saw him as kind and women found him handsome.
Scott enjoyed contemplating the beautiful scenes of the desert that were never the same. It filled his senses and attracted him more each day as if sand had started to run into his veins. This was a rare thing to happen, except if you had been born with this feeling as was the case of Omar and his father. But it had happened to Scott in some mysterious way and because he loved the deserted lands and its people so much he was loved back.
He was totally accepted by the people and even went to battle against the highwaymen that threatened the lives of innocent and humble people. In these fights, Scott had risked his life more than once and some new friends had risked their lives for him. Among them was Habibdul, a young man prepared for the hardships of this life and who Scott considered like a best friend, or even better, a brother.
They traveled together, ate together, sang war songs, danced, and courted pretty girls. But neither of them talked about settling down yet.
"Pretty soon I must be heading to the palace."
"Really? You have been there a while ago. Are you getting soft and longing to sleep on satin sheets?"
"I don't mind that at all. Even better if I get a satin-bodied girl to join me."
They both laugh at the suggestion. The sheik would never permit Scott to take one of his girlfriends to the palace. At least not to share his bedroom which was all he offered the girls anyway.

"Seriously now, brother. Why do you have to go? I thought you would head South with us to trade coffee."

"Maybe next time. Now I really must go to the palace. If I miss my sister´s wedding I am afraid she will have the royal guards after me."

"Oh, it is right. Your sister is marrying the prince. So I wish her much happiness and I part from you knowing you will be having a good time."

"But then, both of us always seem to find a good time on our way, isn´t that so Habibdul?"

"I guess it is a gift we have."

They laughed again and even if they said that as a joke it was not far from the truth. Life was good and these two strong decided men knew how to enjoy it for sure.

I MISSED YOU, SON

One more reason for Michelle to accept the invitation to go early to her daughter´s wedding was that she knew that Scott would appear there sooner or later. All his life Scott had been protective of Bethany and in the most important moments of her life, Bethany could count on his presence for sure.

Then, when he arrived at the palace Michelle gave him a long hug and told him how much she loved and missed him.

"I miss you too, mom. The perfect solution would be for you to move here like Bethany."

"Or for you to come back home, son."

"I will go back, mother. You don´t have to worry about that. There is something about the land where we are born that always attracts us."

"I am glad to hear that, Scott. Because I am too old to acquire new habits in a strange country."

"Now you are just fishing for compliments, mom."

"Don´t be silly."

They were still teasing each other when Bethany joined them and took her family to have lunch in a fine restaurant downtown.

The occasion allowed Scott to pay close attention to his sister. She talked about simple things as flowers for the wedding, clothes and bridal cake. But he observed her gestures, the tone of her voice and he read her soul in her eyes. Bethany watched Scott closely too and she was satisfied to notice how happy and calm he was. It was as if his adventures in the desert gave him a necessary fulfillment.

Scott, on the contrary, was not completely satisfied with what he saw in Bethany's eyes. There was a concern there very uncommon for a bride to be.

When they returned to the palace, Michele excused herself because she wanted to give a chance for her children to talk. Bethany took Scott to her favorite bench facing the garden's fountain and he was direct with her.

"Are you having second thoughts about Omar, little sister?"

"No, Scott. What I feel for Omar is like fuel to my life."

"Good. I am glad. I like him a lot. Especially because I am sure that he is crazy about you too."

"We are already married and I feel blessed because of it. The ceremony here is only a formality. One demand from the royalty status."

"Right. Then, if the marriage is not the problem, tell me what is bothering you, Bethany."

"How did you know?"

"How not to know. There is sadness in your eyes."

"I didn't want to worry you."

"Too late for that."

"I feel ungrateful to let such a small thing worry me."

"So, there is a problem."

"It is more like a premonition of something bad. It is because of Omar's family. Not all of them, of course. Iasmin and the girls are so nice. But the old man gives me the creeps. And his son threatens me."

Scott becomes very alert when he hears that.

"What are the threats?"

"I don't know. Omar says it is a matter of misunderstanding the language. But my heart tells me different."

"Listen to your heart. And count on me."

"Thank you, Scott. I feel so relieved now that you know."

Bethany squeezes his hand and he only looks deeply into her eyes. It gives Bethany all the reassurance she needs because she knows that her brother is a man of action.

That same day, Scott hires detectives to find out more about Malouf and Khaleb.

Chapter 37 – Royal wedding

The thing about one royal wedding is that it seems that all the country's population is celebrating with you and not only the guests. On the day of the ceremony, people went to the streets and as Omar and Bethany rode their car slowly among them on the streets, they threw petals o roses at them and shouted 'saeada' to them, which means 'happiness'.
At the palace, the noise was not smaller. Loud music, laughter, and happy chats were heard all around. The place that was already beautiful was now sparkling with the decorations for the wedding. Trucks and trucks brought in delicious foods that were to be served to the aristocratic and noble guests for a week.
The couple received many hugs and greetings that touched their hearts even more than the Jaguars, Ferraris, diamonds, and gold watches that were among the presents that they received.
When the time for the speeches arrived, people had wonderful things to say about the couple. It was a memorable day. Nothing could spoil it, not even Khaleb's attempt to do so. He had entered the line of people waiting to greet the bride and he whispered in her ear, "It is not over yet."
By hearing that, she decided that the guy couldn't be normal. She put it down to a demented mind and forgot about him, at least for the day, as she proceeded to greet the guests of her wedding.

HONEYMOON

This time they decided to be traditional in their choice of a destination for their honeymoon. They took the jet plane and went straight to Paris. They had invitations to visit almost every Designer Clothes Store located in the city. They were almost like children going from one to the other and buying clothes, accessories, and perfumes for each other and for their families. Bethany's assistant was in charge of collecting all the items and sending them home.
There were invitations for dinners in their honor at prominent people's houses. But they declined those politely, with promises to visit again soon. Their nights were reserved for the thirst they had of

one another and even if they locked themselves in the hotel´s honeymoon suite quite early in the night, it was very common for the sun to come up before they had gotten any sleep at all. They would then feed each other breakfast in bed and sleep until noon. The afternoons were perfect for swimming at their private pool on the roof or going shopping to stop only for a snack in one of the famous French bakeries.

"Omar, I don´t want to go home tomorrow."

"Neither do I, my love. Shall I rearrange our flight?"

She gave a long sigh and got even closer to him on their bed. His warm, muscled body welcomed hers.

"It is just a manner of speech. I know that we have commitments at home."

"We have already had two honeymoons. And both of them were wonderful. Why don´t we arrange to have one per semester from now on?"

"Oh, that is delightful! Where can we go for the next one?"

"You choose, my princess."

"What about Greece?"

"You have impeccable taste. Greece it is."

"Omar, you make me so happy. I don´t deserve you."

"But you have me. I am all yours and every thought of mine is to find ways to make you smile."

"I am happy as I never imagined to be possible. I love to be your wife. I am all yours too."

And they sealed their love words with the total surrender of their bodies to the touch of the beloved one.

The next morning, Omar surprised Bethany with the change of plans since they were not to fly home that afternoon anymore, but would stay for another week completely devoted to each other, proving that Paris was indeed a perfect place for the people who were in love.

PERMISSION TO DIG

When the married couple returned to the palace, Scott was still there because he wouldn´t leave while his mother was still there. He also had unfinished businesses to attend to since he was waiting for the first reports his investigators would produce about Malouf and

Khaleb. They had left right after the wedding along with hundreds of guests.

The nights became happier with Scott´s cheerful presence. He told them about the landscapes he had seen, the exotic food he had tasted which included snakes. Also the stories and music he had heard during his travels.

Sheik Mohamed was satisfied to see that the young man appreciated his country and so was Omar. Michele enjoyed the feeling that Scott was happy but she couldn´t resist teasing him.

"Snake, son? Why on earth would you eat that?"

"It is not a big deal in the deserts, mom. It really tastes like fish. And you won´t find fish in the middle of all that sand."

That produced laughter all around. Bethany had a dreaming look in her eyes when she commented on her brother´s adventures.

"I wish I could have joined you around a fire to listen to the storytellers and the singers. That is the pure culture of these people. I considered it the richest one. They are true artists because there is no sponsor behind them. All they do comes from their hearts."

"You are so right, little sister. I tell you what, if Omar produces the fire I will bring the artists. Of course, only if the sheik agrees."

"I not only agree as I see it fit to sponsor them. Bethany inspired me to encourage these talented people to keep alive our country´s best traditions."

"And I will see to it that a small stage is set on our garden and there will be so many candles that a fire won´t be missed."

"Thank you, Omar. I will look forward to it."

"Everything you wish, my love."

"Now, since I started asking permission to the sheik, I might as well go all the way."

"What is it you wish, young man?"

"Well, Sheik Mohamed, it has caught my attention that the Bedouins have some stop places that they use often. These stops became famous because there one caravan can help the other when they trade medicines or supplies."

"It is true. Even the Bedouins have their organization system, Scott. It surprises me that you would notice that. It proves that you have a real interest in my people. I feel glad. So, what is it that you need my permission for?"

"Very recently I have become a man of means, thanks to my sister's generosity."

"Nonsense that you should say that. It is only that you are our dad's rightful heir."

"Thanks, Bethany. Anyway, I would like to invest a part of it where people most need help. So if you authorize me, I would like to dig some wells for these nomad travelers."

Sheik Mohamed even stood up when he heard that. He was so excited that it was hard not to admire his vivid appearance. There was an air of authority about him but also some quality that challenged the admirer to join him in his dreams and projects for his country.

"Scott, I can't believe my ears. This has been a project in which I invested many hours of research and was about to see it come true when the war prevented it. I have all the drawings from the best engineers in this country."

"Wow, it is great news."

"Omar, my son, I have to thank you. Not only have you married a woman superior in looks and talents, but also you have brought to us a family of people whose virtue is incomparable. Scott, if you are serious about it, I must start to think of you as my second son."

"It is an honor to me, Sheik Mohamed."

"Michele, I must congratulate you. To have one admirable child could be put down to luck. But two, as Bethany and Scott, must be recognized as the excellent product of good parenting. Please, allow me to shake your hand."

"With pleasure, sheik. Because then I can return the compliment to you about Omar."

"I am enchanted."

He then took the party to his office and showed them some of his most treasured plans of improvements to his people's lives. Everybody paid close attention because they all knew that soon they would become a reality. And that was due to the fact that they had joined forces now.

A PRIVATE TALK

When Scott had a moment alone with his sister he told her about the investigator's discoveries.

"It seems that Malouf has been acquiring an enormous quantity of land in Australia."

"Australia?"

"Maybe it was as far as he could go from watchful eyes."

"Is it possible that he bought those lands with his savings?"

"No. It is prime land and filled with cattle. There are also real estate properties in Khaleb´s name."

"Interesting."

"You were right about their malice towards you. Nothing worse than a banker entering the family from their point of view. There is not much you can hide from a banker when your intentions are dishonest."

"I see. But I didn´t expect that. I was naïve enough to believe that they were loyal to the country and preferred the old traditions like neighbor families´ alliances through marriage."

"The truth is that they are only loyal to their own interests and schemes. Do you want me to talk to Omar about it? Or even the sheik?"

"Not yet. We must investigate further. If it comes to denouncing their devious actions, we must have proof."

"You are right. And I want you to be very careful, Bethany. It is some scum men we are dealing with here. They have the guts to rob their own family. I don´t know what else they are capable of doing."

"Don´t worry, Scott. I feel an aversion for them from the first day we met."

And so it was decided to continue with the investigation and keep alert.

Chapter 38 – Habibdul and Youssef

For the first function at the palace, Scott had invited Habibdul and Youssef to perform. The caravan supposed to trade coffee suffered a delay and had to come to the city to solve the problem of the baskets that would carry the grains. It gave the perfect chance for Scott to have his best friend singing his songs for his friends and family. The storyteller was Youssef a very old man that had learned great tales from his great-grandfather. He had a sweet smile and a voice that seemed to embrace your soul.

The main garden of the palace was radiant because of dozens of lanterns and candles and the small stage looked very exotic. Comfortable armchairs had been placed all around it.

When the artists appeared onstage everybody greeted them with applause and then there was a respectful silence.

Youssef started to say,

I will tell you the story that a hurt soldier told my great-grandfather while he was trying to mend his wounds. This is the story of the sultan of Nonwater Land. His name was Sharanim. He had three brothers that were also his best friends. When it was time to battle they went side by side to defeat the enemies. All of them became powerful and rich men and when the age to settle down came, each one took a beautiful wife to form their families.

Sharanim's wife was a beautiful woman and he usually showed her off at parties and told everybody that he was the luckiest man on earth. Her long dark hair matched her mysterious brown eyes. And he was satisfied for a long time. Until one day when his younger brother, Hassan came to visit him bringing his new wife. People say that the woman's red hair put Sharanim's heart on fire and the truth is that he cornered her at dark places inside his palace and touched her body in a sinful manner. At first, being young and afraid, she accepted his advances but after the third or fourth time, she complained with her husband.

Hassan immediately went to ask his brother about this matter and was told to meet him at one of the palace's towers. His anger didn't help Hassan to notice the danger around him and he was thrown from the tower by two of the guards while his brother watched him fall to a tragic death.

That same night, Sharanim took the redhead beauty to his bed and enjoyed her body as he wished. Later he had sent word to the others that he had taken the widow under his protection out of the love he felt for his unlucky brother that died in a tragic accident.

People had him in high consideration for that. He also kept his brother Hassan's lands but people thought it was just natural. Because the widow didn't agree to any of that, she was kept in chains.

Then Sharanim went to visit his brother Jamal who had married a blond woman that came to the desert from distant lands. Jamal complained that she wouldn't get pregnant even after being married to him for one year now. Then Sharanim decided to help them and he went to the woman´s bed every morning after his brother left for work. He didn´t feel ashamed of his sinful acts and even threatened the life of the woman if she told her husband about what they were doing. When a week passed and the time arrived for Sharanim to return home, he couldn´t control his lust anymore. He poisoned his brother and took the widow with him. She didn´t fight because she feared him. For that reason, there was no need to keep her locked, but she became very sad, a shadow of her old self.

When Sharanim invited his last brother to visit his palace he had already made plans to kill him and take his wife. He used the excuse that they should share Jamal´s lands to attract his brother to his trap.

When his brother Ebrahim arrived, Sharanim could have no idea of how his wife looked like because she was covered from head to toe. He didn´t mind a bit because what moved him by now was an intense desire to commit adultery and murder. He had lost all self-control and the idea of taking all his brother Ebrahim´s money also appealed to him. He had become a slave of his disordered emotions.

So, when his own wife said that Ebrahim had gone on a horse ride and the woman was still in bed due to a headache, his mouth watered and he went to her bed. He was a strong man and then he couldn´t understand at first, where the strength of the woman was coming from when she held him and put a knife through his heart. In the last minutes that he had to live, he recognized his brother Ebrahim´s face when the woman´s shawl that covered his head fell to the floor.

The fact is that Sharanin´s wife, feeling distraught and disgusted by her husband´s behavior had sent word in advance to the brother-in-law telling everything.

She never repented her actions because she thought that Sharanin had met the death he deserved for being a man who had drowned into lust.”

There was a small silence that followed the end of his narrative, Then people stood to applaud Youssef. He bowed and thanked them. Next, it was time for Habibdul to perform.

“Now it is my great pleasure to sing for you the song I was inspired to composed after listening to this story many times. It goes like that:
Your lust
Will cause the loss
Of people´s trust

But you don´t mind
Lustful beast
But you don´t mind
Lustful beast
Your lust
Will make your treasure
Turn to dust
But you don´t mind
Lustful beast
But you don´t mind
Lustful beast
Until finally
You will not be missed
Lustful beast.”

Another round of applause showed how much people enjoyed the song. After that, everyone was invited to a tent where they could meet the artists in person and talk to them while enjoying the refreshments prepared for the night.
“So, little sister, was it as you expected?”
“Much better I assure you. The story made me shiver. And then Habibdul expressed what we were all feeling through his wonderful song.”
“Come with me. Habibdul is talking to Omar and I want to introduce you to him. He is my best friend in these parts.”
“I will be honored, Scott.”
Michele was telling Youssef how much she had liked his story and how he had been able to transport her to the scene.
All in all, the night was a success and they were looking forward to the next show that would take place in two days.

SAVING HIS LIFE

The next night was very calm and Omar had invited Scott to join him and Bethany to savor some coffee that Habibdul had gifted them with.
“Oh, I just love the coffee when it is grounded on the same day. It tastes delicious.”

"If it pleases you so much, my love, maybe Habibdul won´t have to travel so far to sell his grains. I will make an offer he can´t refuse."
"Omar, that coffee is supposed to supply an entire village. Even my little sister wouldn´t be able to drink it all. Right, 'coffee maniac'?"
"Wrong, 'sun addicted'. I will just serve the coffee to the visitors like you."
"I see you both keep inventing titles for each other."
"No offense intended, honey. It started as children´s play and it´s a habit that won´t go away."
"Don´t worry, Bethany. It humors me. I always wished to have a sibling. It is the bond of friendship that you have with Scott which I most admire in brotherhood. I hope we don´t have an only child."
"Me too. I want to see many of our children running around this palace."
"Anyway, at least I have my cousin Khaleb who has been kind of a substitute for a brother."
Bethany and Scott exchange a worried look that Omar notices.
"What is it? You both look concerned."
"It is not a concern, Omar, it is more like curiosity. Bethany and I were just wondering how was it when your cousin saved your life."
"Ah, that. He was really brave that day."
"Can you tell us the details, my prince?"
"Of course I will tell you, my love. Well, I was alone at the palace´s library when five guys wearing hoods entered the place. They all had swords in their hands and they told me to be quiet or else they would kill me. I couldn´t just sit there, so I reached for a sword of my own. It was hanging on the wall and I knew it was not as sharp as theirs because it was used only for decoration of the place. But it was a form of defense from those guys that I knew were serious about hurting or killing me. I grabbed the sword in a reflex but it angered them more and as they were approaching me one of them produced a gun. I knew by then that all hope was lost. Right at that moment, Khaleb opened the door suddenly and entered the library. When he saw the armed men, he screamed 'guards', 'guards'. It made the intruders run away. That is how he saved my life that day."
"Wow. What a terrible scene. I can´t stand that your life was in danger, Omar."
"It was long ago, Bethany. Since then we have improved our security system."

“I am glad to hear that.”
“Tell me, Omar. On the way out, didn´t the intruders hurt Khaleb?”
“Not really.”
“Not even a scratch?”
“Nothing, Scott. I guess we were both lucky.”
“Did he have a machinegun? I mean, to scare five armed intruders it would take at least that.”
“Khaleb was not armed. I guess his shouts for the guards scared the guys.”
“Were they caught?”
“No. It really surprised us how they were quick to disappear. These people have much practice as evildoers. Now let´s drop this subject. Look, it has made Bethany turn pale.”
“I am all right, Omar. But I agree with you that we can talk about something else.”
And they went back to talking about coffee and the travels for trade.

OPINIONS

Later, Scott found a moment alone with his sister, and they exchanged impressions on that story.
“Imagine that, Bethany. The villains only saw Khaleb´s face and ran away.”
“Strange, right? They didn´t run from Omar and he had a weapon.”
“It doesn´t make sense. Also, the five men just evaporated in the air.”
“It seems to me like somebody facilitated their escape, little sister.”
“Or maybe they didn´t even have to bother escaping. They just took their hoods and walked around calmly, as they were instructed and paid to do.”
“Of course. You are brilliant, Bethany. They were obviously part of the staff here. And it brings back the name of our main suspect. The only one who could take advantage of this situation…”
“Khaleb.”
It was clear that they all had the same enemy, although Omar thought about him as a hero. It wouldn´t be easy to prove him guilty because he was treacherous. But Scott was far from giving up.

Chapter 39 – Garden feast

The Sheik Mohamed had doubled his guests for the second storytelling event due to the success of the first one. People were chatting happily and admiring the garden while the artists got ready. They wore colorful clothes that enhanced their act and as soon as they appeared the applause began. People then sat down and paid attention, first to Youssef's words.

"It is time for me to tell the story of Nazal, the man who cooked at the sultan's palace. He made delicious dishes and heard many compliments about them. Even if he had received much help to prepare the food, he took the compliments all to himself.

His wife often told him, "Don't be a fool, you couldn't have done all that by yourself."

"But the thing is, I did."

He didn't mind lying about it because pride was taking the best of him.

Nazal went as far as fishing for compliments and to accomplish that he sent the kitchen apprentice to ask if everything was to the sultan and the guests' taste.

When the boy came back running in happiness and cheerfully saying, "They love our food…" Nazal would slap his face and speak in an angered tone, "It is my food they are enjoying, not ours, you piece of garbage."

Sometimes guests brought food as presents and Nazal's futility made him say that he had cooked them too. Anything from pies to bread or meat that arrived at the palace, he told everyone that he had done it.

He started to dress up before he went to the kitchen and after a while among the smoke and the juices and greases from the pans, he became ridiculous.

But his sense of self-importance and his weak mind didn't allow him to realize it.

He started to feel superior and more important than other servants of the house and many times he said to them, "If you didn't have me to feed you, soon you would be no better than stray dogs."

One day, a very exotic pudding arrived as a gift and was served for dinner. A little after that, one servant came and asked Nazal, "Who made that pudding? The sultan himself wants to know."

"I made it, of course, you fool."

The man knew that it was not true because he received the pudding at the gate. Anyway, since he hated the cook, he just said, "Then the sultan wants you to come to the dining room."

Nazal was so vain that his chest seemed to inflate. No admiration of him and his cooking talents would be excessive and he expected nothing less than glorious words of compliment, and who knows, maybe even a raise in his salary.

When he saw the upper part of a man's body inclined on the table where the puddings poison had caused his death, it was too late for Nazal to acknowledge his mistake.

Nobody expected him to confess his guilt, so they didn't think much about his screams of not having cooked the pudding.

The sultan just said, "What snakes we have in our own houses." And then he signaled for the guards to take Nazal to be punished with death for having tried to kill the sultan and succeeding at killing his cousin.

When they told his wife about the consequences of his pride, she simply stated that because he had no ears to listen to the need of others, his big mouth had been the cause of his death. She had known him well."

Exclamations of surprise were heard all around and people stood up clapping their hands. Now it was time to listen to the song that the story had inspired Habibdul to create. And he didn't make them wait. This is what he sang:

Be proud all you want
Oh you
Proud one
Be proud all you want
Oh you
Proud one
Vanity is your real food
You will never change your mood
Your end will be no good
Oh you
Proud one

People joined him singing the chorus and it made Habibdul proud. It is the top emotion for the artists to have the audience joining them in their art.

This time some dancers and instrument players had joined Habibdul and Youssef. This way there was music and dancing all around in the enjoyable garden feast.

ONE STRIKE OF LUCK

Bethany had no idea of how to help Scott in the investigations about Malouf and Khaleb. She couldn't just start asking too many questions without raising suspicions.
But her luck did not fail her and one morning during breakfast, Omar asked for her advice.
"My love, do you recommend that we invest in commodities or stock for the rest of this semester?"
As Bethany explained the advantages of each one, Sheik Mohamed felt impressed by her skills.
"Omar, aren't you lucky that you married a competent banker and we can profit from her advice?"
"We sure are, father."
"It is in my nature, I think. Grandpa taught me that sometimes we have to allow money to make more money for us."
"I remember Worthgold saying that."
"Did you know him well?"
"We had businesses together for a while. All very profitable."
"Grandpa never made a bad investment. He thought in numbers, not in images. It was his gift."
"Which you seem to have inherited from him, Bethany."
"It is a great compliment. Thank you, sheik."
"Omar, I tell you what. Why don't you ask Bethany to look into all of our investments and accounts?"
"I am glad to do it."
"It could take a while, father."
"I suppose so, son. Take as long as you need, Bethany. And we will follow your recommendations for the necessary changes."
"Won't it be too much work for you, Bethany?"
"Not really, Omar. I will do it during my morning hour at GBW. The Global Bank branch that we opened here became kind of the headquarters for me. It is totally equipped for all the transactions."
"That is settled then, my love. When would you like to start?"
"Today."

"That is a Worthgold all right."
"A Worthgold al Malik, father."
"Better yet, son."

WITHDRAWALS

"It is absurd the amounts in these withdrawals that Malouf took from the sheik's account, Scott."
"How bad is it?"
"There are dozens of them. He took two million dollars, five million, and sometimes ten million. They sum to over a hundred million dollars."
"That is around the value he has invested in Australia."
"By the looks of it we can conclude that first, he deposited the money in his own bank account, then he used it to buy land."
"It shows that he is an amateur thief. His bank deposits prove his guilt and they are enough to send him to jail, Bethany."
"I don't think the sheik will want his family in jail, but at least we can stop him from doing it again."
"Wait a moment, little sister. If the man doesn't go to jail and only receives a warning from the sheik, he will become your declared enemy. It is very dangerous to upset such a man."
"But what alternative do we have?"
"Let him steal away. Let's put it down to loss. Consider it a donation in the family."
"That is not a real solution, Scott. And I will not be guided by fear. Malouf already hates me as it is."
"Let me give a look at those papers, will you? If you remember well I took courses specializing in bank fraud."
"Of course I remember. Here are the papers. Have fun."
"I sure will, little sister. I will look for Malouf's tail to pull in these documents."
"I hope you succeed, Scott. There is nothing I despise more than thieves."
"Maybe murderers?"
"Oh, Scott. Do you think it is possible?"
"I would say by now that it is wise to take small steps. We don't know these people and what they are capable of."

Bethany nods slowly and wonders how devastated the sheik would be to find out that he has been robbed by his late wife's brother. Life had some cruel turns.

BANK REVERSAL

"Is your brother sick or something, Bethany?"
"Why do you say that, Omar?"
"When you both arrived from the bank he locked himself in his bedroom and we haven't seen him since."
"I am sure he is fine. Maybe he had a headache or a cold."
"It is just that we have a Storytelling event tonight and I don't know whether to cancel or keep it."
"Keep it, Omar. He would have told us if he needed to cancel it."
"You are right, Bethany. I will tell my assistant to get things ready, then. I will see you for dinner, my love."
"Yes. See you in a couple of hours. I will check on Scott and also on my mom. She went shopping with Iasmin and the girls."
"That is my aunt, all right. On the day of her arrival at the palace and she has the energy to go shopping."
It brings a smile on Omar's face to think of that and he kisses Bethany tenderly before they part.
When she knocks on Scott's door he shouts 'come in' and returns to talk on the phone.
"As simple as that? Wow! I thought so. Thank you, John, I owe you one."
Bethany is curious to see him so happy with the phone conversation.
"What have you found out so far, Scott?"
"As I told you, Bethany, this is an amateur thief. He collected the sheik's signature for those withdrawals, but he didn't collect Omar's."
"What do you mean?"
"I mean that it is a joint account. Without Omar's signature, the transactions aren't valid and they can be reversed. Not all of the sheik's accounts are like that. I suppose Malouf was unlucky to have chosen that one."
"How come the bank paid the amounts if there was one signature missing?"

"Let's say it was all in the family. The sheik's signature has weight as does his word. People obey him and worry about the details later. But I phoned Malouf's bank and was informed that he has a deadline to provide Omar's signature on those papers."

"Is that the man you were talking to on the phone just now?"

"No. That was John from our lawyer's team back home. I asked for his advice in this case. He said that the best way to do it is to have a letter signed by Omar saying that he disagrees with the transactions. With that, the amounts will suffer an immediate bank reversal."

"So, I just have to tell Omar the truth."

"I wouldn't."

"Why?"

"Because then it will become clear to the uncle that you had a participation in this. If Omar confronts him it will be like a declaration of war."

"What do you suggest."

"Let Malouf suffer and lose. But stay out of it. Tell Omar and the sheik that some of their money was transferred but not invested properly and you advise them to bring it back so that you can invest it well. Then, invest it immediately, as you are doing with other incomes."

"You are a genius, Scott."

The next day, after few explanations at breakfast, Omar signs the letter that Scott had prepared and handed to his sister.

It was very fast to have the money back. They also knew that the ownership of the Australian properties had been frozen for lack of payment. The ball was in Malouf's side of the court now.

Chapter 40 – The sisters' tale

By now, a large group invited by the sheik attended the storytelling events. His best friends, authorities, and business partners that happened to be in town in the days of the feast. It is impressive how every tasteful people can appreciate a well-told story.

And Youssef didn't let them down when he told one of his great-grandpa's favorite tales.

"Today I will tell you a story I learned when I was only a child:

There were once two sisters, Lalah and Leleeh who married two brothers and lived in neighbor houses.

Leleeh's husband liked to study and he spent most of his day reading books and papers. They were young when they met and Leleeh expected him to become a respected teacher someday. This idea made her feel superior to her sister and despise her since Lalah's husband didn't have patience for books and spent his time trading cheap merchandise such as old clocks or small vases.

Being always outside and in movement, Lalah's husband became very strong and healthy. He was a simple and happy man and his entrance at his home was full of laughter and hugs. Soon he was throwing one of his kids in the air and inviting all of them to join his fun. Also, he was lucky to find some beautiful things amid the trinkets that he bought and sold, like some shining curtain for the kitchen or a nice bracelet for Lalah.

When Leleeh witnessed all of that day after day, she felt so envious that it made her sick. Her own husband looked pale and thin. He was serious and quiet. Never the ambitious type, they lived from a small allowance the school paid him to translate some books. He never became a teacher because he was too shy. Leleeh kept bragging about him, but as the years went by it didn't make sense anymore.

In time, Lalah's husband had saved enough to buy valuable merchandise and his profits kept raising. He had built more rooms to the house and his children and wife wore the best clothes.

Leleeh became resentful and she frequently called her sister's children lazy, ugly and dumb. Lalah couldn't accept that, so she stopped visiting Leleeh and inviting her over.

This decision was not well received by the envious sister.

She now had an insatiable desire for everything that Lalah owned. She longed for her dresses and rings. She watched the flowers in her sister's garden and the thought of planting her own never entered her mind. Instead, she had a necessity to deprive Lalah of each joyful thing. She often stepped on the flowers during the late hours of the night to destroy them and cause pain.

Being in favor of simple solutions, Lalah asked her husband to build a big fence between the houses.

It enraged Leleeh greatly and because she didn't have access to her nephews anymore she started to offend her own husband saying to him how disappointed she was because he was a failure. And she used her poisonous words to disturb him until one day he just left. In a state of uncontrolled mind, Leleeh kept imagining that her sister was laughing at her behind that fence. It was far from the truth because Lalah kept busy with house chores. She loved to cook for her family and she also sewed her husband's clothes. She had no time or inclination to mind her sister's business.

By now, every time Leleeh heard the laughs on the other side of the fence she believed that they were mocking her.

And she started to plan her revenge on her innocent and unaware sister. She was discontent with her poverty because without her husband's income she had to sell the house furniture little by little and even so live like a miserly.

Leleeh went to the town's market and suggested to the woman who sold rugs that Lalah was her husband's lover. She pretended to be her friend and to wish her well and told some stories about seeing Lalah with the man.

A week later Leleeh did the same thing with the woman who sold clothes. She made her so suspicious that the woman even cried and sobbed about this misfortune.

Without even knowing it, Lalah had lost her reputation.

In a month, five or six women hated Lalah with all their heart and Leleeh made sure to put them in touch with each other, so they could get their sorrows out of their chests talking about the plight common to all. But they did more than that. They got together one afternoon and cornered Lalah on an empty street and beat her so bad that she stayed on the floor drowning in her blood.

Leleeh desired to deprive her sister of her happiness so much that she didn't mind if Lalah lost her life in the process. On the contrary, she felt victorious that her plan to fool those women had paid off.

When some men found Lalah on the floor, she had fainted from the pain but they managed to take her to her house. Leleeh pretended to be sorry for her and moved to her house with the excuse of helping take care of Lalah. Being there, she wore Lalah's clothes which had been objects of her covetousness. She also ate like a pig and ordered the kids around. Lalah's husband was so sad about the situation that it was only natural for Leleeh to comfort him with very long embraces. She found many occasions to rub her body against his and when her sister died a little while later she moved to his bed immediately.

Leleeh had succeeded in taking everything her sister owned. But she was still discontent because she was addicted to the envying more than to the obtaining. She wouldn´t do the house chores, she abandoned the garden, and didn´t care for the children. Leleeh found the man very noisy and never joined his laughter with his kids. Her pleasure had all been in hating and envying. She never felt guilty about what happened to Lalah. In fact, she still felt joy when she thought of her sister´s misfortune and considered it well deserved.

Since Leleeh never took care of herself she soon had a disheveled appearance. The children hated her and the man found out that she was bitter and mean. When he sold the house and moved to another town for a fresh start he left Leleeh behind.

In her urge to inflict pain upon her sister, Leleeh had weighed down her own soul.

With no means to support herself, she soon became a beggar. Leleeh wandered the streets looking like the madwoman she had become. It was common for boys to throw rocks at her just for laughs. And people often saw her trying to peek inside their houses finding things to envy. And she would grief when she saw their prosperity.

She suffered for the rest of her life and the truth is that she had brought this upon herself."

There was an explosion of applause from the audience, followed by the reverent silence when they were presented with Habibdul´s song.

Envious woman
Stubborn as a mule
Your mirror has a hole
Right in the middle

You search the neighbor´s life
Your eye is like a knife
Envy is all you grow
Your own life you throw
Envious woman

Stubborn as a mule
You have no decency
With this, we all agree
Envious woman.

IMPRESSIONS

These performances always kept people chatting vividly afterward. It was not different with Bethany and while they sipped delicious mint teas, she exchanged impressions with Michelle and Iasmin.

"I got impressed by that verse of the song that says that her mirror has a hole in the middle."

"Why, my daughter?"

"Because she refuses to look at herself."

"Wow. Now I understand it better. By doing so, she can never improve herself."

"Yes, Iasmin. That is exactly what I grasped from this tale. All she minds about is the next persons´ life. It is horrible that there are people like that."

"Don´t you think it is only an old tale, Bethany?"

"No. I believe that art represents life. It is supposed to capture our attention and make us understand our own emotions better. There is always room for improvement in our character."

They kept on talking until Amal and Nadia took Bethany away from the older women because they wanted to be introduced to Habibdul.

He was not only a talented artist but also a very handsome man and it hadn´t escaped the young women´s eyes.

TEACHER YOUSSEF

After Bethany left Omar´s cousins chatting with Habibdul and Scott, she joined her husband and his father who were in a group talking to Youssef.

"Bethany, my love. You will be glad to know that Youssef has just accepted my father´s offer and will become the teacher of young artists in the art of storytelling."

"That is wonderful. I congratulate you, Sheik Mohamed for the brilliant idea. And Youssef for saying yes."

"Thank you, Bethany. When I witnessed such great talent I recognized that it is a treasure that must be preserved. We will start by recording all the stories Youssef can remember. It will be kept in our National Library. The next step will be for him to teach the next generations how to tell a story in a way to capture our attention one hundred percent."

"Well, I never thought of myself as a teacher. But I will try my best not to disappoint."

The elderly artist was truly humble. Bethany was glad to know that he was now under the sheik´s protection. Soon he would become wealthy and in no need to cross the deserts looking for means to survive. Hopefully, from now on, only his stories would travel far.

Chapter 41 – Last performance

And here were the guests gathered for the last performance of the series in the palace. Youssef waited for everybody to take a seat after the warm wave of applause and then he began.

"I will now tell you the story of the camel merchant Selim. He worked very hard and had a good number of animals, around thirty. This allowed him to provide a good life for his wife and two sons. He was a talkative and happy man, so one day he was invited to have dinner at one of his customers' house who was a wealthy man. There, Selim saw expensive objects and rugs made of exotic fabrics. The food was also sophisticated and the people at the house treated him well.

But instead of leaving content from the pleasant event, he left with a burden on his shoulders because his spirit now desired those expensive material possessions.

Selim decided he would do everything in his power to become rich. The first thing he did was double the number of animals he owned. Now, in order to feed all those animals, he had to cut on his family´s food. They also couldn´t afford to buy clothes or shoes anymore. Soon they looked like the beggars on the streets, but Selim told them to be patient because one day their family would be a very rich one.

Dreaming of money and studying the means to obtain it, Selim raised the price of his camels. This made people go elsewhere to purchase their animals.

After months of starving, his wife left for her mother´s house and took the children with her. Selim felt relieved because he didn´t find joy in their company anymore, they had become an expense, a real burden.

Sixty camels ate a lot, so Selim started to sell his house´s furniture to be able to feed them. In a short time, he was sitting in an empty room, but he didn´t seem to realize it because his mind was busy dreaming about gold and jewels.

Then his luck seemed to return to him when a foreigner approached him and decided to buy four of his camels. The man paid the price in full but Selim wasn´t satisfied by that. He had seen the man´s purse full of gold coins and he wanted all of it. So he distracted his customer and took the purse. Had he not been so greedy, the man wouldn´t even bother to return for it. But he left him without even the money to buy food for the long journey ahead of him.
When Selim saw the man from a distance he prepared to greet him with a sharp knife. After killing him, it was easy to bury the man in the backyard.
All the trouble he had had was worth it because he got to keep the money, his four camels back and the man´s horse. Nobody complained about it because the man was a stranger in those parts and had not been missed.
Selim decided to follow this line of action because it had paid off so well. He prepared some knives, blenders, and even a small gun and hid them among his things while he waited for his next victim.
Instead, a search party came to question him since the man he had killed was the sheik´s own younger brother. They knew he had traveled to buy camels, so it was natural to look for him where they were sold.
When they saw the horse, Selim couldn´t deny what he had done. After they put a knife to his throat he confessed everything and showed them the bag of money and the place he had buried the body.
It didn´t prevent his violent death and after all his greed on this earth, his last thought was that he sure hoped there was gold waiting for him in heaven. His avarice had plunged into his heart and not even death could separate him from his earthly desires."
When Habibdul started to sing he was able to capture their imaginations once again.
When you become greedy
The self-control you lose
Your acts become barbarian
The bad instincts you use

You are greedy for money
You are greedy for gold
Crimes you have committed
Bad lies you have told

You keep your greed, no matter how much you save
Then, goodbye to you I wave
Because your greed will take you to the grave

FIREWORKS

That last night of storytelling was very special. Youssef and Habibdul received medals of honor from the sheik's hands. They were touched by his speech that ended like that, "These medals are for your contributions to the improvement of culture and education in this country."
And then there were fireworks, music, and dancing to celebrate life, most of all, and the richness of making new friends.
People left the palace with the feeling of having taken part in a very prestigious event. It was one of those entertainments that you would not easily forget because it caused an impression in your spirit.
They looked forward to more opportunities like that, and the sheik assured them that he would not let a long time pass without inviting the same artists to the palace again.

AMAL AND HER MOM

"Talking about education, I will soon part with my sweet girl Amal since she is going abroad to improve her education. Just as her cousin Omar did."
"Really, Iasmin? You have not told me about that."
"It is because I was hoping that she would change her mind, Michele. But she has made up her mind and the college sent her the acceptance letter."
"Well, congratulations Amal."
"Thanks, auntie. My mom feels fear, but I keep telling her that she shouldn't. It is a great school and the campus is wonderful."
"Which school is that?"
"The same one my cousin Omar went to."
"Well, that is really close to the apartment I will be living at."
Michele tells them all about Bethany's place and how she wanted her mom to live there.

"That is such a coincidence. Maybe I won´t worry so much if you keep one eye on Amal from time to time."
Michele looks thoughtful for a moment. Then she says,
"Even better. Why doesn´t Amal come to live with me?"
"Really, auntie?"
"Of course, Amal. We could keep each other company. And we will have bedrooms for your mother and Nadia to visit as much as they want."
Iasmin has tears in her eyes when she hugs her generous friend.
"That is such a relief. I was going to fly there to help Amal find a place to live. My heart was suffering to think of her staying at a school dormitory. I didn´t have a clue where to start looking. But now that she can stay with you, Michele, I assure you that I feel as if a stone has been lifted from my chest."
"I believe you, Iasmin. But listen to me… You have to come all the same. This way you can visit her college and see her bedroom in the apartment. Then you can picture her at those places when you are back home."
"I couldn´t impose myself. You are already doing so much."
"This will only work if we drop the ceremonies. You have become dear to me, Iasmin. And the same goes to Amal and Nadia."
"How nice! I accept that but just because I love you too."
"So, tomorrow we make many plans."
And it was indeed a happy solution for them all because it gave no space for loneliness.

FACES BECOME KNOWN

Some people have their fame through magazines and videos. It was not the case with Omar and Bethany. Their faces became familiar because they went in person to visit and help the needy of their country. There were weekly visits to hospitals, homes for the elderly, and orphanages.
They also went to people´s houses in different areas and listened to their problems. A group of secretaries and assistants was always with them, taking notes and making sure that the urgent things got done within the deadline appointed by the couple.
Naturally, the paparazzi made sure to have their pictures on the media constantly. But for the people who had seen them in person, it

was almost like recognizing a member of the family on the news. The difference is that this was the royal family. However, nobody doubted their devotion for their people, and the more they expressed their love and care, the more they were loved back.

SO LONG, BETHANY

A long warm hug was given to Bethany at the airport by her mom. It was a difficult separation, but now things had improved because Michele was not going alone anymore. Three happy faces surrounded her. Iasmin, Nadia, and Amal were very talkative and excited. It was contagious. Bethany knew that her mom saw it as a blessing and a challenge to see this girl through college as she had done with her own children. Education was very important for Michele, maybe because she hadn't been able to finish her own.
"Well, Bethany, to tell you the truth I was feeling a little down for having to face a return trip all by myself. Now I am so happy because my three friends are joining me."
"I could never have guessed things would work out so well, mom."
"It is all because of you, sweetheart. By your marriage, you gave us new family members. It feels so good Bethany, because since Nancy passed away I haven't felt closer to anybody else."
"I know mom. It is hard to find true friends. I am glad for you because these are sweet girls and aunt Iasmin is a dear."
As they finished talking the others approached. They had been to the newsstand and were now ready for the long trip since they had bought tons of magazines and candies. Scott had said his goodbyes at the palace because he had a busy day ahead purchasing goods for his project of building wells.
Omar also came to Bethany's side and embraced her.
"What were you talking to the pilot about?"
"I told him, my love, that a flight without turbulence will mean a large bonus for him."
"Is it really up to him?"
"I guess we will now find out."
They wave to the others and stay watching as the jet plane takes off.

Chapter 42 – Oasis

Omar told Bethany he had a surprise for her. It was a trip to the Al Maliq Oasis that he had planned to distract her from the departure of her mom.

"An oasis? It sounds so romantic."

"I am glad that you think so, my love. It would take us two days to get there by horse. But the helicopter will take us there in just a few hours. What do you say we leave tomorrow and stay the rest of the week."

"I think it is wonderful. This way I will have time to pack. What do we take to an oasis?"

He laughs heartedly and she finds herself in his arms all of a sudden. "Whatever you want, I guess."

"Omar, be serious. I have no idea what to expect."

"That is one reason for me to take you there. You will meet people who never lived in the city. They have a simple life but you will find them sincere and loyal. That land where the oasis is located belongs to my family for centuries. My mother loved to go there with my father and me. She used to say that in that place we were all hers."

"How lovely! Thanks for sharing it with me."

"How could I not? You have become a part of me. The essential part."

By learning that the place is isolated from civilization, Bethany decides not to take western clothes there. Her instinct tells her that Omar desires her to dive into the roots of who he is and she intends to enjoy every second of the experience.

The next day, when the helicopter approaches the oasis, Bethany has a view so splendid that she is out of breath. The palm trees and other vegetations outnumber the dark green tents that are pitched together. There are natural swimming pools that make the place look like a very exclusive country club, but in this case, nature worked out the design as it pleased.

"Omar, this place is a paradise."

"I have to agree with you."

"The ground seems to be so fertile. How is it possible if we are surrounded by the desert sand?"

"I guess it is the same concept that your brother wants to explore in favor of the people. Getting the underground water."

"I see."

"Only in this case, it happens naturally."
"There are children playing there."
"Fifteen families live here. It is a small village but they manage well. My father has offered many times to bring them to the city but they always refuse. I guess they are happy here."
"I am sure they are."
When the helicopter landed, a crowd stopped at its door and they all greeted Bethany and Omar with large smiles.
When Omar leads his wife to the largest tent a woman comes out dressed in a djellaba made of wool. She introduces herself as Jamile and tells Bethany that she will be of help to her. Bethany thanks her politely and accepts some fresh tea from her hands. Omar also takes a cup and sits down in one of the cushions placed all around a low table. There are also beautiful carpets and thick curtains made specially to shut the sunlight out.
Bethany sits on a comfortable sofa and stretches her legs while Omar approved of the menu choice for the day. He also enquired Ibrahim, the other servant about the provisions that had been sent the previous day.
"Everything arrived in order, my prince."
"Good. If we want for anything else we can always send the helicopter."
"That is for sure, prince Omar."
"Well, Bethany, if you are not too tired I suggest that we have a look around this place while it is not so hot."
"I feel fine. I would love to explore the oasis with you."
And there was much to see and learn. Because it was a bright sunny day, the men were busy filling the troughs with water for the horses and camels. Women had to do house chores and mind the children. Despite the fact that they were all very busy, they seemed happy and had a smile to offer along with explanations to any doubt that occurred to Bethany. One thing she was curious to know was about the fertile ground and how it could be so since they were far from civilization and its solutions such as fertilizers. She was then told that they used the animals' manure which was efficient and without the chemicals' effects.
When she saw the horses so well-kept it made her realize that Omar's love for these animals was assurance enough that any of them that belonged to him would be outstanding.

"Tomorrow morning, we can take the horses and visit some intriguing caves made in the rocks by the desert winds."

Bethany looked at him in surprise. It had never crossed her mind that they would leave the oasis.

"But only if you want to, my love."

"Of course I want to, Omar. I am all in for this adventure. I want to experience all the emotions of these parts."

"I was hoping you would say that, Bethany."

Next, they followed Ibrahim to the nearest pool of natural water, which made the oasis so picturesque, and Omar dismissed him with a wave of his hand.

"Do you want to refresh a little before lunch?"

"I don't have my swimsuit, Omar."

"That is why I made sure we are left alone."

"How nice!"

They entered the crystal-clear water together as prince and princess of that place and he whispered in her ear that he hoped she would conceive a baby right there in the heart of their land and in the middle of rear nature. She was delighted by his idea and soon they were in each other's arms with only birds and colorful little insects to witness their love.

TRIBESMEN

The tribesmen that lived in the oasis were direct descendants from the al Maliq family. They had many skills but above all, they were outstanding riders.

Just as Omar was. Bethany looked at that handsome man riding a magnificent horse and she just couldn't believe in her luck to be his beloved wife.

That morning they were heading to the caves and the group consisted of ten men armed to protect them. Bethany had become an excellent rider too and she enjoyed feeling that the horses had quickened their pace when they were near their destiny. These animals were of a brown color, except for Omar's horse, which was of a dark yellow, a kind of golden color that befitted the prince. During all the stay at the oasis, Omar had decided to wear only the traditional white robes and now they were flowing around him. The prince looked imposing and majestic but Bethany had no idea that so did she.

THE CAVES

As Omar gallantly helped his wife dismount her horse, her eyes were immediately attracted to the most beautiful formations in rocks that she had ever seen.
There were holes and curves that allowed the sun to shine through them and create incredible drawings on the floor.
And then, Omar took her inside one of the biggest caves and it was very fresh inside. The soft wind there surprised her and when her eyes were used to the dimness, she could explore the beautiful inside. When she touched some rocks, they felt like glass in her hands.
"This place has always brought me much peace, my love."
"I can understand why. It is extraordinary, Omar."
When Bethany had seen enough of this cave, she went to the smaller ones and found out that the wind produced a soft sound in some of them. It was like a soft whistle or a very little bell. She felt the urge to hug her husband and just stay silent by his side enjoying all that.
As soon as Omar felt she was finished exploring their surroundings, he took her back to the large cave.
"It is not wise to ride back now. The sun is at its hottest now and I don't want your memories of today to be of an intolerable hot and dusty desert, my love."
"That could never be, Omar. But I am glad to stay here longer."
"Good. This is a great place for a picnic." After saying so, the prince clapped his hand and immediately two tribesmen entered carrying cushions and a large picnic cloth that they laid on the cave's floor. Some torches were placed around the couple too. After that, they brought in different loaves of bread, meats, and delicious sauces. There were also many fruits and sweets.
"Oh, this could feed an army. Should we invite the men, my prince?"
"They brought much more for themselves, sweetheart. Don't worry. They are sitting at the entrance of the cavern to guarantee our safety. A couple of them have gone to the top of the Mount and they will be having their lunch there, while they look around."
"It sounds fun."

"These people enjoy adventures."
"Me too."
"OK, pretty princess, I will take you up there later."
"Thanks, husband."
They enjoyed the delicious foods and juices while Omar told his wife about the times he had visited the caves as a boy. She encouraged him to tell her about the smallest details and what he had felt then. It brought him memories of happy times with his mother and father. When he made a small pause, it was as if he looked into the past, and his peaceful face proved that it was a happy one.
"Honey, it is so cozy in here that I wouldn´t be surprised if we took a nap on these soft cushions."
"I was hoping you would feel that way, my princess. Come here to my arms."
When she happily did as he told her to, Omar´s cologne filled her senses and his strong arms showed her that she would always find a home with this man. No matter if it was in a palace, a cave, or in the middle of the sand. As long as he stretched his arms and she could cuddle there.

Chapter 43 – Pregnant princess

The same day of the couple´s return to the palace, Malouf had also arrived for one of his frequent visits.
It caused such a distaste to Bethany that she almost asked Omar to take her back to the oasis. But then she decided to control her emotions and not to say anything. She knew that life was not made only of vacations and paradisiac places.
During dinner, the sheik was happy to hear his son tell the news about the oasis and the nice people who lived there. Then his attention went to his brother-in-law and he wanted to know where Malouf had been for the last weeks.
"I came from Australia."
"That is quite far. Were you on business or vacation?"
"Vacation."
Oh, so the old goat was going to play the innocent. Bethany knew that, by now, his misfortune had already exploded in his face.

He was careful in his choice of words and he kept looking at Bethany as if expecting some reaction that would prove that she had had some participation in the matter.

"Land there is cheap if you know where to look for. Maybe I could interest you in buying some farms."

"No, thank you. Too far for my taste. And anyway, Bethany is responsible for all our investments from now on."

"Is that wise?"

The petulant man. Do robbers get to give an opinion? Bethany almost couldn't hide how much she despised him.

"It is the wisest decision I could ever make. We have had huge returns so far."

"I see. And I guess land is out of the question."

Bethany didn't even blink because she knew that he was watching her and evaluating her reactions to his words.

"All offers are considered. In GBW I have a group specialized in evaluating which are the best options of investments. I would only ask you to bring your proposal during business hours."

"Of course, it is rude of me. I will let you enjoy your dinner."

"Thank you, Malouf. It is considerate of you."

He became red because her tone of voice implied just the opposite.

The next two or three days Malouf tried to bring back the subject of Australian's lands only to see Bethany dismiss it. He was defeated and he knew it. He looked at her with all his hate but then it stopped mattering.

Bethany had found out that she was pregnant. She told Omar and he was so satisfied and proud that he spent hours telling her how much he loved her. He would touch her belly, carry her in his arms around their room, ask her to sing for him, and insist that she rested.

He told his father about it and the sheik gave Bethany a crown made of gold that had belonged to Omar's mother. It was a very touching moment.

When Bethany called Michele to tell her the great news, she could hear her mother laughing and crying at the same time.

As for Scott, the moment he heard the news he went to buy bikes and toys for the future nephew or niece.

Those were happy moments and the pregnancy months passed quickly.

BABY BENJAMIN

"Now you can have one idea of how much a man can be crazy in love with a baby, little sister. The way Omar acts with Ben is exactly how your father did with you."
"Ah, Scott. Thank you for telling me that. I don't know if I enjoy watching Ben more, or if I enjoy watching Omar with him."
Brother and sister were sitting at a soft low sofa watching Omar talking to Ben and carrying him in his laps around the room to make the two-month-old sleep. But Ben kept staring at Omar and showed no signs of being sleepy.
"Is it true that the sheik bought Benjamin a castle in France?"
"Yes. He says that everybody who is somebody has a castle there to spend the vacations."
"I guess if Benjamin gets spoiled, all of us will take the blame."
"That is so right."
Everywhere they took Benjamin there was a trail of happiness after him. The baby's first visit abroad was to the proud grandma. But they also took him to parks, zoos, and gardens around the world. The little family was quite famous by now, but they had a unique way of ignoring the fame and diving into their happiness.

FIRST BIRTHDAY

There was not one room in the palace without balloons or decorations for Benjamin's first birthday party. Because he was the future sheik of his country and the whole political world was aware of that, presents started to arrive at the palace. They were from presidents of many countries and soon two rooms were filled with expensive toys, pieces of art, and jewels for the little prince.
Bethany had dressed him exactly like Omar and they both looked gorgeous.
The cake was taller than a man. The party started in the morning and kept going until the darkness of the night allowed them to enjoy the fireworks. Benjamin's name was formed again and again in the ski by the modern fireworks that his grandpa had purchased for the occasion.

Prince Benjamin Worthgold al Maliq was healthy, happy, rich, and surrounded by many people who loved him. His mom and dad would always fight to guarantee that nothing went wrong in his life.

Chapter 44 – Khaleb is everywhere

Bethany was happy to have her brother often at the palace. Not only he was keeping one eye on her, but also he enjoyed discussing the progress of the wells projects. He had already installed five of them in different regions and people there were happy to have better access to water. The first one was launched with the presence of Sheik Mohamed himself.

Unfortunately, Khaleb was also a constant presence in the palace. He was with them during meals or entertaining important guests. He followed the royal family to inaugurations and functions. He had opinions about everything and they were not always smart ones. His attitude didn´t seem to bother Sheik Mohammed or Omar but it was starting to give on Bethany´s nerves. When Malouf also joined them, it was common for Bethany to have migraines after she received so many looks of pure hate.

Khaleb had told some sad stories to the sheik and asked to have a place as one of his counselors. His uncle couldn´t say no to him, but instead, invited Khaleb to live at the palace for a while to acquire experience.

His arrival marked the beginning of struggles in Bethany´s life.

Khaleb was indeed the fly in the soup. He had a way of finding Bethany alone and then he would say horrible things to her and even shoot some coward threats.

"Omar must be tired of you by now."

"That is none of your business."

"Funny looking baby you have there."

"I don´t care about your opinion."

"Many babies die before they are one year old."

"Don´t be disgusting, Khaleb. Anyway, Ben already complete one."

"I bet he would like to have a farmer as a cousin."

Oh, so he wouldn´t drop the subject of the Australian farms. It was indeed a fortune that he and his father had lost in this attempt of robbery. Bethany decided to ignore him and walked away.

As always, Ben was the heart of the palace and everyone wanted to be with him. It was common for the proud grandfather to pick him up at the nursery and take him to the gardens or to the library to show him pictures in the books.

Omar and Bethany also took Ben to the swimming pools a lot and he loved it. His giggles were heard from a distance.

So, when the sheik entered the nursery and started playing with the baby, Bethany smiled and went to take a long bath. The babysitters were also around Ben, just in case he needed a change of diapers or a bottle of milk.

So, when Bethany returned to the nursery, she was startled to see Khaleb holding Ben, instead of the sheik. He saw the look of concern and offered an explanation, "Uncle was called on the phone, so I offered to watch the baby."

"It was not necessary. His babysitters are very capable."

"I told them to take a break."

"You shouldn't have done it."

Bethany took Benjamin from his arms and heard Khaleb's cruel talk.

"You know, Bethany, I got the impression that your baby is very weak. Many accidents can happen to such a small child."

"Get out of here, Khaleb."

He went immediately because Khaleb recognized that she was furious. It was enough for now.

DECISION TO TALK

Because Khaleb was now threatening her baby, Bethany decided to talk to Omar about him. That same day she took Omar to the office to tell him all about Malouf and his son's bad deeds.

"Omar, it saddens me to bring to your attention that your relatives have been robbing you. Malouf and Khaleb found means to fool your father into transferring much money to their account."

"My father is no fool, Bethany."

"Of course not, Omar. Bad choice of words. I am sorry. They tricked him. It is common for rich people to become a target. Malouf and his son are far from honest. They hate me and Khaleb says bad things about Ben."

"My cousin loves the little prince, Bethany. I am sure you are mistaken."

Bethany didn´t expect this. It was like talking to a wall. He didn´t believe anything she said and his answers showed his bad mood. It had been so different when Bethany had confided in Scott. Her brother had supported her and offered his help at once. But Omar had reacted in a different manner. And then, came the question.

LOVE AND TRUST

"Bethany, don´t you love me anymore?"
"Of course I love you, Omar. What makes you ask that question?"
"Khaleb tried to prevent me. He said that the problem with foreign women is that they quickly get bored with our ways. They start finding problems with the husband´s family and soon they are getting ready to leave."
"What did you answer him?"
"I got really mad and told him to shut up. I said he had a trauma because of his mother´s behavior and that I was sure of your love, Bethany. I forbade him to say another word about you."
"What a relief! I couldn´t stand it if you did not defend me from his false accusations."
It was disheartening for Bethany to find out that Khaleb had been poisoning Omar against her. Because she felt so close to her husband she thought that nothing could ever come between them. But it looked like she had underestimated her enemy and now she was receiving sorrow as payment for her mistake.
"I thought the accusations were false. But now you are doing exactly what he said. Why are you accusing my uncle Malouf of theft?"
"Omar, you must believe me. He made your father sign authorization papers and he took a lot of money from the bank account."
"Probably to pay some staff. My father shares a lot of his workload with his advisors and uncle Malouf has been helping him for decades."
"Right. But the money went to his personal account."
"How much?"
"Many draws that added up to one hundred million dollars."
"And that was all?"
"That I had knowledge of, yes."
Omar looked very upset and it was as if his words were hurting himself more than her ears.

"Bethany, when you gave billions of dollars to Scott I was not against it. I thought it was noble of you and I loved you even more because of your generosity."

His words wounded her because they made sense. She thought it was better not to say anything.

"Now in my uncle's case, couldn't you have the benefit of the doubt? He is an old man, not an able finance specialist like you. I am sure he is not a robber. Malouf committed some mistake."

"Please, Omar. Let me explain it to you."

"If you don't mind, Bethany, I would rather not talk about it anymore."

She looked at her husband and saw the pain in his eyes. It was the saddest conversation they had ever had and she agreed with him that it was best to end it.

STRATEGY

What Bethany couldn't know was that Omar had developed a fear of losing her. Khaleb's constant telling him that Bethany didn't love him and would soon leave him had affected Omar.

As she saw Omar leave the palace without giving her a kiss for the first time since they were together, Bethany decided she would not have any of that.

Khaleb had not kept the money and he would not keep the advantage of separating the couple too.

She had many servants working on her bedroom and preparing it for a romantic night. White petals of roses covered the whole floor. On the bed, there were red petals. Bethany ordered a hundred candles that made the room look like a sunrise. There were scented oils burning in little pots. And then there were Bethany's clothes. They were transparent robes of soft black silk that made her look beautiful and mysterious.

Omar entered their bedroom to find a scene from dreams. She didn't allow him to talk because as soon as he entered, she ran to him and her mouth covered his in passionate kisses.

"Oh, Bethany, my love!"

"My prince, my husband. I love you!"
And she made sure to tell him that she loved him again and again. They didn't sleep at all that night. Servants left the dinner at their door and Bethany served her husband in bed. The next day, she asked Omar not to leave the bedroom and he was happy to stay with her. They rested during the morning and after lunch, they took their time caressing and loving each other.
At night, Bethany asked Omar to stay with her the next day too. He asked with a smile, "Why, my love?"
"Because I need you."
It was enough to convince him. Bethany sent for Ben and they played with the baby all morning. Then, when the babysitter took their son to his bedroom, the couple had a romantic lunch and they fed each other in the mouth between kisses.
Later, they entered the bathtub together and Bethany sang love songs in a sensual voice that pleased Omar intensely.
That night, Bethany had only one question for him.
"What is worrying you?"
"I am afraid that you stop loving me."
"I will stop breathing first." She gives him a long kiss and feels his immediate response. "Do you believe me, Omar?"
"Yes."
And he showed her that he believed.

GRANDMA

Omar and Bethany took Ben to visit his grandmother and Scott was invited to fly there with them. Michele was throwing her grandson another birthday party, and this way Scott could participate.
"You know, mom, when this project of the wells is over I will be ready to come home."
"Wow. That is great news, son. I am tired of missing you."
"Then it will be my turn to miss you, brother."
"Don't worry, little sister. I will visit you a lot. Also, I will take mom with me."
"That is great to hear. I wish we could all live together."

"We are together now. Let's make it memorable. Wait until you see the cake I ordered for Ben."
Benjamin was a source of happiness to all of them. The party was a success.

Chapter 45 - Sudden death

Their return to the palace was very well-received by the sheik. If Mohamed had missed his son in the past, now he made clear that he almost got sick when he parted from his grandson. He declared that Ben was the reason for his joy and the light of his life.
Sheik Mohamed also made it very clear the length of his appreciation for his daughter-in-law and often he compared her beauty and wit to his late wife's.
They had become close friends and he offered his advice to Bethany in the same quantity as he asked for her opinions. This relationship made Omar very happy because these were the two people he most loved in the world. Except for Benjamin, who was the winner of everybody's heart. Ben was number one for all of them, which only caused a stronger bond to take place.
The night of their return there was a banquet for dinner, Omar and Bethany sat at each side of sheik Mohamed. That night, Khaleb was sitting beside Omar, across from Bethany.
It was almost like watching a child playing with a new toy when you saw the Sheik Mohamed with one of the objects of his collection of new technologies.
That night he was proud of a glass made of two layers to keep a cold liquid between them. When you poured your drink in, it became cold without the necessity of adding ice.
He was explaining all of this to Bethany, "You see, the advantage is that your juice, for example, will not become watery as sometimes happens when you add ice."
"Oh, that is great! I hate when that happens to my drink."
Omar and Ben were both playing with their food since the dad was feeding mashed potatoes to the one-year-old boy, while the last one

was throwing peas and carrots at his daddy. Bethany didn't even pretend to be mad at them for this behavior because they were just too cute to be frowned upon. She returned her attention to her father-in-law.

"Here. Take my new glass, Bethany. You will taste the most perfect juice."

"Thank you. Here is mine. I haven't touched it yet. And I didn't put ice in it either."

"Don't do that, uncle."

"What, Khaleb?"

"Don't exchange glasses. You know… Because of the germs."

"Now that is one argument I haven't heard before. He is right, Bethany. I have taken a sip. Give me back the glass."

"No way! You are the healthiest man I know. I am already drinking it. Mmmm. It is delicious."

"I told you. I will order more of these glasses for all of us. This one came from Japan."

"They amaze me due to the number of new things they launch each year in Japan."

"It is true, Bethany…" As the sheik was trying to say, Khaleb interrupted him again because the sheik was starting to taste the orange juice.

"Don't drink that, uncle."

"Khaleb, don't be rude. Why shouldn't I drink my juice?"

"Maybe you prefer a fresh one. Or some iced tea."

"What is it with you and drinks tonight? Don't interrupt me again." And he turned the glass, drinking all at once. "We have to go together to Japan, Bethany. I want to show you and Omar some industries that use robots on the assembly line…

They kept talking and Bethany noticed that Khaleb looked defeated. She wondered what he had wanted to accomplish by calling the sheik's attention to him more than once. Maybe he felt jealous of the treatment the sheik gave her. Certainly, he had wanted to have the Japanese glass himself. But it was useless to fight for attention because, after Omar and Ben, the sheik's affection went directly to Bethany.

She thought about commenting this with Omar but Ben was so cute making faces to his dad and Omar was throwing him in the air and making him laugh so much that Bethany forgot all about Khaleb and joined the fun.

The next morning there was a moment of panic in the palace when the maid found the sheik dead in his bed. His heart had stopped during the night. The doctors assured the family that he had not suffered because it happened so fast.

Even so, Omar was devastated. And soon all the country joined his grief, for Sheik Mohamed al Maliq had been loved by his people with devotion.

Bethany showed her grief through her tears and the hurt in her eyes. Even the baby became quiet as if he sensed the sadness.

The country stopped its commercial activities for one week. Only emergency services worked. They were mourning for a great leader. Thousands of people attended the funeral.

THE SHEIK AND THE SHAIKHAH

The coronation of Omar and Bethany was a beautiful ceremony to which attended people from all around the world.

From then on, there were many decisions to be made and official meetings to attend. Some changes were made and among them, Khaleb asked to be transferred from counselor to a military position. It was a relief for Bethany because this caused him to move to the soldiers´ quarters and she saw very little of him. After his uncle died, Khaleb´s face looked unsettled and Bethany was surprised because she couldn´t imagine he had true feelings for the sheik. Life was really full of surprises.

Scott´s investigators had found out that since the farms´ fiasco, Malouf and Khaleb had started taking percentages from commercial deals made by the sheik. They had already gathered around twenty million dollars.

“That is a form of bribe, Scott.”

“I agree. They are low. Are you going to tell Omar?”

“No. Omar is so sad by the loss of his father that I don´t want to upset him further. Besides, he wouldn´t believe me anyway. We have to remember that Malouf is the brother of his mother.”

“So, what will you do?”

“I will let them do it. It is like giving crumbs to pigs. Maybe if they are satisfied they won´t bother us.”

"This kind of person is never satisfied, little sister. They are greedy ones."

"I know. I wish they would go away."

"Why would they leave? They have many cows to milk here."

"Unfortunately, there is nothing I can do at the moment."

"I still think you should tell your husband."

"Maybe soon."

What bothered Bethany the most is that in order for Malouf to make his sordid deals, h took Omar away from her a lot. There were many trips to meet with 'business partners' and 'investors'. These meetings were in an old-fashioned way and women were not allowed to participate. It saddened Bethany that Omar would still take part in those.

But the loss of his father had made him cling to his uncle as a fatherly figure and he couldn't see that it was not having a good effect on him. The poisonous old man was eager to imply that Omar was not half the man Mohamed had been and neither was he a strong leader.

Bethany used all her influence to keep Omar at her side and she took him to the presence of the poor and the simple people because they were not afraid to show affection and loyalty.

She also insisted that once a month, Omar took her and Ben on some trip away from everybody they knew. He always felt at peace in those moments. And that is how life was happening for them, one day at a time.

Bethany knew that as soon as the mourning period passed Omar would become the extraordinary sheik he was destined to be. With shaikhah Bethany by his side, that was for sure.

BEG TO DIFFER

Khaleb was really the stone in Bethany's shoe. He started with jokes about how nice it would be for Omar to have one harem at the palace.

And then he started to bring women to have lunch or dinner with them. Sometimes they were semi-naked. It was impossible to ignore and it was cause for another argument between Bethany and Omar. As soon as they were together she brought up what was bothering her.

"I won't accept this type of woman at my table!"

"What kind of women? Dressed in Arabian clothes?"

"Of course that is not the problem. They don't dress with decency."

"What do you expect? Khaleb is single. It is normal for him to be attracted to young women."

"Omar, have you gone blind?"

"No. I see the girls. Very nice looking."

Bethany knew that his rude answer was a reflex to her rude question. That is why she hated fights. People always went too far. So she immediately stopped talking and a silent tear ran down her face. She remembered days when Omar only had eyes for her. And now he had complimented vulgar women in an offensive tone of voice.

Point for Khaleb in this subtle war he had initiated.

"Bethany, I am so sorry."

"No. You are the sheik. Your cousin is right, you are allowed to have your harem. Just, please tell me when you will start it, so I will have time to pack my things and leave."

Omar saw her walk away with her head down and her shoulders shaking. She was right, he was a blind fool.

That night, Bethany received a thousand roses from her husband and Khaleb was forbidden to bring any company to the meals.

Chapter 46 – The last threat

As the days went by a distance took place between Omar and Bethany. It was as if they couldn't communicate with each other openly. Omar had a vast land of sorrow inside him caused by his mourning. He thought it best to spare his wife from the dark that called to him. And he closed up, even more, when he listened to his uncle telling him that he would never be a great leader like Mohamed if he lct a woman interfere with the country's affairs.

It was shocking for Bethany to recognize how much Omar had changed in such a short time. One day, Malouf suggested the purchase of farms in New Zealand during lunch.

"Please, I have asked you not to discuss business during meals."

"So, as a counselor, I can only talk to the sheik if you give permission, Bethany?"

"That is not what I am saying."

"Time is pressing. I need to have Omar´s signature in order to beat the competitor who wants to buy the farms."

"The farms are not a good investment at the moment."

"Shut up." Omar`s furious scream reverberated around the big table surprising even the guests who were distracted with their own conversations at the other end. There was a heavy silence because nobody knew if his order was directed at Bethany or Malouf. But then it became clear to all.

"Tell me more about the farms, uncle."

Bethany became very red and her spirit gave a little jump as if Omar had slapped her on the face. She ate silently and it was the longest meal of her life. Instead of leaving the table and making Malouf´s victory more obvious, she just disconnected from the surroundings. She took the opportunity to search inside her what those investments meant to her. Nothing. Bethany had not married Omar for his money, so if he wanted to let his uncle rob him blind, she would not interfere. Part of a person´s learning process was to make mistakes. Omar would have his share of them because there was nothing she could do. She could read the ache in Omar´s eyes and in his gloomy behavior.

But she could not accept his abuse because it would not create a healthy environment for raising her child. Then, after lunch, Bethany went to GBW Bank and transferred all of Omar´s investments back to his old bank. She signed documents that excluded her name and signature of any of his deals.

When the bank called Omar with the news, he went straight to Bethany´s office and he saw that she was very pale and fragile.

"Bethany, it was not necessary to do that."

"For me it was."

"I told Malouf that I will pass the farms deal."

"That is your decision to make."

"Isn´t that what you wanted?"

"What I want is for that to be the last time that you shout at me. What was that? Do you need to prove your superiority?"

"Oh, Bethany, forgive me. I was so arrogant."

"I don´t recognize you anymore, Omar."

"I am still the same man, Bethany. I am your husband. The man who loves you."

"That was a strange way of showing it."

"I am only human. I need you."

"Then let me in. Let me be there for you."

"I want to. Let's start over. Please, undo the bank transfer."

"No. It will only cause more unnecessary tensions. With Malouf getting your signature, very soon there will be nothing to invest, anyway."

"Now I am offended, Bethany. It is billions of dollars we are talking about."

"I think he won't go for less than that." She was being direct calling Malouf a thief now. Omar's eyes got icy and his voice followed.

"Won't you undo the transfer, Bethany?"

"No. I lost the interest." This sentence was like a payback to the slap she had felt from his words. Because it was a blow to him. It was as if she was taking back her love for him.

"Right. Have it your way, Bethany."

The truth is that they were both hurt and shouldn't be taking serious decisions right now. But neither of them could think straight after exchanging so many bitter words. Omar left suddenly and it occurred to Bethany that it was the first time they had gotten together without exchanging at least a hug or a kiss. It saddened her to think that maybe it was the first of many days like that.

BUSINESS TRIP

It was not a surprise to hear that Malouf was taking Omar with him for a business trip abroad. She had nothing to say about that, and it made Omar mad.

"Won't you ask me to stay?"

"Will you?"

"No. I can't. You see, as a sheik, I have responsibilities."

"Right."

"Won't you say more than that?"

"What do you want me to say, Omar?"

"I don't know. Say that you care. Say that you will miss me."

"You know I will."

He sat by her side looking defeated.

"I wish you would fight for me to stay."

"What is the point? Even when we are side by side, your mind is so distant from me. And your heart is becoming cold."

"Please, don´t say that, Bethany. I love you."

"I know you do. But this is not the life that we dreamt of having together. One life in which your uncle interferes so much."

"He is a counselor."

"Retire him."

"It would hurt him."

"So, instead, you hurt me."

He stays silent because he knows that she is right.

"Well, Omar. As long as you are happy."

"I am not happy, Bethany."

"You know, Omar, I am sure that even your own father didn´t wish you to have this life. Taken here and there by other people´s interests. Distant from your own wife and son."

"I know, Bethany. I feel like I am diving in a dark well."

"Then, come here to my arms."

"I am afraid that you will drown with me."

"I won´t. Let me be strong for us. And then one day it will be your turn to help me when I lose my mother. That is life, a sequence of good and bad days. But we don´t have to face it alone. We are a couple."

"Do you still love me?"

"More than anyone except Ben."

"I love you too, Bethany."

"Then, stay with me."

"I can´t cancel the trip, my love. But I will postpone it a couple of days."

"It is enough."

And they share their souls again. Omar shares his grief with her only to find out great comfort in her words, in her loving eyes, in her arms. They lock themselves from the world and renew their promises and dreams.

When Omar finally leaves, he says to her, "As soon as I return my uncle will be transferred away from the palace to attend some matters of our tribes in the east of the country.

Bethany's eyes shine so strongly that he wishes he could cancel the trip altogether. But there are some politicians waiting for him as well as investors. So, they part after a long kiss and loving words.

COUSIN KHALEB

After a few days that Omar had left Khaleb finds a way to talk to Bethany in private.
"Well, well, well… I think it is time you pay me back the money you stole from me and my father."
"You mean the money that you stole from Omar in the first place, right?"
"It makes no difference for him. He hadn't even noticed that it was missing."
"But I noticed. Be glad you are not in jail. Although it is never late for pressing charges."
"Omar will never allow that."
"Don't be so sure."
"Why don't you spare yourself of a battle in which you are the loser and just give me the money?"
"Listen Khaleb, you will never have so much power as you have had till now because I will personally guarantee that you have no access to this palace or its businesses."
"Wow, Bethany, how can you be so naive? I have lived in these parts all my life and you are a newcomer here. You think that you are superior to me but you are not. You are pretty stupid to think that you can be equal to me. You are not a worthy enemy. You are dust under my fingernails. There are people here at the palace who are totally loyal to me. You have no idea who they are."
"I am sure you have bribed one or two persons, Khaleb. I am not so idiot as you think. But if it is necessary I will change all the housemaids."
"Well, while you are at it, maybe you will see the end of your life, Omar's life, or even the baby's. Ben is so helpless."
"What do you mean, Khaleb?"
"I mean, for example, the most powerful person in this country, the poor old uncle Mohamed, the great sheik. It took not more than few drops of poison to kill him."

"Why would you do such a thing, Khaleb? Are you out of your mind? The Sheik Mohamed never meant any harm to you. On the contrary, he was always so nice to you."

"Oh, Bethany, Bethany. You are so right in your conclusions. But the thing is… The poison was not intended for him but for you. It was only his bad luck that he wanted to exchange glasses with you that day. If you try to remember the details you will recall that I tried to prevent that."

Bethany was struck by surprise and by how mean he was. Her life had hung by a thread. And an innocent man had died.

She felt defeated. There was nothing she could do against him and Khaleb read fear in her eyes.

"Surrender. Give me the money. You know you have to. Because I have my men on the trip with Omar too. Maybe he is drinking or eating something poisoned right now."

"You are disgusting."

"But I win."

"Yes. You win. I will give you the money in a week."

"I give you two days."

"So be it. Now leave."

He walks out very confident and Bethany sits down and cries sobbing bitterly.

Chapter 47 – Fleeing

Bethany got in touch with her brother and he came to the palace immediately. It was lucky for her that he had not left for one of his trips to the desert. Scott had bought an apartment for himself a few blocks from the bank and the truth is that he was keeping an eye on her since they had found out that Omar's relatives were thieves and crooks.

So, when he took his sister's hands and read despair in her eyes, Scott knew that something very serious had happened because Bethany was a strong woman and he had never seen her so distraught.

"Oh, Scott, I am so glad you are here."

"What is it, little sister?"

And then she told him everything that Khaleb had said to her.

"So he is a murderer, after all."

"Yes. And he is a coward too. He threatened Ben's life."

"The nerve of the man. Where is he now?"

"I don't know. Why do you ask?"

"I will deal with him. Let's see if he is as brave as he says he is."

"No, please, don't go after him. Listen, Scott, I don't want you to fight Khaleb. He is treacherous and also, some people here are paid by him to do evil. I just need your help to get away."

"What about Omar?"

"He won't listen to me, I have tried. I guess it is a quality he has… He sees the good in people and he doesn't accept the truth about his family. I admire him for that but now Ben's life is at risk and I will take no more chances."

"You are right. I will make the arrangements for us to leave tomorrow. That is the day you are supposed to pay Khaleb, right?"

"Yes. But I will not give him one cent. That would not solve things. His mind is so sick that he could just go ahead and kill me. Why should I give him financial power to pay more traitors or by more poison?"

"I agree with you. And even if he didn't kill you, once he got the money he would just ask for more. I must go now. Prepare one bag for Ben and another one for you. Make sure to wear simple clothes because we don't want people to know who you are."

"Where will we be going?"

"First we will go south and after that, I will arrange for us to leave the country. I have contacts at the southern border."

They talk a little more and then Scott goes to plan for the escape.

Bethany also hurries to have things ready for the long trip. It was a relief to count on her brother. If only Omar had the same blind faith in her. She sighs deeply because she knows that in order to save her son's life she will be heartbroken from the separation from the man she loves.

SOME CALLS

Because Scott is a very rich man it takes him no time at all to purchase weapons and goods for the trip ahead. Besides, he is in a situation in which he has made many true friends over the last years and he is not too proud to ask for their help. The main aid to his mission is Habibdul because he knows the desert like the palm of his hand and he has a gift that Scott has witnessed more than once: Habibdul can smell danger from a distance. It is as if he has a sixth sense for these things.

And then Scott makes one last call that is essential for their departure from the country.

He tells everything to the person on the other end of the line and waits for the shock to settle.

"What do you need, Scott?"

"Listen carefully…"

After he hangs up, Scott knows that Bethany has now a lot in her favor. He hopes all these efforts will be enough to save their lives because from now on, he is at great risk too. If anyone tries to kill Bethany or Ben, they will have to run over him first.

Moreover, Scott knew that there was a great chance for him to have to face his brother-in-law's wrath. But it was so worth it. He wasn't afraid at all. Omar had done what he believed was right when he defended his family. He could not condemn his behavior. That was the rule worldwide, each one protecting their kin. But Scott also did what he thought was right. Each one used their minds and feelings to make their decisions. Omar had achieved great respect as a sheik. Like a man who had to be obeyed at any cost since his word was law. He was a real leader and a good man. But he had not chosen Bethany as his priority. Some part of Omar had needed a submissive wife who should not bother him with details like threats to her life. So, Omar was left with a huge population who gave him recognition and obedience, but Scott knew that they were just strangers and could not fill the sheik's heart as Bethany could. Smiles and bows from subjects in the anonymous crowd had no value or meaning to give peace to a man's heart.

But it was Omar's problem and Scott had enough of his own to worry about.

If ever a confrontation came, though Scott didn't fear it and so far was very prepared for it, if the occasion presented itself, surely Bethany's heart would be broken.

Because Scott had contributed to his brother-in-law's success with extensive donations for the poor people's access to water, he felt hurt by Omar's ingratitude. He could only start to imagine how Bethany felt by his rejection of her complaints. She had changed all her life to be with him.

And Omar had made clear who was dear to him: Malouf and Khaleb. As for Scott, the preservation of your sister's life was his utmost priority. She had a home in his heart and he would never be empty of her. Scott would die with her if he had to. He thought his brother-in-law felt that way too. At least he had seemed so passionate to the outside observer. But it seemed that blood spoke louder than marriage.

Scott was ready to go reaping Ben's cute smirks and Bethany's tender looks of thanks. Because he had entered this war to win.

ROYAL LOOKS

As the caravan took its distance from the city, Bethany felt as if a dagger was being placed in her heart. She never expected to be separated from Omar and she only did it because she felt sure that it was the only way to save her life and even his own.

Now that Bethany knew about the Sheik Mohamed's murder, deep down she knew that Khaleb would not rest until he saw her dead.

The first day went by slowly and the heat was intense. The rustic clothes bothered her skin and the thick scarf over her long hair felt like an oven melting her head. She was not one to complain and she knew that everybody on this journey had to endure one discomfort or another. But Bethany was also a very practical person who went for simple solutions. At the end of the day, while Ben was sleeping inside the kart, Bethany took her brother to a distant spot from the camping area. He could read her features and knew that she was suffering because she missed Omar so much.

"Please, brother, lend me your knife."

"Come on, Bethany, there is no need to feel so hopeless. Don't do something crazy."

"The only crazy thing I am about to do is to kick you many times if you don't hand me that knife. How can you even imagine I would do a foolish thing? I have Ben to think of."

Scott felt relieved by the familiar way she was talking. They had teased each other since childhood and he saw proof of her strength and beautiful personality. He handed her the knife.

"Ok, Bethany. Be careful. It is very sharp."

Then she cuts her hair completely and he watches the long curls fall at their feet. Then she puts the keffiyeh back in place and that scarf doesn't seem so suffocating now. He feels proud of her because Bethany was not a person who would say empty words and do small gestures. By undressing of her royal looks, she proved that she put Ben above any vanity.

"Better, sister?"

"Fresher."

"But you look like a little monkey, you know. That is your title now: Little monkey Bethany."

Her eyes contained all the thanks a person is capable of. In these hard moments of her life, Scott made her smile, taking her to a sweet trip of their childhood games. She was so lucky to have him as a brother.

"And your title is big gorilla. Now, let's find something to eat because I am starving."

Arm in arm they go back to the tents and when they sit down to eat, still there are smiles on their faces.

Chapter 48 – Dangers ahead

After a week had passed on their trip through the scorching desert, Bethany got used to the slow rhythm of the caravan. It was a relief to realize that Ben was not suffering the effects of the trip so much because he was always protected by the shadows and well-fed. Adjia had proved to be of great help since she loved to play with Ben and his laughter could be heard by his mom while she had her meals or talked to her brother.

Then one day, there was a change in the scene. They were near some rock formations and a dozen men dressed in dark robes climbed down and approached them. It was clear that their intention was to plunder.

Immediately Habibdul and his men reached inside the coffee grains' bags and took out the most impressive machine guns that Bethany had ever seen.

The outlaws seemed to be impressed too because they took some steps back and stayed quiet, just watching the caravan pass.

Scott rode beside Bethany's wagon and shouted to her, "Isn't money a marvelous thing?"

"I didn't know you had bought these weapons, Scott."

"Aren't you glad I did? Now, stay in the back of the wagon. It is not safe yet."

Habibdul and some men heavily armed went to meet the men and after taking their weapons that were mostly knives and old guns, made sure to tie them with ropes.

Many hours later, when they stopped to eat Bethany asked Habibdul if those men wouldn't die under the sun, being tied like that.

"No. We saw two other men on top of the rocks. They will untie their friends. I just did it to give us some advantage because it would be bad to travel with them following us. But now that they lost many weapons and saw that we are not defenseless, they won't dare to come after us."

"So, they are basically cowards."

"Indeed they prefer to attack families and elderly people."

Scott had said to his sister that he trusted Habibdul completely. She felt lucky to have him on their side because he was skilled and unafraid. What turn of events! She had to leave her home and subject herself and her child to these dangers. What people did for money was outrageous! She was very scared. Especially for her baby. If they hadn't been armed, what could those men have done? Would they be taking Ben back to the palace and away from her? She discussed it with her brother, but Scott calmed her down. He said that these men were not connected with the palace. They were like pirates of the sand and they attacked everybody. Sometimes they had a word with the head of the caravan and if he agreed to facilitate their work, he would share their profits. They were not only cowards but also lazy.

Even after being reassured by Scott, Bethany had a hard time sleeping that night.

LONG-DISTANCE PHONE CALL

Omar was ready to leave the palace when he was told that there was an urgent call for him. He decided to take it.

"Where is Bethany, Omar?"

"I really don't know. She went away with Scott. They are probably in the middle of the desert right now."

"I know exactly where she is."

"Then you must tell me. You don't know what dangers she could face. And she took Ben."

"Is she facing more dangers than she did in the palace, Omar? Where they tried to poison her drink and killed your father instead?"

"What are you talking about?"

"Bethany told Scott and he explained to me all the evil that Khaleb had done."

Omar was so startled by this news that he urged even more to know Bethany's location. After all, Khaleb was tracking her down.

THE TRUTH

Because he had changed his plans, Omar had his uncle brought to his presence, before he went after Bethany.

At first, when he learned that she was gone, Omar had agreed with everything Malouf was saying because he wanted to gather more information and find out if his uncle had spooked Bethany in some way because she always complained about Malouf. But now it was time for a direct talk.

"I have news, uncle."

"What is that, Omar?"

"Well, Khaleb was captured by Scott's men. He confessed that he poisoned my father."

Omar decided to lie because he wanted to watch Malouf's reaction. It didn't take more than that for the truth to surface.

"But that was an accident, Omar, I swear. It was me who bought the poison, but it was not intended to kill anybody."

"What was it intended for?"

"It was only to keep Bethany drugged so that she wouldn't have the strength to interfere with our businesses."

"Are you out of your mind, uncle?"

"Well, she had already caused such a loss for us when she undid the Australian farms deal."

"Which you wanted to buy with stolen money, right?"

"I always deserved more than your father was willing to pay me."

"Don't talk about my father, you lowlife."

"Please, have mercy. What will you do with Khaleb?"
"I will hunt him down like the dog he is."
And then, Omar had his guards take Malouf to prison and went out of the palace with a terrible look on his face.

ALMOST THERE

"Bethany, we will be separating from the caravan any day now. Get your things and Ben's ready."
"Won't we go to the village with them?"
"It is too dangerous to stay with them now. Our men have spotted searching groups around the caravan. And it is not necessary anyway. I have arranged for transportations to pick us up at the 'Chill Caves' in two days."
"What a horrible name, Scott."
"It is because the caves' entrance looks like giant eyes on a giant horrendous rock face. But we will not be entering the caves. Helicopters will be waiting for us there."
"Are you sure?"
"More than I am sure of my breathing."
"All right, then. I will get a few things and put them all in a small bag."
"Good. Soon this nightmare will be over."
As Scott walks away, Bethany approaches Adjia and decides to let her know about the new plans.
"We will be parting sooner than I thought, Adjia."
"I will miss you so much. And the little prince."
"So you know who we are…"
"Yes. I recognized you from your pictures in many magazines. But don't worry, I didn't tell the others."
"Thank you. You know, in such a short time I feel that I can trust you. Maybe it is what happened between my mom and Scott's babysitter Nancy. A true friendship happened when they were least expecting it. You are so sweet with my son that I think of you as a friend, Adjia."
"I am honored, shaikhah."
"Please, don't call me that. The truth is that I am in danger."
"Sure, madam. I will do as you say."

"Adjia, would you like to come to live with Ben and me? You could keep babysitting him and I will give your parents enough money to start their own business and not depend on anyone else. This way, you will also be free to find someone your own age and marry for love."

"Oh, that would be so nice. But I don't know if my father will agree. He gave his word."

"Why don't you ask him? Tell him I will reward the fabric merchant too. So there will be no complaints."

After almost an hour of talking to her parents, Adjia comes back with good news.

"My father says that my cousin Tania can take my place. Her family is even poorer than us and it will be the best solution to provide for them and to set me free. Also, we could never refuse anything to our shaikhah. Oh, sorry! I forgot not to say it aloud."

"It is okay."

"So, there is no need to pay."

"I want to. Tell your father that he will receive fifty thousand dollars and the same amount goes as a present to the new bride. That should settle things."

"You are so generous, madam. Thank you so much. I will feel so much better knowing that my family is provided for."

"Scott will see to the details. You all can count on it."

Bethany knew she had done the right thing when she saw the happiness in Adjia's face.

VIOLENCE

Khaleb caught up with Habibdul's caravan that was heading south and treated them with his usual violence. Now his group consisted of twelve men because he had divided the others to search in every possible direction and report to him. With him were the men he trusted the most because he had paid them to be loyal to him. Khaleb was following a lead from some men who had heard a baby crying inside a wagon on this caravan. But he was disappointed and confused not to find Bethany and Ben among the travelers. He was about to leave the group when one of his men showed him some baby clothes he had found in one of the wagons. It was one of the items that Bethany had left behind when Scott told her to pack a smaller bag. She didn´t think of burying or destroying them in the big fire they used for cooking. And that was lucky for Khaleb.

Being sure that they were nearby, he started to interrogate the people about the place where Bethany had left the group. Because he was so cruel, he got his answers.

At full speed, he went after her and there was a look on his face that showed that his mind was not stable.

All he could think of was his desire to kill Bethany and he didn´t even remember what advantage he would have from that act. Moreover, he didn´t care for the consequences when Omar found out what he did. He just needed to do it, there was a lust for her blood in his system. So he forced his horse even more and his men followed him through the deserted night.

Chapter 49 – The rescue

Habibdul and his armed men walked in front of the small group. Then Bethany with Ben in her arms and Adjia followed them and Scott was the last one. They arrived at the caves and Bethany thought that they were really ugly.

Everybody was exhausted but then Habibdul summed their feelings with a relieved exclamation.

"Here they are!"

And so it was. Three big helicopters that could fit twenty people each were right ahead waiting for them. Bethany noticed that they were those kinds of military choppers that traveled long distances.

"Are they taking us all the way home, Scott?"

"No. Only to the neighboring country, where we shall take a jet plane. Someone from the embassy is on board to facilitate the permissions."

"Now I am impressed."

And she really was. But nothing could have prepared Bethany for the surprise she felt when Michelle came down from one of the choppers.

"Mom!"

Her scream of delight made her mother open her arms and Bethany just had time to put Ben in Adjia´s arms before her mother squeezed her in a comforting embrace.

"Oh, Bethany! I am so glad to see you!"

"Me too, mom. Scott, I don´t believe that you phoned mom."

"Of course I did. We needed all the help we could summon."

They were interrupted by an alarmed Habibdul.

"You better get on board. Some horses are approaching us in all velocity."

Bethany felt as if a cold hand was pressing her spine. She looked at Scott at once.

"Don´t worry. Habibdul and his men are heavily armed and pointing at them. Just get inside."

Michelle went back into the helicopter with Bethany right behind her. Then, from her seat, she stretched her arms to take Ben and that is when she heard Khaleb shout,

"I am pointing at Ben."

And so he was. He had a rifle on his hand and it was aiming directly at Ben´s head.

Every one of Habibdul´s men, including him, were pointing at Khaleb, but he didn´t seem to care. He was very cold and gave his orders,

"Come with me, Bethany, and your baby shall live."

"Don´t do it, sister."

But Bethany was already jumping from the helicopter and as her body shielded her son, Adjia gave the baby to the desperate grandmother.

Khaleb was now aiming at Bethany´s head and a heavy silence was all around them. When he dismounted slowly and took her arm, Michelle gave a scream and Ben started to cry. Bethany gave her son what she thought was a last look because she knew how obsessed Khaleb was and allowed him to take her inside the fearful cave.

Many armed men came down from the helicopters when Khaleb was out of view with his hostage and because they outnumbered Khaleb´s men and also had more powerful weapons, they forced them to drop their weapons and surrender. Habibdul went around catching the guns and his men helped him tie them up. Even so, nobody felt victorious since a tragic ending could happen in the cave.

Scott followed Khaleb to the cave.

"Go away, Scott. I win."

"I dropped my gun. I just want to be with her."

"If you want to watch your sister die, that is up to you."
"Then you can kill me too. Won´t that be nice to you?"
"Don´t think that I won´t."
Khaleb was walking sideways with his rifle touching Bethany´s head while he forced her to enter the cave with him.
"I know you will. It will be a bonus to you."
Khaleb gave a strange laugh and Bethany was afraid that he would shoot her brother too.
"Go back, Scott. I need you to take care of Ben."
"I rather die with you, little sister. Omar can take care of his son."
"You bet I can."
And because this was a day full of surprises, Omar came out from the shadows and punched the riffle from Khaleb´s hand. Bethany fell to the floor but she was not hurt. It was all that Scott needed to jump and grab the riffle. All the while Omar was punching his cousin in the face and kicking him with all his straight. Khaleb just whined on the floor trying to defend his face because he already had a broken nose and now Omar was punching his mouth and making him lose most of his teeth.
Bethany tried to pull Omar back but he wouldn´t move. Habibdul and some men had entered the cave due to Scott´s signal but nobody would interfere with the sheik´s affairs.
Then Bethany screamed to Omar, "Stop, Omar. Please, stop."
She looked at her brother pleadingly and Scott told the men to separate Omar and Khaleb. Bethany hugged her husband and whispered to him, "You would never forgive yourself if you killed him."
Omar seemed to come out of a daze.
"Bethany, my love. Are you all right?"
He took her in his arms and started to walk out of the cave. Then he said to Scott, "Are you coming?"
"In a minute. You go ahead and take the chopper. I will be in the next one."
"Scott, don´t kill him. We are not murderers like him, brother. Let him rot in jail."
"Of course, little sister. Just go to mom and Ben. I just want to ask Khaleb something."
She nods at him and drops her head on Omar´s shoulder.
"Well Khaleb, here we are."

"You can't kill me. You promised your sister."

"And I value my word. Now, Khaleb, it has caught my attention that you are very interested in money, farms, and expensive things."

"I am like any other man."

"Maybe you are. Probably not. But what happens is that I am a very rich man. So I bought the most expensive machine gun in the world. And I did it thinking about you. Now my question is: have you ever seen one of these?"

One of the men stepped ahead holding a brand-new weapon. Khaleb was already sweating but when the gun touched his face he started to tremble visibly.

"Well, my little sister was braver than you. And by the smell of it, you should be ashamed."

Khaleb was sobbing openly now.

"You promised, Scott. You did."

"But I am keeping my promise. I am walking out of here with my best friend Habibdul and taking a helicopter to join my family."

"So, can I go?"

"First, Ibrahim needs to show you how this machine gun works."

"No… Scott, I beg you."

"It was not nice to meet you, Khaleb. Fortunately, nobody else will ever have to suffer your presence."

When Scott and Habibdul stepped out of the cave, they heard the shooting. It didn't even make them turn their heads.

"Are you sure you don't want to come with me, Habibdul?"

"No, brother. The desert calls me."

"Then, I thank you again and hope to meet you soon."

They hug and Habibdul says to his friend, "`Till we meet again, Scott."

"`Till we meet again, my friend."

UNPUZZLE

When Scott arrived at the airport a little later, his family was not preparing to board the jet plane. The trip was too much for Bethany right now and even Michelle and Adjia had taken such a scare that it was decided that they all should rest at a nice hotel nearby.

Scott thought it was a good idea because after so many days in the desert a long shower would be welcome and he was sure that

Bethany would get a deserved rest in a nice bed, even if she had not complained at all about the hardships of their journey.

Omar kept his arm around her shoulder all the time and she had Ben in her arms. Everybody looked like they had come out of a war and in a way, they did.

Scott stared at Bethany and she finally asked, "And Khaleb?"

"Dead."

Relief showed in her eyes. Then the concern appeared.

"Did you kill him?"

"No."

As relief replace the concern again in Bethany´s eyes, Scott looked at Omar. He seemed pleased that the problem had been solved without his interference. They never talked about Khaleb again. It wasn´t necessary after all.

Many hours later, Ben was peacefully sleeping in his bedroom and Adjia was watching him with loving eyes. The other adults gathered at the hotel´s restaurant for a nice dinner and talk.

"Please, explain to me how mom got involved in this mess, Scott."

"Well, Bethany, if there is something that I learned from my childhood is that our mother is not a weak person who stays mopping in the corner of a room and regretting imaginary problems. I saw her fight for the right to visit you in an unfriendly environment. I have witnessed her capacities to make things better as much in work as in our home."

"Oh, son." Michelle was touched by his words and Scott held her hand showing his affection.

"I also concluded that mom would go crazy if she tried to contact both of her children to no avail for many days. She could decide to come over to the palace, and with Malouf there I didn´t know if she would be safe."

"I agree with you, brother."

"My uncle is in jail now."

Everybody looked at Omar and allowed the good news to calm them. Scott continued with his explanations.

"So I thought the best solution was to ask for mom´s help and then tell her what we needed."

"The helicopters," Bethany concluded.

"Yes. And a contact from the embassy to ensure our leaving the country without passports."

"That was smart. But how did you know where to find us, Omar? I mean, you saved the day." The remembrance of the violent scene made Bethany shake all over.

"I called him."

"You called him? Why mother? I had asked you for secrecy. I know that things turned out okay and I have nothing against him, but I am curious about your reasons."

"It is simple, Scott. Omar is not the enemy. He is just dumb."

"I paid a big price for that." Omar gave Bethany a look of regret. "Forgive me, my love."

"Of course I forgive you, Omar. It was hard to believe such a story. Even for me, it was pretty unbelievable."

"But you were right all the time."

"It is just that the way they acted and talked to me was proof enough of their evildoing. I never wanted to run away from you, Omar. It is just that with the threat of poisoning over our heads, I was afraid we could be murdered before I could convince you of the danger in the situation."

"You did well, Bethany."

"Fortunately, Scott didn´t think twice and rushed to help me. Thank you, brother. I am indebted to you."

"You owe me your love, little sister."

"And that you will have for as long as I live."

They looked at each other with the recognition that it was true. Nobody mentioned that Scott had volunteered to die with his sister because Michelle had already been scared enough. The group went early to bed because they were physically and emotionally exhausted. Also, they had an early flight the next day because Bethany needed time away from the palace and Omar had agreed to join them.

Chapter 50 – Take me home

Some weeks had passed since the rescue and Bethany still didn´t feel like going back to the palace. There were functions there to attend and other royal compromises but she just didn´t feel up to it. One day, Omar suggested that they could go for the celebration of Ben´s birthday which was near.

"Omar, I am so sorry. I just can´t."

"Why, Bethany? It is our home. Ben will be the sheik one day. We have postponed our return long enough."
"I know. You are right but even so, I feel sick when I think of going there. I was threatened beyond my forces there."
"It is all over now."
"We don't know that. There were some maids and other staff who received money to act against us."
"I see."
"And your uncle was making a lot of money from illicit deals. Maybe he still wants revenge."
"Nobody has access to him in jail."
"I know, Omar. Please, just give me a little more time."
"Sure, my love. As long as you need. And as for the staff, I will arrange for new people to work for us. To the last of them, gardeners, maids, cooks... It is our son's security we are talking about. I promise you I won't save efforts to guarantee it."
"Thank you so much. I love you for that!"
"And I love you with all my heart. I will prove it to you."
So they stayed longer and Omar went by himself once a month to take care of his country's businesses and to ensure a safe environment for his family. Bethany missed him a lot on these occasions and still, she wouldn't go with him.

NIGHTMARES

One night, Ben cried a lot because he had a fever. The pediatrician told them that it was just a cold and after prescribing some medicine everything was fine. But after that night, Bethany started to have bad dreams and she would wake up sweating and crying. Omar didn't know how to help her, so he just held Bethany and rocked her back to sleep. They both wished to return to normality and to taste peace and happiness again. But some sort of trauma was making Bethany suffer and Omar felt very guilty and sad.

AT THE BEACH

Michelle suggested to the couple a stay in her beach house because she believed that the beautiful and quiet place would be good for them. They thought it was a good idea and Ben would benefit from the beach. And it was really good to sit in the shadows and watch Adjia and Ben playing with the sand and the toys.

On these occasions, Omar and Bethany had long talks in which they talked about their love and their dreams for the future. Everything was almost normal except for the nightmares that kept making Bethany suffer.

THE BEST VISITOR

When Scott arrived for a visit over the weekend they were all pleased to see him. Even Ben surprised his parents because he wanted to be in Scott's lap all the time.

"It seems that I am his favorite," Scott couldn't avoid teasing a little.

"You are everybody's favorite, brother."

"And you are mine, little sister."

"So, Scott, are you sure you want to travel with me next month?"

"Yes, Omar. It is the last water well that will be installed. Then I will feel that I made good when I gave your father my word to complete his project."

"You made my father very happy. And I think of you as a true brother. You can ask me for anything."

"The same goes here, brother-in-law."

The next day, Scott invited his sister for a long walk along the beach because he wanted to talk to her.

"So, little sister, have you given up on being a sheikhah?"

"Oh Scott, I don't know."

"You sound desperate, Bethany. What is bothering you?"

"I think I am still in shock."

"I don't think so. Quite a while has passed and you are far from being a weak person."

"And still I haven't got the strength to go back to the palace."

"I see. You have your reasons. Why don't you share them with me?"

"I don't feel safe there."

"Mother told me of your nightmares. What is it that you dream about?"

She took a while to answer and Scott waited patiently because he knew that Bethany was searching in her soul for capacities to deal with her fears.

"In my nightmares, someone is always pointing a gun at Ben."

"I understand."
"I feel like I am being dramatic and a burden to everybody."
"But see, Bethany, you aren't. Because someone really pointed a gun at your son. It is not drama, just a caring mother's normal reaction."
His answer made some tears appear in her eyes and when he held her, Bethany could finally cry all the despair she had felt.
"There, there. You can blow your nose in my shirt if you want to."
And this made Bethany laugh.
"Scott, you have the gift to make everything lighter. I love you so much."
"Me too, little sister. My life improved a lot when you were born. There was suddenly an extra color to it."
"Thanks for saying that, Scott."
"You are welcome. Now, Bethany, tell me what makes you insecure to live in your palace."
"Maybe it is a silly reason."
"It wasn't the last time."
"Well, it is just that Malouf was making a lot of money from those deals. Also, he and his son paid some staff to betray Omar and his dad. I know that he is isolated in prison, but I keep thinking that someone goes there to give him food. What if he pays for an act of revenge on his son's death?"
"I see your point, Bethany. I will check with Omar, but I am sure that your husband is not as naïve as he used to be. The guard must be of his highest trust."
"I guess you are right."
"But I also agree that you should stay here a while longer. I mean, Ben loves the beach, right? And Omar is giving you the time you need, isn't he?"
"He has been wonderful. And so have you. I am lucky!"
When they return to the beach house, Omar senses that Bethany is much more relaxed and for the first time after long, she has a peaceful sleep.

THE JAIL

"Wow, I am impressed! It is true what they say about jails: they are disgusting. But this one beats all. Maybe because they have a pig inside."

"Why did you come here to make fun of me? Haven't you had enough? You and your sister took everything I had."

"Don't be ridiculous, Malouf. A thief does not own anything. It is just right to give it back to its lawful owner."

"I am an important man. It was just fair for me to have the means to present myself properly."

"Well, since you declare you are so important, I think it is only fair that you drink from the sheik's own glass. Mohamed wouldn't mind, he always had a generous heart."

"What do you mean?"

"I mean that my friends here brought you a very special drink that is not unfamiliar to you."

Three men step up from the shadows and when Scott gives the order, the guard opens the cell and they enter.

"I will not drink poison. You can't make me."

"Of course I can't. I am just a curious visitor from distant parts. I already saw the jail, now I will go on to see the towers. Take your time, Malouf. Make a toast or two. These guys have a whole bottle of your own poison to feed you with. Sorry I can't stay."

Scott stepped away and two guys held Malouf while another one poured the poisoned drink down his throat. They were to repeat it until the bottle was dry.

When the sunlight hit his eyes, Scott took a long breath. It was nice to get out of the underground jail. He took a moment to study his reaction, to search his conscience about what he had just paid a big sum of money to accomplish in secret. He concluded that he was feeling fine. So he started to whistle and went away to have a pleasant time with his old friends Youssef and Habibdul.

LOVE WINS

The news of Malouf's death put an end to Bethany's nightmares. Omar told her that his uncle had a heart attack and died just like his father. They both thought that it was kind of Malouf's destiny to have the same faith of the sheik. And while Mohamed was always remembered, Malouf was not missed at all.

Life was full of joy again and laughter could be heard everywhere the happy couple went.

Then, one day, Bethany asked Omar, "Please, take me home."

“Of course, my love. But why now? So suddenly?”
“Because I am pregnant and I want our baby to be born in our home.”
“Bethany, you make me so happy.”
“You are my life, Omar.”
And they knew that their future life was full of promises because they had arrived at that stage where one could only think of making the other happy.
And so they did.

THE END